His Reluctant Marchioness

Lustful Lords, Book Five

SORCHA MOWBRAY

Published by Amour Press 2022, First Edition

Copyright © 2022 by Sorcha Mowbray

ISBN Print: 978-1-955615-15-0

ISBN ePUB: 978-1-955615-14-3

Cover design from Fiona Jayde Media

Chapter Images from Illustration 13209099 / Victorian Vines © Freeskyblue | Dreamstime.com

All rights reserved.

No part of this publication may be reproduced, stored or transmitted in any form or by any means, electronic, mechanical, photocopying, recording, scanning, or any information storage and retrieval system without the prior written permission from the author, except in the instance of quotes for reviews. No part of this book may be scanned, uploaded, or distributed via the internet without the permission of the author and it is a violation of the international copyright law, which subjects the violator to severe fines and imprisonment.

This novel is entirely a work of fiction. The names, characters, incidents, and places portrayed in it are the work of the author's imagination and are not to be construed as real except where noted and authorized. Any resemblance to actual persons, living or dead, events or localities is entirely coincidental. Any trademarks, service marks, product names, or names featured are assumed to be the property of their respective owners, and are used only for reference. There is no implied endorsement if any of these terms are used.

Prologue

May 1843

Amy Amelia VanBolton bounced on her toes as she waited for her mother to get her coat. Excitement bubbled up, nearly spilling over as she imagined all the grand adventures she would have in London. She would meet lords and ladies, take tea, and stroll along Rotten Row. And the balls! She would dance and dance until her feet fell off. After what seemed like an eternity, they stepped out on to the deck of the *SS Great Western* for an evening stroll with her father. The ship's tall masts stretched up as though reaching for the stars as the sails billowed in the frosty night air. Most passengers had retired for the night, so it was peaceful but for the chugging of the steam engines pushing them ever closer to their destination. They walked toward the stern of the ship where they had agreed to meet.

"Have you thought about where you'd like to go first in London?" her mother asked as they walked.

Amy smiled, her exhilaration nearly boiling over. "I think I'd like to attend a Vauxhall Masquerade."

Her mother gasped and laughed. "Try again, my dear. You are just sixteen. There will be no masquerades or balls in your future for a few more years. Besides, I'm quite certain those types of entertainments are no longer held there. But perhaps we could arrange a more sedate daytime visit."

Amy sighed. "Very well, I suppose a daytime visit will have to suffice. But no balls, mother? Not even one?"

Her mother smiled indulgently. "Perhaps one ball."

Amy squealed. "It will have to be the most elegant of all the balls!"

Her mother chuckled. Ahead, they heard male voices. "That must be your father and Richard."

As they moved closer, the heated tones carried to them. Her mother drew up short and then stepped in front of Amy as though shielding her. They paused and listened for a moment.

"I've told you, Richard, I shall not be involved with that type of establishment." Her father's voice sounded angry.

"We stand to make so much more money by adding such entertainments to our clubs. And I tell you, the men would spend even more time and money in our establishments if we offered them." Richard pressed.

"We make plenty of money. I have no need of more."

Richard snorted. "*You* may have plenty, but I do not. I have debts that must be paid. I need to create more income since you refuse to loan me further funds."

"I'll not fund your disastrous habits. We've been friends for years. I cannot watch you throw everything we've worked for away. You must stop your gambling." Her father urged.

"What I need is more money, Ted. They've threatened to hurt me!" Richard yelled. Silence hung heavy for a few heartbeats, and then Richard groaned. "Why can't you understand? I have none of what you have. You stole Alicia from me at university. Everything you touch turns to gold, and you have a beautiful daughter to marry off to your advantage. I have nothing but this business and my disastrous habits."

Her father growled. "Alicia was never yours. She didn't even know you existed. Everything I touch turns to gold because I work hard and make smart choices. There's no magic to it. And as for my daughter, she will be afforded the same choices I had and shall marry for love. She is *not* a bargaining chip."

Amy cringed into her mother's back, their skirts meshed together, as they listened to the argument. Her mother turned around and took her by the shoulders. "Amy, I want you to go to our cabin and lock the door. Do not let anyone in until your father and I return. Do you understand me?"

Amy stared at her mother as the voices grew louder and angrier. Her blood thrummed through her body, making it sound as if her heart beat in her ears. The words faded, but the furious tone of the conversation permeated everything.

Her mother shook her lightly. "Do you understand what I am telling you?"

Jerked back to the moment, she nodded. Then her mother spun and rushed around the corner to where the men were arguing. Amy huddled there, terrified to see what was happening but terrified that if she did as her mother bade, she'd never see her parents again.

"Ted, Richard! Stop this at once!" she heard her mother shout over the two men's arguing voices.

"Go back to the cabin, Alicia. You should not see this." Her father's voice came low and urgent.

Amy peeked around the corner just as Richard punched her father in the face. "Stay, Alicia. You should see who the better man is. The one able to defend you and protect you."

He punched her father in the stomach. "The one you should have chosen all those years ago."

"I love Ted. I've always loved him. But had I never met him, I would not have chosen you, Richard." Her mother's crisp voice cut through the sounds of fighting. Amy knew that tone. She only heard it when she was in deep trouble with her mother.

Richard roared, and then suddenly she heard a yell and then a scream. "Richard! What have you done?"

Amy peeked around the corner, no longer able to control the need to see. To her horror, she saw her father flail back over the rail, his shirt soaked in blood, and her mother grabbing his coat to save him. As she watched, Richard stepped up behind them. He reached out and pushed her father again, causing him to fall over the rail.

"Ted!" her mother cried out as her father splashed into the water. Fury mottled her mother's face as she faced Richard. "You unscrupulous bastard!" Then she turned to storm away but made no progress as Richard grabbed her arm.

"Where do you think you're going?" he demanded.

"To tell the captain to stop the ship." She tried to wrench away from the enraged man.

"The hell you are. You will say nothing if you want you and your brat to live."

Alicia gasped. "Stop this, Richard. This needs to end now."

"You will marry me, Alicia. You will marry me and give me all the money I am due. The clubs were my idea, not his! And you belong to me now."

"Never!" she cried and leaned back to pull away again.

Richard hauled her against him and tried to kiss her. Her mother must have bit his lip because he drew back, a trickle of blood dripping down his chin. Before her mother could sweep past him, he hauled his arm back and slapped her. "Bitch!"

Amelia whimpered as she watched, unable to do anything to help her mother. Then Richard drew a knife from somewhere on his person and stabbed her mother in the stomach. As she cried out, he pulled the knife from her body. "It could have been different, Alicia." And then he pushed her mother over the rail as well.

Amy gasped, but stifled her cry. Or so she thought, until Richard turned and caught her looking around the corner. "Amy, come here this instant."

Without further hesitation, Amy spun and ran to her cabin. She heard the thunder of feet behind her, but she raced as though the devil himself was behind her, and in truth, he was. Richard had always been kind to her, overly solicitous of late even. But she'd never feared him until this moment. As she slammed the door of her cabin shut, she slid the bolt home and then found a chair to place underneath the handle. Then she turned and huddled in the far corner of the room to wait. And hope.

Perhaps she had been mistaken about what she'd seen? Maybe someone from the crew had noticed her parents falling over? In the end, she knew neither of those things was true and that she was utterly alone now. Richard had killed both her parents and then pushed them overboard.

She was on her own. There was no one to save her. No one to comfort her.

She sat there for hours, shivering as tears streamed down her face. Every so often, the door handle would rattle, though he never said a word.

As the night dragged on, her swollen eyes drooped. She thought if she hid in the cabin until they docked that she could slip away in the hubbub of everyone disembarking. Whatever she did, she had to escape her father's partner

Morning broke gray and cold, which matched the bleakness that had taken hold of her during the night. She could hear people moving about in the hallway and knew she had a limited opportunity to slip away unnoticed. Pulling her cloak tightly around her, she pulled the hood up to cover her hair and edged the door open to peek into the hall. She couldn't see Richard anywhere, so she dashed out and fell in behind a family headed to the deck.

"Come along, children. We must stay together." The mother spoke over her shoulder as they all marched ahead. Out on the deck, passengers and crew were scurrying everywhere. In the throng, she spotted Richard and ducked behind some trunks that were waiting to be off-loaded. She noticed another small group heading toward the gangplank and decided it was now or never. She dashed over and tried to keep her head down as she blended in with the group. She was almost to the dock when she heard a voice shout out behind her. "Captain! There she is!"

Not waiting to hear what story Richard had concocted for the captain of the ship, Amy dashed into the masses on the dock and made her way as far from the *SS Great Western* as she could manage. She ran until a stitch in her side forced her to slow down. But still, she pressed on, determined to put as much distance as she could manage between herself and

Richard. After what seemed like an hour of walking, she finally thought it might be safe to stop. She pressed up against a wall and caught her breath. She'd left everything when she fled, but at least she was alive. Well, not everything. She pressed the metal lump that hung between her breasts into her skin. She at least had the small pictures of her parents nestled in each half of the gold locket her father had given her for her tenth birthday. Her stomach rumbled loudly, reminding her she would need to do something about food soon.

With a sigh, she pressed on, walking through the London streets she had so looked forward to seeing. But that was before. Before her world had been shattered by one man. Now, all she wanted was to go back to the time when her parents were alive, and she wasn't alone and hunted by a man who wished to kill her. Or worse.

Chapter One

February 1863

Frank Lucifer donned the black mask he'd been given and walked into the main hall of The Market. It was ridiculous, really. The mask couldn't hide his identity since so many people there knew him. But it gave him a sense of anonymity that allowed him to seek what he needed tonight. Heading to Philipe, he made his request for a blonde who would also be masked. Specifically, he asked for someone who would tend to his needs without concern for her own pleasure. But not one of the ladies of the house, if at all possible. He preferred a woman who acted from honest desire, not practiced movements she could execute in her sleep. Philipe assured him that a woman would join him in the green room shortly. And with that, he headed upstairs to find said room and settle in for an evening of pleasure. *His pleasure.*

Lucifer found the room and entered, leaving his mask in place. He poured himself a drink and sat down to wait for someone to join him. Perhaps a quarter of an hour later, there was a soft knock at the door. "You may enter," he called out.

The door opened, and a woman stepped inside. She stood nearly as tall as he was, with long blonde hair that swept around her elbows and a mask that obscured her eye color from where he sat. "Good evening, my lord," she greeted him and shut the door.

"I'm no lord. Sir, will do just fine."

"Very good, sir. I see you've already poured yourself a drink. Is there ought, else I can get you?"

"You may come here and sit with me. Pour yourself a drink if you'd like." He waved a hand at the wing-backed chair across from him. Normally, he would stand when a woman entered a room, but tonight he was tired. Bone tired. Perhaps it had sunk all the way to his soul. Could one be soul tired? He suspected the answer was yes.

Dressed in a long silky robe that fell in gathers from a ribbon tied at her waist and heeled slippers, she crossed the room, poured herself a scotch, and then sat down. "And how may I entertain you this evening?" she asked, her head tilting to one side as she allowed her gaze to drift over his body in a slow perusal. She was no submissive flower here to see to his needs. No, she was a woman who was prepared to take stock of what was on offer.

"I'd like to be taken care of. I'm looking for a woman to see to my pleasure without concern for her own needs. I want my cock milked of my seed until my bollocks are shriveled husks."

She lifted her head and smiled. "Then you've come to the right place."

The masked blonde woman tugged on the ribbon and let her robe fall open as she sat across from him, sipping her scotch. A corset encased her voluptuous curves and pushed up her breasts until they teetered precariously at the edge of the garment. Below that, her pale thighs were sheathed in silk, held up by garters. She stood, allowing her robe to flow down around her into a puddle of silky material before she stepped towards him.

"Why don't I help you get more comfortable to start?" She reached up and peeled his jacket over his shoulders and down along his arms until he had to lean forward to allow her to strip the garment off. Next, she worked on unbuttoning his waistcoat and removing it until all that remained was his fine linen shirt. All the while, she treated him to a close personal inspection of her assets. "There," she said, "Now you look more at ease."

Reclining back in the chair, he picked up his whiskey and took a sip. "Very nice."

She smiled. "I'm here to please." She moved to retake her seat but stopped when he spoke.

"I meant your breasts. They look plump and lovely on display like that."

She continued on her original course to her seat, picked up her own drink, and looked over at him. "Now, tell me what exactly it is that you're looking for this evening—besides shriveled bollocks?"

He chuckled, though he was unable to keep the sardonic edge out. "I don't lack for want of female companionship. But for one night, I'd like to not have to worry about the woman's pleasure. To be the one whose pleasure is the priority." *To be cared for.* But he refused to speak those words and further humiliate himself. It was bad enough he had such *feelings*, but to speak them aloud? *Never.*

She nodded. "That sounds simple enough." She tossed back the last of her drink and set her glass aside. Curious to see what she intended, he lounged back, almost slumping in his seat, sipping his own drink. Then she slipped out of her chair, onto her knees, and crawled across the thick green Aubusson rug towards him. Upon her arrival at his knees, she reached up and gently nudged them until he spread his thighs, making room for her between.

"Why take so many women to your bed if you find it exhausting to see to their needs? There are many other ways to sate one's own desires." Not waiting for his reply, she reached up and unfastened his trousers, slowly opening them as he watched. His whiskey glass dangled from his fingertips, all but forgotten for the moment.

"It is less about seeing to my own desires and more about business. A properly pleasured woman is far more likely to share bits of information she shouldn't. The fact my own desires are met is merely a boon." He shrugged one shoulder as she reached inside and pulled his cock out. He thought about sipping his whiskey, but seeing her blonde head tip over his groin distracted him from his drink. When she stretched her pink tongue out and licked the tip of his head and then swirled it around the entire circumference, his semi-hard cock rose to attention.

"Yes, I can see that you're ready for some singular attention." She laughed, a soft husky sound that sent tingles running down his spine. Then she opened her mouth and encompassed the head entirely. He sucked in a breath as the warm sensation engulfed him, and then she slid lower and lower down the shaft. Before he knew it, her lips were at the base of his cock as her hands snuggled his balls in a firm but teasing grip.

Then she pulled up and off and smiled up at him. "Seems you do like to challenge a girl."

He laughed softly but enjoyed the idea that she found him—his length——pleasing. Then she returned to her previous efforts, swallowing the head of his cock, sliding all the way down the length and back up. Over and over again. She continued to work his cock until it grew harder than he ever remembered. Before long, he was close to spilling into her divine mouth.

"Stop." A low growl escaped him as he beat back the need to come.

She looked up at him but shook her head and returned to sucking his cock. As she worked his length in and out of her mouth, stroking him, cupping his sack, and playing with him, he knew it wouldn't be long. Couldn't be, because he'd never been so aroused. As the pleasure grew more intense, his fingers tensed on the glass in his hand. And then the tingling sensation in his groin coalesced into a deep knot of pleasure that seemed to shoot out of his body as he exploded in her mouth. The glass slipped from his fingertips, thumping dully on the rug as bliss zipped from his cock to his limbs, and he surrendered to the pleasure she'd wrought. She swallowed every drop as she continued to work his length until he'd grown soft and exquisitely sensitive.

Then she rose to her feet, picked up his glass, and walked back over to the bar. He couldn't help but admire her beautifully rounded derriere, emphasized by her nipped-in waist. There she refilled their drinks, pouring him a whiskey and herself a scotch. As she returned to her seat, she passed him his drink. He sat with his trousers open, his flaccid cock lying there unattended and ignored for the moment.

A sly, almost challenging, look entered her dark eyes. "If you're able to return to full staff, you may dictate what occurs next, if that appeals."

He always enjoyed a challenge, especially one that came from such an enticing source. "Alone in a room with a woman who can do what you did with your mouth, I can promise you I shall be ready shortly."

She let her head fall back as she laughed, exposing the enticing length of her throat. "Well then, in the meantime, you've said you pleasure these women for business, yet your business is not that of the flesh but of information. Is the information they share so valuable you must sell yourself?"

He closed his trousers, unexpectedly uncomfortable with the conversation. The notion that he sold himself in such a fashion deeply disturbed him since his own mother had been a prostitute in a house of significantly lower standards than The Market. He'd sworn never to treat a woman as his mother had been, as a means to an end. Riled by her suggestion, he picked up his whiskey and drank. He swallowed and took another moment to form his response. "As I explained earlier, I don't not enjoy my time with these women. I prefer the transient nature of the encounters, as I am not the kind of man who would take a wife. And I refute the notion that I have sold myself. I'd very likely bed these same women or other women just like them. I give as much as I receive."

"Truly? Do your tastes in women vary so widely?" Her brows rose, giving her the appearance of being skeptical.

"I can find something to appreciate about all the variations of a woman's form. But you are correct. I have my personal preferences." And the woman across from him met many of those requirements. She was tall, no stranger to physical activity if the musculature of her form was any indication. But she came with full curves, hips for a man to wrap his hands around, and breasts that might take hours to fully appreciate.

She offered him a half smile, one almost tinged with bitterness. "A connoisseur of women. How unfortunate."

"Is it? I've yet to hear any complaints from my bed mates." He tried to keep his comment nonchalant, but her comment rankled him further.

Before the discussion could continue, she stood up and walked over to the bed. Once there, she turned down the covers and prepared the bed for them to occupy it. She wore no bloomers, and his cock reawakened as he watched her bend over. When she returned to where they sat, he pulled her towards him and sat her in his lap so that she straddled him.

From there, he reached into her corset top, lifted her breasts out, and began sucking on one nipple and then the other. Slowly working his way back and forth between the two tips until they both hardened. There were parts of pleasuring a woman that he thoroughly enjoyed in their own right. And this was one of his favorites, particularly with her voluptuous curves. As she wiggled on his lap, his cock revived to a partially engorged state. He reveled in the weight of her pressing against him, the soft moans of bliss that escaped her, and the way her hands clung to his shoulders, urging him on. Releasing her nipple, he grabbed her backside with both hands and squeezed. "You have a magnificent arse."

"Thank you," she said, though he was pleased to note she sounded a bit breathless.

Then he spanned her waist with his hands and lifted her off of his lap. Upright, she pulled him from the chair, and they made their way to the bed. Having taken back control, she stepped in to his body. Reaching up, she laid a hand on his pectoral. "Not a stranger to hard work, I see."

His nostrils flared as he waited to see what she might do next. Then she moved around him, letting her hand trail behind her. As she pressed her chest into his back, her other hand came around him. She lowered her arms and gathered the hem of his shirt in her hands. Then she slowly lifted until more and more of his skin was exposed.

Finally, he had to lift his arms so she could fully remove his shirt. He heard the material plop onto the floor before her hands returned to her inspection of him from behind. Her breath caressed his skin in soft puffs as she leaned over his shoulder to look down at his chest. She wasn't quite as tall as him, so her view was limited. But what she couldn't see, she seemed content to explore with her hands. He sucked in his stomach as her fingertips drifted over his belly. He wasn't as lean as his brother, who had a tendency to enjoy fighting and sparring, but he was not a paunch-laden profligate who ate, drank, and fucked himself into a stupor.

Her lips grazed his shoulder, and then she was moving again, her hands falling away as she circled back around to his front. Her breasts remained exposed, begging for his touch. So, he moved to tweak one nipple but was thwarted by a smart smack to his hand.

"I did not—" She seemed to cut herself off. "My apologies. Please touch me if you wish." She replaced his hand on her breast.

He was curious about her response, but then his fingers found her pebbled nipple, and the thought fell away as easily as his trousers did under her influence. He stepped out of his pants and stood before her, fully naked, with his cock in a semi-hard state. He rolled one tip and then the other, listening as her breath caught.

Absorbed in her minute reactions, he was caught off guard when she pressed him backwards until his legs bumped against the bed. She continued the pressure on his chest. "Sit back against the headboard."

Doing as she wished, he sat and waited to see what she would do next. Unhooking her corset down the front, she slowly removed it as he watched. Left in nothing but her garters and hose, she was a magnificent sight.

Moving sleek and slow like a predator, she crawled on the bed and up between his thighs until she found his cock—now jutting out as if seeking her attention. There she began to suck and stroke him, laving him with her tongue like a lollipop. With such attention, it took little time for him to move past simply hard to throbbingly erect. Pulling her mouth off his length, he drew her up until she straddled him. And then she sank down on his cock, making her lovely, luscious tits fully available for his enjoyment. She rode him, sliding up and down his length as he leaned forward to rub his beard over one nipple. She moaned as her quim squeezed his cock. Bloody hell! She was a menace to his self-control. He'd thought to pleasure her, but he had never had a woman who solely sought his pleasure without servicing her own needs first. And he had to admit—he found the experience to be amazingly irresistible.

As she slid up and down his shaft, he reveled in the lush curves that engulfed him until, once more, that tingling sensation began in his groin and ripped right up into his gut before radiating out through his limbs. And just as he was about to shoot, he pulled her off to spend on his own stomach as his toes curled, and he groaned low and long.

After he was done, she cleaned him up with a nearby rag as he caught his breath. She had done all that he had asked, having seen to his pleasure without thought of her own. It was instinctual to offer her a little pleasure in return; besides, he needed to know what she tasted like. With an urgency he couldn't credit, considering he'd just released, he sat up, pushed her back onto the bed, and spread her thighs.

Amelia Ketting, better known as Mistress Lash, lay back on the bed as the masked man spread her thighs and wedged himself between them until his bearded face aligned with her pussy. Once there, he spread her open and drew his tongue from her damp hole all the way over her clit. As he licked over and over again, following that same line, her body came alive, tingling at every sensation. Every swipe of his tongue. He was proving to be a generous lover despite his claims of wanting to have his own pleasure serviced this night.

He continued to work over her clit, dragging his tongue over and over it and then sliding down to delve deep inside of her before repeating it all again. Every scrape of his beard against her tender thighs, every drag of his tongue over her clit, had shivers careening along her spine. As she grew closer to orgasm, she slapped one hand on her head to ensure that her wig didn't slide away and the other on his head to make sure he didn't slide away, either. Pleasure rippled out from her groin, down her legs, and up her body to tighten her nipples. She rode the crest until she exploded in his mouth, grinding herself against his magical tongue until the last vestiges of her orgasm had passed.

She wondered if perhaps there might have been more between them if she could have gotten to know the man. He seemed so aware of her needs and desires. But alas, she was acting the role of a nameless woman tonight. She was not Mistress Lash—though that had been a close call when she'd nearly forgotten what role she played. And he was merely an incognito patron of The Market. This would be their first and last encounter.

Chapter Two

It had been two fucking weeks since Lucifer had been with a woman. Not just a woman, but *the* woman. The one who had apparently ruined all women for him. At least for the moment. He refused to believe this could be more than a fleeting infatuation. Pulling out a sheet of paper, he carefully set pen to paper. He'd thought through the structure of the offer he wished to make for the last week. Frankly, he'd thought of nothing else but the mystery woman he'd met at The Market. He did not know her name or how to find her, but of course, Madame du Pompadour would. And right now, he needed to have her again. To see if he could fuck her out of his system.

He clearly laid out his terms. He wanted to see the woman at least once a week for the next six months. They would wear masks, and their identities would remain secret for as long as they both agreed on that point. They would meet at The Market for their assignations for as long as they remained anonymous. If at any time, either or both wished to reveal themselves, they could. At such time, if they chose, they could select another location to meet for the remainder of their contract. At the end of the term of their agreement, they could then decide if they wished to continue their arrangement or not.

He included the terms with a brief note to Madame asking her to pass the request to the lady in question. Should she be agreeable, Madame would set it all in The Market's normal contract format, and they would both sign. He looked forward to the arrangement being solidified quickly. Until then, he'd be left to seek his satisfaction alone, as he had done since their one night together. Once he'd cleared her out of his system, he hoped to return to normal business activities. Until then, he realized he would have to find someone he trusted to take over his role in the information trade. The question was, who?

Contemplating his choices, he handed off his missive to Gordie to see delivered and then hied himself to his brother's townhouse.

A short while later, Lucifer stood in Flint's study with a drink in hand, attempting to appear indifferent despite being curious as to the reason for his summons.

"How are things going at Lucifer's?" Flint asked as he settled in his wingback chair across from him.

His club was a point of pride for him. He'd scrabbled, stole, fought, and connived—on occasion—to build a successful gaming hell. He took a sip of his whiskey before responding. "Everyone is gambling and losing as normal. And I met a woman I can't seem to get out of my head."

"Really? Who is she?" Flint sipped his drink.

"I don't know." He frowned, his frustration surfacing more quickly than he cared for. "I met her at The Market, and you know how Madame can be about protecting her client's identities." He sighed. "I've extended an offer for six months, so I might have an opportunity to excise her from my head."

Flint chuckled. "I'm afraid to say I have my doubts about your likelihood of success in that endeavor."

"I'm not like you and your friends. There is no capacity for love within me. I doubt there is a woman alive who could banish the darkness within me. And frankly, I'm not sure I would want a woman to try. It might very well kill her. Or me. In either case, it would not end well."

"If I can do anything for you, for any reason, you know you need only ask. I owe you my life and my happiness." Flint's gaze bore into him with an uncomfortable intensity that made Lucifer want to squirm.

Of course, Lucifer highly doubted he would request assistance for anything from his half-brother. Without question, the man had a far rougher edge than the average lord, and he'd not flinched in dealing with the ruffians that had threatened his wife, Ros. He'd even shot one man in the arm, but there were few situations in Lucifer's world that his brother could actually offer assistance with. "And how are things in your world, brother?"

Not surprisingly, Flint displayed a wide grin. "My world is perfect. My lovely wife keeps me quite in line, and I cannot complain about her methods. My mother is doing well despite our father's death, or perhaps because of it. The more I learn, the more I wonder how she survived that marriage for so long."

"Have you found a slew of other siblings that you were unaware of?" Lucifer chuckled nervously. How would he feel if there were more of him? More bastard children that had grown up without a father or even a mother, in truth.

"No new siblings, but far too many peccadilloes and some very questionable investments."

Lucifer sipped his drink and contemplated what their dead father might have been up to. "Certainly nothing truly nefarious, I would think."

Flint raised his glass and mimicked him. "Nothing nefarious—yet—as you suggested. However, he was moving money around and somehow managed to fall behind on payments to many of his creditors. It was shocking, considering the family coffers contain more than enough to manage the debt. He'd also revised his will to recognize you as an illegitimate son."

"Did he now? That's a rather surprising move, considering the efforts he put forth to ignore me as a child." Lucifer ignored the bitter bile that churned in his gut. His fury over his father's past actions stemmed more from his mistreatment of his mother than anything the man had done to him. His mother had been left pregnant, penniless, and in disgrace by a man who possessed more than enough income to see her comfortably settled, if forgotten, in some out-of-the-way corner of England. Instead, his father and his grandmother chose to desert his mother, driving her to sell her body to survive.

Flint shrugged. "I suppose the old man was feeling his age. Regardless, I have already acknowledged you as my brother to anyone who's interested. Along with that, I wanted to make an offer to you. I would like to bestow on you the use of one of the family titles. I was thinking of the Marquess of Portridge. It's one of the older marquessates we hold and comes with a modest estate near the border with Wales that is quite lovely during hunting season."

Lucifer shook his head without hesitation. "While I am sure you would love for me to help financially by taking over the maintenance fees of said estate, I have told you before, and I'll say it again. I have no use for a title."

Flint tipped his glass toward Lucifer. "Actually, the estate comes with a small income each year to help with its maintenance; so no, this is not an attempt by me to reduce my debt. This is merely about me acknowledging you as my brother and establishing you on some footing within the family structure."

"And yet I'm afraid I shall still pass. I do not need a title to know that you are my brother. I'm quite comfortable with who I am and my place in this world."

Flint grunted in acknowledgment. "I am more concerned about the rest of the Ton and how they will treat you as word spreads of our connection. A title would give you greater legitimacy in the eyes of society and could even open certain doors for you."

"I have lived my life this long without those doors being open and have no concerns over the need of them in the future. If I had need of them, I'd simply kick them in. As for the Ton, I have little to no interest in their opinion of me. My answer remains a no."

The pair continued the rest of their visit, sipping their drinks and discussing several bills that were up for vote in Parliament. By the time Lucifer made to leave, they had solved most of the world's problems and grown closer for the effort.

Chapter Three

Amelia sat across from Madame du Pompadour in stunned silence. She couldn't possibly be hearing her correctly. But her employer extended a sheet of paper across the desk toward her and continued saying the very words that simply didn't make sense. "As I've said, he has made a very fair offer in terms of time and expectation. But he is unaware that you are also a member of my staff. So, there is no financial compensation enumerated. You chose to participate that night as a client and not a staff member, so that is how he has framed his offer. If you would prefer to be compensated, I can inform him of your employment here."

Amelia stared at the contract for a few heartbeats as she considered everything that had occurred that night between them. Admittedly, she'd thought about him frequently. More than thought about him—she'd pleasured herself to memories of what they'd done together. How he'd crawled between her thighs and licked her pussy until she was mindless with bliss. Few men had endeavored to provide that service to her, and none so well as he had.

Her heart pounded in her chest as she wiped her slightly damp palms on her cotton day dress. Finally, she reached out to take the document and tried her best to ignore her trembling hand. Was it fear? Or perhaps excitement? She decided not to examine the cause too closely. Curiosity pushed her past any reservations as she pulled the contract closer so she could read its contents. Clearly, Madame du Pompadour had personally drawn up the agreement because Amelia recognized the flowing feminine scrawl, but the words reminded her of the man she'd met. She scanned the page and considered what he'd offered. It was short and succinct. But strangely, there was no demand about her seeing to his needs. Was he suggesting a mutually beneficial exchange of pleasure? It certainly was intriguing based on her one experience with him. He knew his way around a woman's body and was not afraid to utilize that knowledge.

She looked up from the page and took the pen Madame du Pompadour had placed near her side of the desk. Without offering a word of explanation, she signed the agreement. It was truly an easy choice, all things considered. With that, she rose and turned to go.

"He'd like to see you this evening," Madame du Pompadour said, stopping her exit.

Amelia resisted the urge to smile as she turned around. "What time?"

"Midnight." Madame picked up the signed contract and tucked it in a drawer.

"Very well. I can accommodate that request. Is the little dungeon available?"

Madame considered for a moment. "I believe it is unspoken for."

"Very good. Is it still set up with the Medieval theme?" They had hosted a party for two of the Lustful Lords a few nights earlier. Baron Lincolnshire and Earl Dunmere had a few friends attend a themed party where a few of the girls of the house had joined, dressed in peasant costumes that left little to the imagination. The party and the costumes had been well received, by all accounts. Perhaps she'd borrow one from the house for her assignation with her mystery lover?

"It is, but I can have it reverted to its normal state," Madame offered.

"I think not. Let him know appropriate attire is required. I shall visit the wardrobe room to garb myself accordingly. Thank you, Madame." With that, Amelia headed upstairs to search out her clothing for that night.

Lucifer walked into the room he'd been directed to at The Market. While it was not one he'd had occasion to enter before, it was downstairs near the dungeon, which he was familiar with. Upon entering, the tunic bearing a rampant lion, hose, and crown he'd been provided immediately made sense. The room's walls appeared to be made of stone, a similar finish to the dungeon. To one side, there was a wide and rather tall chair that was well padded with velvet cushions—obviously his throne. Beside the throne sat a table with two pitchers and goblets. Centered on the far wall was an enormous bed with a canopy and drapes that would keep the cold out if this had been a proper castle. On the other far wall sat a fireplace that had a fire crackling merrily. There was a divan set near the fire and, should they be required, a set of manacles on the wall.

He smiled and closed the door behind him, letting anticipation for the night ahead seep into his body to make the blood thrum through his veins. He'd spent the afternoon with a semi-hard cock after receiving word that his proposal had been accepted. The custom mask he'd had made while he'd considered whether to make the offer to his mystery woman fit snuggly to his face. It was similar to the black ones distributed by The Market, except that it was custom molded to his face, lined with black velvet, and most importantly, boasted slightly wider eye holes to allow him a greater field of vision.

He poured himself a drink, pleased to see that the pitcher was, in truth, filled with whiskey and not wine or mead as he had feared, and considered his seating options. Deciding not to rush things, he opted to take a seat on the throne. It was perhaps a choice that went against the grain, considering he'd just turned down Flint's offer of a title, but he was, in effect, the ruler of his domain, and he'd earned that title with his own intelligence and hard work. One might think a common street thug wouldn't be comfortable taking a king's seat, but then how many common street thugs scrabbled their way out of the gutter and into the questionable fringes of polite society? Precisely one that he was aware of. Him.

There was a soft knock at the door, and then it opened without waiting for his response. His train of thought choked in his head as he took in blonde hair braided into a thick rope and draped artfully over one shoulder. Next, he noticed the sheer cream linen that caressed her deliciously curved figure, which he remembered with an apparently excellent recall. She closed the door and curtsied. "Good evening, milord."

He chuckled to himself. Obviously, they would be role-playing this evening, and he mentally rubbed his hands together at all the deliciousness that could lead to. The notion pleased him. "Good evening."

"The housekeeper said you had need of more fuel." She rattled the coal in her bucket and then padded over to the fireplace with bare feet.

As she stepped in front of the flames, the transparency of her linen chemise became even more obvious. His cock thickened and grew at the sight of her luscious curves defined by the light. "That and more."

She set the bucket down and turned to face him. "What else may I do for ye, milord?"

He realized the string that should hold the neck of her bodice closed was not tied. With her movement, her blouse now gaped open, displaying the valley of her breasts. This contrasted the simple bit of fabric and lacing that bound her waist in such a way as to cinch it in, making her breasts look even more round and inviting compared to the span of her waist. Though, she was no waif. No, she was more robust peasant woman than a woman who might blow away in the next stiff wind. While thin and delicate may have been *de rigueur,* he found her lush curves and healthy proportions to be far more pleasing both to the eye and to his hands as he had fucked her the last time they were together. "Come here, wench."

She did as she was told, crossing the room to where he sat on his throne. He reached over and poured a goblet of what he assumed was red wine for her from the second pitcher. "Have a drink of wine with me." He held out the goblet to her.

"I don't think Mrs. Heler would approve of such a thing. She might beat me for not doing my duties." She hesitated, just out of his reach.

"I assure you, Mrs. Heler will not so much as lift a finger to scold you for doing as I ask." He responded with an easy confidence that came from knowing this was but a little fun and that if anyone might dare to lift a finger to hurt this woman, he would hunt them down and flay the skin from their hides one stroke of the lash at a time.

As though she could read his rather dark and surprising thoughts, her dark eyes widened before she stepped closer and took the goblet. Looking about and seeing again that one of two possible seats for her was across the room by the fire, he opted for the other available choice—his lap. He reached out and clamped his hand on her wrist. "Come sit with me."

"Milord," she exclaimed as she plopped down on his lap.

"That is much better." He sat back, giving her room to settle in on his lap. "How is it I have never seen you here before?"

She took a sip from her goblet. "Today is my second day here. Me ma insisted I was old enough to work at the Lord's keep now."

"You look to be ripe with womanhood." He grinned and cupped her breast through the thin linen. He could feel her nipple pucker and bead up at his touch.

She offered him a sly smile. "The prior's son has oft said the same to me."

Lucifer's brow lifted. "Has he then? When was this?"

"Just last week when..." her words trailed off.

"When what?" He found his voice came out rougher than he'd expected, as jealousy of a fictional being surged through him as real as if the man had been standing there.

"When he kissed me in the priory." She grinned. "He held my booby much as you are and kissed me." She sounded breathless as she relayed the made-up detail.

"Did he, now?" Lucifer squeezed her breast gently and then set his own goblet down before taking hers. "Did he kiss you like this?" He leaned in and pressed his lips to her cheek, just below her mask.

She shook her head and laughed. "No, he kissed me here." And she pointed to her lips.

Lucifer placed his lips on hers and pressed them together for a moment. "Like that?"

Again, she shook her head. "No, he slipped his tongue in my mouth."

Lucifer repressed the urge to groan and then kissed her long and deep, syncing up the movements of his tongue and his hand so that they were perfectly timed to grant her as much pleasure as he could. When he pulled back, they were both breathless. "Like that?"

She smiled at him. "Oh no, milord. That was ever so much better."

Lucifer chuckled. "And has he kissed you anywhere else?"

She nodded. "He kissed my boobies once. And even between my legs." She looked up into his eyes, their gazes locked together. "He was ever so good at that."

Lucifer's cock throbbed in his hose at full attention. He needed to be inside her soon, or he would spill, with or without the aid of her warm cunny. "Was he now?" He pulled away from her breast and dropped his hand to her ankle. Drawing it along her leg while pushing the fabric of her dress higher and higher, he asked more questions. "And you liked what he did to you?"

Her voice hitched as she tried to respond. "Oh—yes. I liked the way he made me tingle all over."

He had her skirts pushed up and her bare pussy exposed as he pushed one finger deep inside of her. She was soaked from their little game, much as he was rock hard. His other hand caressed the breast he'd abandoned, tweaking and plucking at the nipple through the linen. Then he leaned over and captured her lips with his again. Adding a second finger, he timed his movements so that he was stimulating her in at least two places at any given moment, be it her mouth, her breast, or her quim. She was so wet and ready for him. It was all he could do to control the urge to lift her up and impale her on his cock. With a start, he realized there was no reason not to do so. This was merely a fantasy, and it was one they both wanted to end with his cock buried deep inside her.

Putting thoughts to action, he shifted her upright and helped her rise to straddle his thighs. As she knelt, hovering over him, he quickly tugged his hose down, freeing his cock, and donned a French Letter. And then she was sinking down on him in a single slow slide that squeezed him tighter and tighter the deeper he sank. "Fuck, your pussy feels so good."

She moaned. "I swore I had embellished the way your cock fills me, but here you are proving me wrong."

Finally, she sat down on his cock so that he was buried to the hilt in her heat. She felt so good it had his head spinning. And then she rose up and did it all over again. As she slowly rode him, he reached up and widened the neckline of her chemise, completely exposing her breasts. He then leaned forward and sucked on one tip as he pinched and plucked the other. Her hands gripped his head, holding him there as she continued her pace. He slid his free hand down and around to grab her arse and squeeze. They continued to fuck like that for a while as he luxuriated in suckling her breasts and squeezing her arse. Then he needed more. "Up."

His demand surprised her, but she recovered quickly and clambered up from his lap. He stood and then bent her over the throne, leaving her backside thrust up high in the air. Behind her, he sank into her heat once more. Determined to bring her as much pleasure as he could, he reached forward and down to stroke her dangling breasts. With a low moan, she thrust her breasts into his hands even as she maintained their rhythm. She felt so good wrapped around him.

Then he straightened up and looked down to find the tight pucker of her backside presented to him. Reaching down and around, he dragged his fingers over her slit, collecting her juices. Then he brought his hand back and pressed a finger against the very tight forbidden entrance. She moaned loudly as he penetrated her rear orifice and sank to his first knuckle.

"Yes, sir! Oh, yes!" she cried out as he started working the digit in and out of her in time with the thrusts of his cock.

The way her pussy tightened around him had him close to orgasm as he continued working in and out of her body. Suddenly, he knew he wanted to fuck her rear entrance at some point. Not tonight, but in the future, he wanted to have her there. She was so tight and clearly had never been entered there. As irrational as it was, he wanted her to bear the imprint of his body for the rest of her days. And he knew taking her there would be a way to do that. "At some point, I want to fuck you here." He wiggled his finger to illustrate his point.

Her response was a low moan of pleasure-pain as he added a second digit to the first. Her quim squeezed his cock in response. But she'd remained quiet.

He continued to pump into her body and prompted her for a response. "Will you let me?"

She panted for breath as he relentlessly shuttled in and out of her body in both holes. "Perhaps…"

He needed her to say yes. "That is not an answer." He slapped her upturned bottom with his free hand and spread his fingers in her arse.

"Yes!" Her cry seemed ripped from her as her body clenched around him. Still working in and out of her, he waited to hear more. "Yes, you can fuck me there. Oh god! I'm coming, sir!" And then her body shook around him, clenching down like a vise on both his fingers and his cock. As he continued working in and out of her, his own climax rushed up from his balls and shot out through his limbs like a firework exploding in the night sky, causing him to roar with the intensity. His body was alive with the shimmers of pleasure as she milked him for his release. As he finally slowed the thrusts of his hips, he pulled out of her and removed the French Letter he'd donned, tossing it into a nearby waste bin.

Needing a moment or ten to recover, he scooped her into his arms, ignoring her protests, and deposited her on the bed where he joined her. Moments later, they were snuggled under the covers. Her breathing slowed, and he let his own eyes drift closed.

Chapter Four

All around Amelia, the smells of sex, sweat, and leather permeated the air while loud moans of excitement mingled with the deep cries of pleasure-pain. Despite all that was occurring, her mind couldn't help but wander to her recent encounter with a mysterious masked man. It had been lovely to shed the accouterments of her trade and merely be with a man. The snap of a whip slicing through the air punctuated the sounds and jerked her attention back to the present. "Careful, Cat. You don't want to cut the man open," Amelia cautioned her apprentice in an indistinct murmur that most occupants of The Market's dungeon would miss.

Cat shot her an apologetic glance as she pulled her whip in to her side. "Yes, Mistress Lash."

A loud moan carried from across the room, drawing Amelia's attention. One of the ladies of The Market was on her knees, sucking a man's cock as another of the ladies set clamps on his nipples. With a soft sigh of ennui, Amelia forced her focus to remain on her apprentice.

She needed Cat to find her inner control. She knew how to wield a whip, but she clearly had yet to tap into that well of self-control that she needed to have to truly become a Mistress. To be able to own the client body and soul.

"Please, mistress, more. I need more," the man chained to the wall in front of them pleaded.

Amelia watched as Cat redoubled her efforts, letting the whip fly in steadier, more frequent bursts. After a few more moments of letting her attempt to service the client, Amelia finally stopped her. "Enough, Cat, he's had enough."

"No mistress, please don't stop," he cried from where he was chained to the wall. "Truly, I need more."

Amelia strode over to where the man leaned into the wall and looked closely at the crisscross of red welts on his back. "No, you've had enough for the night." Glancing back at Cat, she nodded toward the door. "Go see if Simone is around. What he needs now are her tender mercies."

With a nod, Cat stepped out of the dungeon and went to fetch the woman who was to be waiting nearby. When Amelia released the man from the manacles holding him up along the wall, his knees sagged.

"Please, Mistress, just a few more strokes. I promise I deserve them." The pleading whine from a man she knew to be tenth in line to the crown made her weary.

"No, your time in the dungeon is at an end for this evening. Let Simone take care of you. She'll see that you get exactly what you need."

A moment later, Cat reappeared with Simone in tow. Each of them stretched one of his arms over their shoulders and helped the man walk gingerly away from where he'd been chained up for his punishment. As the trio moved away, Amelia looked around the room and took in the sights and sounds around her. The gray stone walls were interrupted periodically by a body that was secured either to the wall or to some implement like a St. Andrews cross. Men and women filled the space, though it was mostly the men who were the willing captives of the women.

It was strange to realize that the very place that once made her happy, no longer touched her in that way. The joy of fulfilling someone's needs and the pleasure of a job well done had lost their luster. Closing her eyes, she inhaled sharply and tried to shake off her melancholy. Without a second look, she followed Cat and Simone's path from the room.

She was done for the night since this had been her last scheduled client. Perhaps she'd send a note to her new lover and see if he was available. Being alone wouldn't do this evening, but she had no interest in servicing any customers. Though she had much to consider with regard to Cat and her own nebulous future. As she headed upstairs to her chamber, she pondered the idea of walking away from The Market and everything that she had built over the years. When she had walked into the brothel, she'd been a naïve girl desperate for work, with no identification papers and a dangerous secret.

Only two of those things had changed.

Walking into her room, she looked about the chamber and realized that even with the fine silks and satins, the touches of gold here and there, and the beautiful gowns hanging in her wardrobe, she was still missing the most important thing. Love.

She reached into a drawer beneath her skivvies and intimate apparel and pulled out a gold locket. For a moment, she merely stared at the intricate filigree details, the delicate scrollwork that curved around the edges. Then she opened it and peered at the familiar faces of a man and a woman. Her heart seized as she allowed her memories to flood in, and then a tear slipped silently down her cheek.

On a sharply drawn breath, she snapped the locket closed and stuffed the jewelry back in her drawer. She could not dwell on a past long forgotten. Instead, she focused on her future. One that promised her a life in a small cottage somewhere near the sea. A place where the wind was as brisk as it was refreshing and where there was no one to give orders, no one to whip.

She wasn't greedy; she just wanted some place tucked away where she could live out the rest of her days. She'd long since given up the idea that she might one day go home. Might one day seek justice for her parents. And love? There was no possibility of love when her life was a tangle of lies and secrets.

With a twinge of regret, she pushed such wasted thoughts aside and busied herself with removing her leather corset and breaches. A soft knock at the door sounded, and she quickly slipped on a sacque gown. "Come in," she called out.

The door opened, and Cat slipped into the room. She'd expected such a visit. Cat often sought her out after a session with a client. "Mistress Lash, I wished to speak to you about my progress."

"Of course," Amelia sat down and motioned for Cat to join her. "You've come far in four months. Though you still have work to do. You are more than competent in the technicalities of wielding the whip. You know how hard to strike, and you know at what interval to do so as well. Where you need to focus is on judging a man's tolerance."

"I listened to his moans, and I watched his physical reaction. What did I miss?" Cat's big blue eyes pleaded with her for an answer.

"You forgot to listen to yourself. You allowed his words to sway your judgment."

Cat considered her words for a moment. "I suppose you're correct. I allowed him to sway me. He seemed so desperate for more punishment. I didn't want to deny him what he needed."

"That's just it, Cat. You are the one who should determine his needs. His sole decision is to place his trust in your hands. To give his power to you so that his burden may be lightened, even if only for a short time. Your problem is that you lack confidence. That's where you're coming up short. If *you* don't believe that you're in control, then how is the man chained to the wall supposed to? You have to know that you can give him everything that he needs when he needs it. Even before he knows he needs it. And that means knowing when he is taking what you are giving, possibly begging for more, because he believes it pleases you. Not because it fulfills his own needs." Amelia fell silent and waited for her apprentice to digest what she'd shared.

Cat tensed up and then rose from her seat and commenced pacing. "I understand what you are saying, Mistress Lash, but *how* do I gain that confidence? Where do I find such certainty?"

Amelia smiled gently. "That is something we shall have to discover. Every Mistress is different in terms of where they gain their confidence. Mine came from a need to make my way in this world without relying on anyone else. My mentor's came from the knowledge that she was deeply loved by her parents and that, in their eyes, she was capable of anything. We shall endeavor to discover the source of yours."

Cat's chin trembled as she halted and drew a shuddering breath. "Yes, Mistress Lash."

Amelia rose and placed her hands on the younger woman's shoulders. "Cat, it will come in time. You've learned quickly, more than quickly. But it takes time to gain the competence to allow yourself to be truly in control and to break free of decades of ingrained training that a woman is the weaker sex."

Cat nodded. "I understand, thank you."

"Very well. Go and rest; try to have a good evening. As I said, you've made excellent progress, and you will continue to do so." Amelia pulled her in for a brief hug and then released her.

Cat attempted a smile before she slipped away.

Alone again, Amelia looked around the room and noticed a note waiting on her table. She crossed the space and picked it up. She immediately recognized the feminine scrawl on the outside of the message. Another note from Her Grace, the Duchess of Shropshire. Ros was a client at one time—someone she had, for a moment, hoped might become her protégé—and someone she now considered a friend. Of course, when they met, she had merely been Mrs. Rosalind Smith. But then she went and married one of the Lustful Lords, Lord Flintshire—Amelia's favorite of the group, if she was honest. To everyone's surprise, shortly after their wedding, Lord Flintshire's father, the Duke of Shropshire, had died of a fatty heart. Amelia opened the missive.

My dearest Amelia,

I hope my note finds you well once again. Flint and I would like to invite you to an intimate dinner tomorrow night. We are officially out of deep mourning and are in much need of a little company and good cheer. We hope to see you at eight o'clock.

Your Friend,

Ros.

Amelia considered the informal invitation and, for a moment, thought to decline. It was already outrageous that a lady, let alone a Duchess, should deign to correspond with her. But a dinner invitation? It seemed a line the Ton would not tolerate being crossed. But then she realized that a night of normal activities away from The Market might be good for her. More and more, she was having difficulty staying focused during work hours. Mostly because all she wanted was to see her masked lover again, but the urge to flee remained a low hum beneath it all. Perhaps unsurprisingly, it seemed her life was destined to be punctuated by a series of escape plots. Would she be as successful this time as she was the last?

Chapter Five

March 1863

Lucifer walked up the front steps of his brother's home, still a little astounded that he was currently hanging on the fringes of polite society. Through an accident of birth, he had a half-brother who had recently been promoted from the Marquess of Flintshire to the Duke of Shropshire, merely because his father passed away and left the title to him. Of course, that same man who died was also Lucifer's father, which made him a duke's by-blow. But that was not something he often acknowledged in any fashion.

With a sharp rap of the knocker on the door, he made his somewhat belated presence known. The butler opened it and admitted him quickly. As the man took his coat, he concluded he was perhaps a bit later than he realized after hearing multiple voices in the front parlor. He paused and sighed. He was quite certain when he'd read the invitation; the invite said that it was an intimate dinner. An intimate dinner—not a soiree—and yet, he heard voices. Many voices. For a moment, he considered taking back his coat, retreating to his apartments above his gambling hell, and hiding for the remainder of the night.

He was in no mood to be entertained or, worse, having to be entertaining for others. But just as he made his decision, Flint appeared. "Lucifer, you've finally arrived."

He ignored the comment, not yet resigned to his fate for the evening. "How are you, Flint?"

"Much better now that I can shed this farcical display of deep mourning and socialize with friends again." Flint grinned.

"Yes, well, no one said you had to actually honor such social dogma. I certainly didn't bother."

Flint snorted. "Can you imagine how the matrons who rule over London society would receive such blatant disregard for the proprieties? Had I served anything less than the minimally acceptable sentence, they would have never allowed myself or my wife into another ballroom again."

Lucifer let one brow drift up. "Would such an outcome truly be so hideous?"

With a chuckle, Flint slapped Lucifer on the back and attempted to steer him into the parlor. "If you would have had the gumption to explain to my wife why she was barred from polite society, then you are a braver man than I."

Lucifer refused to budge.

"Is something amiss?" Flint looked back at him.

"I recall your invitation suggesting this would be a minor affair. It sounds as though you've a herd of cattle housed in your front parlor."

Flint snorted. "While I believe most of my guests would object to such a characterization, I did not mislead you. This is a small gathering of my closest friends. It seems that in the last few years, my circle has rather expanded from the Lustful Lords to include their ladies and a few other staunch friends, such as Lord and Lady Heartfield."

"Nevertheless, I was expecting something less...well, just less. I am in no mood to socialize." Lucifer glowered at his brother, allowing his annoyance full rein.

"Well, be that as it may, you will have to explain this to my Duchess, and I caution you she is far more stalwart in the face of opposition than I."

As they entered the room, Lucifer glanced around to see who else had been included in the invitation. He, of course, recognized Lord and Lady Stonemere, Lord and Lady Brougham, Lord and Lady Wolfington, and of course, Lords Lincolnshire and Dunmere. The infamous Lustful Lords, though most of them were far less infamous now that they were married. He also spotted Lord and Lady Heartfield, as promised. Sitting next to Ros, Flint's wife, was a stunning creature with midnight dark hair and eyes the color of a swirling London fog. Gray was far too tepid a description. Feeling compelled to know who the woman was, Lucifer strode over to his hostess. "Your Grace, it is, as always, a pleasure to be included in such an"—he cast a glance around the room and let one corner of his mouth lift—"*intimate* gathering."

Ros tilted her head and smiled. "Do cease with the Your Grace-ing. I'm beginning to feel like an old woman. And of all my guests, had I told you there would be anyone beyond myself and your brother, you would not have come. So, you have no one to blame but yourself for being surprised."

Lucifer laughed, a dark sound that had been known to curdle men's bellies. "A direct hit, my lady. I'm afraid I cannot dispute what you say. Perhaps you might soothe my battle wounds by introducing me to your lovely companion?"

The mysterious beauty next to Ros snorted. "I'm sure you must know who I am. If not by sight, then by reputation, since we move in similar circles."

Lucifer paused and considered. Again, there was something faintly familiar about her—no, he certainly would know if he'd met such a stunning woman. "Tell me who you are, and we can compare notes."

A feral gleam shone in her gray eyes even as she smiled and held out her hand. "Mistress Lash at your service Mr. Lucifer."

Stunned by the information, he took her hand and kissed it. "I feel it is some dastardly plot at work that we have not heretofore met. But I am glad that this oversight has been corrected."

"Really? And why is that precisely?" She looked one part curious and two parts skeptical.

Thrown off, Lucifer stumbled for a moment before he recovered well enough, or so he hoped. "Why, because now I shall have the opportunity to get to know you better. You, your story, intrigues me."

And just like that, Lucifer watched as dark steel doors slammed shut in her gaze. While her smile remained, her face seemingly as pleasant as before he spoke, it was hard not to see that she had retreated entirely from him.

"Yes, well, I'm sure you would find my story—as you put it—a rather dull and narcoleptic tale." She turned to Ros and inquired, "Now, you were telling me where you found this delightful gown you're wearing."

Lucifer blinked, rather in shock, at both her sudden retreat and his own obvious repudiation.

"Amelia!" Ros whispered in shock as she glanced from Mistress Lash back to him in obvious confusion as to what had happened.

He was somewhat comforted to know he was not the only one befuddled by such rudeness. "Excuse me, ladies. I fear I have worn out my welcome here."

Mistress Lash—Amelia—refused to even look at him in acknowledgment, but Ros nodded even as she looked distressed at her friend's behavior. The dark-haired beauty was quite the puzzle. The question remained, was it one he wished to solve?

Amelia breathed a sigh of relief as Mr. Frank Lucifer stalked away. If he'd stared any longer, she feared he would look past her fashionable clothing and perfectly coiffed hair to see the masked wench he'd had in his arms, or perhaps the saucy maid he'd bent over a desk, or even the harem girl he'd bedded amidst a pile of silk pillows. Regardless of which version of her he recognized, it would all lead to the same problem. Her identity would be revealed, and everything would change.

Watching him from the corner of her eye to ensure he stayed where he belonged, she could acknowledge that the man was far too handsome in a dark and edgy sort of way. Certainly not the classical appeal that Viscount Wolfington offered or the golden beauty of the Earl of Brougham. Instead, Lucifer and his brother shared the same devilish ruggedness that suggested they would be equally as comfortable brawling in a dark alley as sipping tea in a drawing room. His neatly trimmed beard—the one she'd felt against the sensitive skin of her inner thighs—did nothing to soften his rough edges.

"Amelia, what was the meaning of such rudeness?" Ros stared at her, clearly shocked by her behavior.

She inhaled slowly, grappling for some reasonable explanation, or at least one she was willing to provide. Finding none, she shrugged. "Have you never taken an instant dislike to a person for no apparent reason?"

Ros blinked. "I cannot say that I have, well, perhaps, with the exception of my sister's dead husband and stepson. Surely, you are not comparing Lucifer with that lot?"

Feeling decidedly uncomfortable, she continued to try to explain. "Of course not, but the man did put me on edge. All that ridiculous fawning just because we move in the same circles. I am under no obligation to tell him anything about myself."

"True, though you could have been a trifle less cutting in sending him on his way." Ros glanced in the direction the man had retreated.

Amelia shrugged. "Perhaps, but I seriously doubt his ego was so severely damaged. Men of his ilk rarely want for confidence."

"That may be true, but he is a guest in my home and my brother-in-law. Please do try to keep a civil tongue in your head when dressing him down."

Amelia blushed furiously. Her friend was, of course, correct. She was not in the public salon of The Market but instead was a guest in someone's home. "Mea culpa, I forgot my whereabouts and, apparently, my manners. I shall tender my apologies to him shortly."

Ros looked at her queerly for a moment and then nodded in satisfaction. "Thank you. He really is a good sort. Remember all he did to help me with Flint, including risking their newly found relationship."

Amelia smiled despite the panic that surged from deep within her. Lucifer was, without question, a dangerous man to have fixated on you. She hadn't known who he was when she'd taken him as a lover, but the moment he'd stepped into the parlor, she had recognized him instantly. Mask or no mask, he was a hard man to ignore. When he had approached them, her heart had raced, her palms had grown damp, and the need to leap from where she sat and run away grew overwhelming. Ignoring all of her instincts—the very ones that had kept her alive and helped her build her client list—she'd stayed seated for fear that running would draw further attention to herself. It was the same reason she gamely smiled at Ros and pressed on with the evening. "Now, do tell me where this dress was acquired."

A short while later, dinner was served. To Amelia's everlasting relief, Lucifer was seated at the opposite end of the table from her, though she was sure she could feel his dark gaze resting on her throughout the service. Towards the end of the meal, a footman delivered a note to him that caused him to rise and slip from the dining room. Determined to make her apology as promised, she excused herself and followed him into Lord Shropshire's study. She closed the door on a soft snick and turned to find him sitting at the duke's desk.

He set the pen he'd been using down. "Are you lost, Mistress Lash? I believe you passed the ladies' retiring room a few doors back."

"Not at all. I know precisely where I am." She resisted the urge to roll her eyes. "I wished to speak with you for a moment."

He stood up from the desk and moved around it to rest his hip on the corner as he crossed his arms over his chest. "Do you now? That certainly wasn't the case earlier. In fact, you dismissed me quite readily, as I recall."

"Indeed, that is precisely what I wished to speak to you about." She licked her lips, her mouth feeling suddenly parched. It was exceedingly difficult not to notice how his biceps bulged beneath his coat as his arms remained crossed. He was no slothful peer of the realm who lazed about all day. Mr. Lucifer was a man of action, and she should know, having seen him divested of every stitch of clothing. "I wanted—"

"Unfortunately, mademoiselle, I am rather busy at the moment. Perhaps we could have what I am sure is to be a riveting chat another time?" Despite his words indicating he was occupied, he remained exactly as he was, indolently leaning against the desk as though this was his home.

Amelia's temper surged so ferociously and without warning that she nearly lost control of it. That was something she had not done since she was a girl. Clamping down hard on her anger, she tried to smile, but it felt more like a grimace. "I'm sure you can spare me a few moments of your precious time."

"Quite the opposite. I am needed back at my place of business." Lucifer straightened up and strode forward as though he would leave.

Incensed, and thoroughly infuriated at the man's rudeness, she stepped in front of him and slapped a hand on his chest to stay his departure. Though her hand merely rested on dark superfine which covered silk and linen beneath it, she could not ignore either the heat emanating from his body nor the firmly packed muscles of his chest. Muscles she was all too familiar with. Shaking her head to clear it, she pressed harder when he made to continue. "My lord—"

He laughed. "Well, you've certainly missed the mark there, m'dear. I am no lord."

She snorted. "A simple mistake with the pompous way you're behaving, as though a mere woman could ever have anything of import to say."

"Pompous? I thought I was doing the gentlemanly thing and removing my presence, which seemed to so offend you earlier."

"Bloody fucking hell," Amelia cursed under her breath.

"My, my. Such un-ladylike language," he said as his gaze seemed to drop to her lips.

"That would stand to reason, as I am not now, nor have I ever been a lady. Now, cease your prattling, so I may say my piece and let you get on with your ever-so-important business." Her hand remained on his chest as she tried to find the words she had intended to say. "I wanted to apologize for my earlier behavior. It was rude of me."

Her heart pounded beneath her breast as he took a step forward. She immediately retreated two steps backward, which had the unfortunate result of separating her hand from his rather impressive chest.

"I agree. It was quite rude of you." He advanced three steps, causing her to dance back another step. Then he took two more, and she found herself pressed against the door of the study. He closed the distance between them, crushing her skirt as he captured her mouth with his.

Her hands made contact with his chest once more, but instead of restraining him, she bunched the superfine in her hands and pulled him closer. Their tongues tangled as each fought for control of the kiss. Heart still racing, she finally surrendered to him, letting him set the pace. The man was a masterful kisser, the way he reached up and angled her head just so, allowing him to sweep deeper into her mouth. The way his body pressed against hers in a silent domination that let her know who was in charge. All of it, combined with his woody yet musky scent, befuddled her brain as her knees turned to aspic. The man went to her head when they were fully naked. She'd no idea he could be just as intoxicating fully clothed. When he finally withdrew, she gasped for air even as he did the same. A slow grin spread across his kiss-swollen lips. "If this is how you will apologize, please feel free to be rude to whatever degree you wish."

Amelia inhaled sharply. "Now, who is being rude?"

"I was merely appreciating your communication skills."

She growled. "You took that kiss. It was not part of my apology. Now step away, you overbearing oaf."

Lucifer took one step back, allowing cool air to rush in and relieve the heat in her cheeks. Whether as a result of that kiss or her renewed anger mattered little at the moment. With that space, she whirled around and pulled the door open. She was already in the hall when she heard him retort, "Do not deny you enjoyed it, Mistress Lash. There is plenty more of that if you wish to seek it out."

She stormed down the hall and ducked into the ladies' retiring room. She had known that man was dangerous.

He kissed like a sinner and was just as unrepentant as one. Seeing him again at The Market was too risky now that they had met outside of their arrangement. Not to mention, she found this version of him rather disagreeable, not that she was any more pleasant. But he was far too curious about her. If he realized he already knew her, there would be no stopping him from nosing around in her life, and that was the last thing she needed right now.

Chapter Six

How did one tell their not-so-anonymous lover that their time together had come to an end? That it was time for both of them to move on? Amelia stared at the blank page and considered. She could send the message to Madame de Pompadour, but that would be the coward's way out. She at least owed him a direct send-off, not one delivered verbally via a third party.

Dear Sir,

I want you to know that the past month has been exceptional. You have been the single most attentive lover I have ever had the pleasure of being with. Unfortunately, due to circumstances beyond my control, I am unable to continue our arrangement. I shall always regret not having more time with you, but it is time to part ways.

Regretfully,

A Masked Lady

She sanded the letter, sealed it, and headed downstairs to give the missive to Madame. Her hands trembled as she knocked on the door and waited. A few moments later, the door opened to reveal Madame du Pompadour swathed in an elegant sacque made of a vibrant blue silk adorned with ruffles at the hem and cuffs. It was loosely closed with a matching sash at her waist that left her corset exposed in the front. With her hair loosely gathered over one shoulder and tied with a matching ribbon, she made a fetching picture, should there be any unexpected male callers. "You are certainly up rather early this morning."

Amelia shrugged. It would have been early if she had been to sleep. "Unfortunately, rest eluded me as I worried over an issue."

"And you've come to a conclusion on this issue?" Madame opened the door wider and waved her in.

"I have. I am ending my agreement with Sir. I discovered his identity last night and realized that we cannot continue on without him realizing who I am." Amelia licked her lips in an attempt to moisten them as she sat down in a leather club chair.

Madame reclined on her divan near the fire. "I fail to understand why your identity is an issue."

Her employer was one of the few people who knew Amelia's true identity. "He met me last night as Mistress Lash at the home of the new Duke and Duchess of Shropshire. He was intrigued by me, even indicated he wanted to learn more about me. I cannot afford for him to be so curious, and I fear if he realizes I am his masked lover, it will only increase his curiosity."

"A reasonable assumption. Though I warn you, calling off the agreement may be equally provoking. Lucifer is not a man who enjoys being thwarted." Madame tilted her head and lifted her brows in emphasis.

Amelia tried not to crush the neatly penned letter in her hands as her nerves jangled. "I feel confident that I managed to convince him I am too much of a shrew to be of interest." Or, she had until they kissed in the library. Her greatest fear was that their kiss was just enough to renew his interest.

"Very well, I assume that letter you are holding contains his *congé*."

Amelia hesitated. Was Madame correct? Would he be angry over her cutting ties and search her out? She pressed her lips together and considered her other option, revealing herself to him and asking him not to pry. Would he honor her request? Somehow, she thought he wouldn't. As a man accustomed to getting what he wanted, there was likely no scenario in which he didn't pursue her story. She was probably doomed no matter what she chose. She sighed. It may only put off the inevitable, but it felt like the most proactive step she could take at the moment. "It does. But I need to ask you to keep my identity from him. I am certain he will ask you who I am."

"As am I. But, of course, I shall not betray your confidence." Madame held out her hand.

"Thank you. I apologize if he becomes difficult." Amelia rose and stepped across the space to hand her the letter.

Madam snorted. "What man isn't difficult? I dare say they teach them how to be just so in childhood because I have yet to meet one who isn't."

Amelia smiled. "Perhaps you are correct. Nevertheless, thank you."

Madame huffed and shooed her out. "Go, you look tired and must get some rest before this evening."

She went to the door and exited quietly, hoping to avoid any of the house's patrons who may yet be lingering after the previous night's debauchery. The letter was safely in Madame's hands, and Amelia knew she would see it was sent to Lucifer through the house messenger.

Lucifer took the stack of correspondence from Gordie and shuffled through the pile. There were the odd invitations to certain fringe soirees and, of course, the usual bills that resulted from running a business. One particular piece immediately stood out with its familiar feminine scrawl and unusual thickness. He opened the letter, obviously addressed to him, and found a second letter addressed to Sir.

His gut clenched.

He carefully opened the paper and read the words. It was short, rather succinct. And undoubtedly, it was an end to the sliver of happiness he'd found over the last month. Bloody hell! He reached into his waistcoat and pulled out his pocket watch. Opening it, he noted it was three o'clock in the afternoon. No doubt Madame du Pompadour would receive visitors by then. He suspected she had sent it over at just such a time because she anticipated his resultant visit. Rising from his desk, he snatched the offending letter up, folded it, and shoved it in his coat pocket. Striding from his office, he found Gordie hovering near the door in case he should be needed.

"I'm headed to The Market. I shouldn't be long, but there are several supply shipments expected shortly." He moved briskly along the gallery with Gordie, pacing him easily, despite his bulk.

"I'll see to the shipments, Mr. Lucifer," Gordie assured him.

Fifteen minutes later, Lucifer sat in Madame du Pompadour's office inside The Market. "I'll not dally with my query. Who is she?"

Madame smiled indulgently. "Mr. Lucifer, I'm afraid you already know the answer to your question."

"Madame, we both know I shall have her name before this is all said and done." He eyed her with resolve.

"That may be, but it will not be information attained from myself or anyone in my employ. Not unlike the anonymity I promised you when you made your initial request, I have also promised her not to reveal her identity to you. Were I to betray that promise, and word should spread—and it would—I would lose my extremely valuable clientele. They come to The Market because discretion is paramount among our many services." She eyed him with warm eyes full of understanding but also a core of steely determination.

Lucifer glared at her. He knew his face would be a mask of demand tinged with threat. But he did not care. He simply wanted her name. "I shall have her name."

Stauncher men had folded under the very same glare he'd leveled at her, but Madame merely smiled and shook her head. "As I said, that may well be true, but it will not be from me. Is there aught else I may do for you today?"

Thwarted for the second time in less than twenty-four hours, and not liking it one whit more now than he had the night before, he stalked from The Market. He would have her name. Nothing less would do.

An hour later, Gordie had popped his head into his office. "Mr. Lucifer, Perkins is here to see you as requested."

He'd been working with his head down, trying to clear the stack of correspondence on his desk since returning from

The Market. It seemed an endless battle at times. "Send him in."

He didn't bother to look up until Perkins had settled into the chair across the desk from him.

"You wished to speak to me?" The man sat across from him, looking as unremarkable as always. Dirty blond hair, gray eyes. He was about five foot ten inches in height and had an average build that was neither too wide nor too narrow. He was truly an everyman that could meld into and out of most environments without anyone taking note. It had proved to be a profitable skill for him.

"I did. I am looking for a woman, and I am afraid I know little about her. She has blonde hair that I am certain was not her true color. She is of unusual height for a woman, nearly as tall as yourself. And she has grey eyes... I think. In fact, she may be naturally dark-haired, because her eyebrows seemed rather dark compared to the blonde hair she wore the few times I saw her. She is a curvy woman. I'd dare say she could skip a corset and still have that luscious silhouette."

The man across from him coughed and stopped taking notes. "No name?"

Lucifer shook his head.

"So, no name. Any particularly unique features? A scar? A birthmark?" Perkins sat with his pencil poised to note any new information.

He sighed. "Not that I noticed. Though her arms were quite toned."

Perkins made a note but shook his head. "Where did you meet her?"

"The Market." Lucifer waited for some comment or judgment from the man across from him.

"I assume you've spoken with Madame du Pompadour?" He looked up quickly from his notebook.

Lucifer ground his teeth. "Of course. She refuses to reveal the woman's identity, though she knows it."

The man nodded. "Excellent. Do you have anything else you can provide me in the way of guidance?"

"Just this letter." Lucifer pushed the note from his mysterious lover across the desk to Perkins.

He opened the letter, read it, and then refolded it and slid it back across the desk. "I do not see any information of note in that document."

"No, there wasn't anything." Lucifer resisted the urge to pinch the bridge of his nose.

Perkins snapped his notebook closed and stood. "I shall begin my inquiries, though I don't expect this matter to take long to resolve. You will hear from me as soon as I have something to share."

Lucifer nodded. "I appreciate both your discretion and haste in dealing with this." He would know who she was, there simply was no other option. He was too far off from purging her from his mind, let alone his fantasies.

Amelia paced her room and looked at the clock on her mantel for the twentieth time in the last hour. Cat was late, and she was never late. The one time she had missed work, she'd sent her brother with word of her illness. This was not like her very punctual and very responsible apprentice.

Frustrated, she strode downstairs herself, no longer content to send a maid to ask Philippe if he'd seen or heard from her. She found Madame's right-hand man milling about in the public salon, keeping an eye on the early arrivals. "There you are. Have you still not heard from Cat?"

Philippe shook his head. "I'm afraid not, Mistress Lash. But, as I said, I shall send word if and when I do hear from her."

Amelia fisted her hands in her skirts. "The moment you hear from her, please. I don't care if I am with a client or not—I wish to know she is well." There was little else she could do at this point, so she returned upstairs and readied herself for her first client of the evening. She needed to ensure her whip arm was warm and ready to service those who needed her.

Six hours and three clients later, she was dismayed to realize Philippe had not sent word to her. She'd checked with the kitchen staff to be sure a messenger hadn't slipped in the back way, but it was still a no. Nerves had her stomach twisting as she realized she would likely not know anything more until she could visit Cat's apartment in the morning. On a curse, she returned to her room. Worried. Wondering. Where could Cat be?

Chapter Seven

April 1863

Amelia Ketting, better known as Mistress Lash, walked crisply down the foggy London sidewalk as she huddled into her cloak. It may have been spring, according to the calendar, but mother nature cared not a jot. Neither did Amelia. She was too worried about Cat to care one whit for the weather. Her apprentice had left The Market the morning before, as usual, to return to her accommodations in Lambeth. The young woman had her mother to take care of and a brother who needed both her income and her presence.

But last night, Cat had not appeared for work as normal. That left Amelia to handle all of her scheduled customers for the evening—damnation, her arm was weary from wielding the whip all night. She had certainly become accustomed to Cat doing more of the work these days, which left her own arm in less than peak condition. But the real question was, what happened to Cat?

Brow creased with worry, Amelia headed down the street as she tried to imagine what might have prevented Cat from arriving at The Market as expected. She hoped she had not fallen ill... or worse. In the beginning of their apprenticeship, she'd worried about her walking home in the wee hours of the morning alone. But she had assured Amelia that she was used to the walk and far too wily to be caught unawares. Her gut clenched into a knot. *Please let that be true.*

Amelia finally found the building where she remembered the little family had let rooms and stepped inside. The walls were dingy with age, dirt, and coal smoke. The cramped staircase up to the next level made the narrow hallway feel even smaller. According to what she knew, Cat lived on the second floor.

Picking up her skirts, Amelia carefully climbed the creaking stairs. When one board wobbled beneath her foot, she pushed past her disdain for the filthy surroundings and clutched at the banister as though it might save her. In reality, it was far more likely to collapse and pull her off the stairs. Either outcome seemed reasonable, all things considered. Stable once again, she climbed the rest of the stairs and found herself confronted with four doors along the hallway, two on each side. Determined to find out what had become of Cat, she stepped up to the first door on the right. She knocked twice sharply and waited. After a few moments, she heard shuffling inside, and then the door opened to reveal a stooped-over, old man who could barely look up to see her. "Eh? What is it you want?" he demanded rather than asked.

Startled, Amelia stammered a moment. "I'm looking for Catherine Stevens."

"No one by that name lives here." The slamming of his door in Amelia's face punctuated his reply.

Well, it seems the nobility do not, in fact, have the market cornered on rudeness. She harumphed and moved to the next door. There, she knocked twice, once again. A neat, though worn-out woman answered the door, opening it only a crack.

A single brown eye assessed Amelia. "I don't have anything to give."

She supposed it was something of a compliment that the woman thought her well enough dressed to solicit donations, but sad that anyone might ask someone living in such a humble establishment for a farthing. Clearly, they needed every ha'penny they could scrape together. "I'm looking for Catherine Stevens."

The door opened a bit wider. "What do you want with the Stevens girl?"

The promise of success spurred Amelia on. "I'm a friend. I haven't seen her in a few days, and I was worried about her. Do you know which flat is hers?"

The woman eyed her warily and then seemed to come to some conclusion that allowed her to point at the door across the hall. "She and her mum live there. But they're good people. Don't need no trouble."

Amelia nodded. "I come only out of concern for a friend." She dared not say an employee because, truly, she was there out of concern for Cat, not her bottom line. "Thank you."

Then she turned and stepped to the third door. Behind her, the other door closed softly. With another firm set of knocks, she waited once more. Again, the door opened a bit, and another single wary eye appeared. This one, blue like Cat's, though cloudier, more worn. "Yes?"

"Mrs. Stevens? I am a friend of Catherine's. I was worried that I did not see her at work yesterday and wanted to stop by to see how she was." Amelia tried to smile warmly in hopes the woman might open the door and even let her in. She hated to air Cat's business in the hallway of her residence.

The door remained ajar, the eye assessing. "Who'd you say you were?"

"I'm Amelia Ketting." She glanced around and lowered her voice. "I'm Mistress Lash at The Market."

"Oh!" The door popped open, revealing a slightly rounder and older version of Cat. "You're the Mistress what's teaching Cat to be like you? To make all that money without having to spread her legs?"

Amelia smiled, "Indeed I am. May I come in?"

Mrs. Stevens blushed and swung the door open wide. "My apologies. I must've forgot my manners. Please come in."

Amelia stepped into what was a tidy, though rundown, room with a makeshift kitchen in one corner. Across the room was another door that sat closed. "I was hoping to find Cat. I was a bit worried about her when she didn't come to The Market last night. It's not like her not to appear without forewarning me or sending word by her brother."

The woman sighed and suddenly appeared worried. "I had hoped you'd come with word of Cat. When she didn't come home yesterday morning like she normally does, I had hoped she'd stayed with you for some reason."

Amelia somehow choked down her initial panic. Cat hadn't come home? But she'd left The Market! She had checked with everyone, including the butler on duty, and all had seen her leave. Worry snaked through her as she composed herself. "Well, I'm not sure where she is. But I do promise you that I shall find her."

The poor woman smiled sadly. "That is very kind of you."

"Not at all. I've always worried about her traipsing back and forth in the wee hours of the morning, but she was determined to be here for George and yourself. Do you have need of anything before I go? I know Catherine brings her earnings home to you."

The woman shook her head. "We'll manage." And then her stomach rumbled loud and long, as if in protest at her words. Straightening her shoulders, Amelia reached into her reticule and produced a few pounds. "Please, consider it a loan until Cat returns safely. I know she'd worry about you two under these circumstances."

The woman reached her gnarled hand out for the money and then hesitated.

"Please, it will make me feel better knowing I've done something for you and George in Cat's absence. And when she returns, we shall sort out repayment and whatnot." Over her dead body. But Mrs. Stevens didn't need to know that.

"Very well. Thank you kindly, my lady." The woman took the money and tucked it away into the folds of her skirts.

Amelia repressed the urge to correct her. She was, after all, no lady. Certainly not by title, and truthfully not by social standards, no matter which side of the Atlantic Ocean she stood on these days. "Thank you. And I shall, of course, let you know at once if I find her."

"Thank you." The woman nodded again.

Amelia turned toward the door and started to leave but stopped short. "You wouldn't happen to know of any other places she might have gone?"

"No. She is a good girl. She goes to work, comes home and sleeps, and then takes care of me and Georgie as best she can. If she'd gone anywhere, it would be to the market, but Georgie usually goes with her." The woman said, the small bit of hope in her eyes filtering away.

"Yes, I didn't imagine she was gallivanting about much. Thank you." Amelia nodded and left the small flat.

Truly worried now, she hurried down the stairs and outside to hail a hansom cab. It was time to get the authorities involved.

*

Still fretting over Cat, Amelia walked through the front door of a bustling Scotland Yard. Inside, the police headquarters teemed with men rushing back and forth. She stood there as people passed her by, a few even bumping her shoulder as they went.

Warily, she approached the front desk even as she dodged men all but running past. The towering wooden desk loomed over her. Behind it sat a rail-thin desk clerk who looked more harried than a woman with six children hanging on her skirts. "Excuse me, sir. I'd like to report a missing person."

The man continued to scribble and then paused to stamp a page before shifting it from one pile to another on his desk without responding.

Amelia took a deep breath and once more attempted to get his attention. "Excuse me, sir. I'd like to report a missing person," she said louder.

His head jerked up, then he looked over at a rather crowded bench to his right and pointed. "Please wait over there. A detective will be with you when he can."

She turned and looked in the direction he indicated, only to see the crowded bench. With a resigned sigh, she trudged over and squeezed herself down onto a seat to wait. It was a good thing she'd opted for a less extravagant day dress for her visit to Lambeth. A dress with full crinolines would not have permitted her to stand in such a crowded place, let alone fit on the bench she'd been directed to. As the hands of the clock moved slowly past each of the numbers, she wondered if anyone in the entire building had time to look for a missing person—let alone the interest.

After half an hour had passed, she stood and started to look down the hallways to see if she could see anyone who might be able to help her. But every man who rushed by appeared busy and otherwise occupied. The desk clerk spied her and said, "Miss, you have to sit down and wait. You can't just go wandering off."

Frustrated, she turned and returned to her seat, crammed against two other people who seemed rather worse for wear. Again, she waited and watched the hands of the clock tick by. Time seemed to slow down as her worry for Cat ramped up. Finally, after another half an hour had passed, she grew frustrated and stood once again.

This time she stopped the first man that walked by. "Excuse me, are you a detective?"

He looked up as if surprised there was a woman in Scotland Yard, let alone speaking to him. "Yes, I am," he answered hesitantly, as though afraid of what she may do at such an admission.

She pasted on as pleasant a smile as she could muster. "Excellent. I'd like to report a missing person." He stared at her for a moment. Almost as though confused by her words as contrasted by her smile. "I'm sure the desk clerk can help you shortly."

Her eyes narrowed, and her smile faded. "The desk clerk told me I needed to wait to speak to a detective."

"Oh, well, then... I suppose you'll have to wait." And he started to move forward until she reached out and pressed a hand to his arm, stopping him.

"Sir, I don't know you. But I do know that my friend is missing. And I need someone to help find her. Please, can you not take my report?"

He hesitated and then nodded. "Of course, my apologies. Follow me."

A few moments later, she found herself seated next to a desk piled high with papers. He sat down, pulled out a fresh sheet of paper and a pen, and looked at her. "I'll need the person's name."

"Her name is Catherine Stevens."

"And what is her employment?"

"She's my apprentice."

"And what is your business?"

Amelia looked at him warily. "I work at The Market."

He scribbled the words and then looked up. "The brothel?"

Amelia nodded. "That's the one."

His eyebrows lifted, but he said nothing further. Next, he asked, "How long has she been missing?"

"Two days. She left The Market two days ago and did not show up for work last night."

He set his pen down and looked at her. "So, what you're telling me is that a prostitute didn't show up for work one night?"

Amelia's lips pressed together in annoyance. "What I'm telling you is that my apprentice, who is learning a trade from me that does not include peddling her flesh, did not appear for work on a night when she was expected, and she has never failed to appear before without some form of notification. This is *unusual* behavior. When I checked with her mother, she has not been seen since the night that I saw her last."

The man's face pinched in annoyance. "Madam, really? You can't expect me to believe that this person—that Cat is missing. She's simply holed up with a customer somewhere, or with a friend, or who knows. But she's not really missing. Maybe she didn't want to come back to work anymore, and she didn't want to tell you?"

Amelia shook her head. "No. She would never have done that. She would never leave her mother and her brother, who need her. They depend on her and her income. Only something nefarious would keep her from them."

He spread his hands as though helpless. "I'm afraid there's just nothing I can do for you, ma'am. She's a woman of her own devices, clearly. I would be wasting Scotland Yard's resources, which are limited, by looking for her. If you find something more significant that suggests foul play, then please come back and tell me. But, for now, this is a non-issue for the police. My apologies."

"Unbelievable," Amelia snapped. "You mean to tell me because of what she does for a living, her being missing is of no interest to Scotland Yard? She pays her taxes, just like every other person in the city. She deserves to be treated with respect and looked for."

"I'm sorry, ma'am. I'm afraid there's nothing I can do. If I told my Superintendent that I was looking for a prostitute who's been missing for a mere two days, I would lose my job."

"Bloody hell!" Amelia stood. "I should have known better than to try to come here for help." And with that, she turned and stomped out of the room and out of Scotland Yard.

It seemed nobody was going to help find her friend. Which meant she'd just have to do it herself.

Chapter Eight

Lucifer's heart pounded in his chest as if it might break free at any moment. He held a note from Perkins, indicating he had a name. The man was due to arrive at any moment, and Lucifer wasn't certain he could physically wait. Mindlessly, his fingertips tapped over and over, ring finger, middle finger, index finger. He hated that this woman had such a fierce hold on him. But he knew he needed more time with her to douse his fascination. Perhaps having a name would do what being inside of her had not?

The door of his office swung open and spat out Perkins.

"Sit." He stilled his restless fingers.

"Thank you, Mr. Lucifer." Perkins settled into the chair and pulled out his notepad. "I went back to The Market to see if I could pick up a trail—"

"Her name, Perkins. I don't give a fuck how you found her."

The investigator blinked slowly. "Very well. Her name is Amelia Kettering."

Bloody hell! Of course, she was. He was a bloody fool for not figuring it out right away.

"And?" Lucifer demanded, his thirst for knowledge mixing with his frustration at the relentless need to know more.

"That is her name."

Lucifer growled and leaned forward. "And what else?"

The man looked unruffled, despite Lucifer's threatening stance. "Well, as I was saying, I returned to The Market to see if I could find her trail and after a few discrete inquiries and motivating payments, I discovered that the woman who had made the arrangement with you was none other than Mistress Lash. It took a bit more digging to find that she is also—"

"I bloody well know that Amelia Kettering is Mistress Lash. What else did you find out about her?"

"You merely requested that I discover her identity." The man shrugged.

Failing to hide his disgust at the unusually basic job Perkins had done, he sat back. "Very well. See Gordie, and he will ensure you are compensated for your time."

"Thank you, Mr. Lucifer. Please let me know if I can be of further service." Perkins stood and exited the room as quickly as he'd entered.

Lucifer leaned back in his chair and considered that the very intriguing Mistress Lash was the woman tantalizing his desires. Considering her letter came just after they met and kissed—again, how had he not recognized her then? She had obviously deduced his identity and sought to avoid his discovering hers. The question was, why?

Why did she not want him to know her identity? Why did she wish to avoid him so desperately? Had he done something to offend her, either during one of their interludes or when they met at his brother's dinner party? He couldn't fathom what had driven her to push him away, but he knew one thing. It would not stand. It was time for Amelia to discover just who she was dealing with.

Determined to confront the woman as soon as possible, he stood and headed to The Market once again. A short while later, he was just walking up the front steps of the grand edifice of the brothel when movement out of the corner of his eye drew his attention. He turned to get a better look at the feminine form and was startled to discover it was the very woman he sought. He pulled out his pocket watch and checked the time to be certain he was not mistaken. No, the trusty timepiece reinforced what he knew. It was bloody early for someone in her profession to be dressed and venturing out. Not unlike his staff, the ladies of The Market had a tendency to keep hours that aligned with those of the Ton, which meant seeing her outside at half-past nine in the morning was quite unusual. What could she be about?

Regardless, he was determined to catch up to her and have a chat about what the hell was going on. Walking quickly behind her, he was surprised to discover that, unlike most women with any refinement, and he most certainly counted her among that number, she had a long loping stride that was elegant yet efficient. There was no question that she was a woman in vigorous health, which he supposed must come as a byproduct of her occupation. Having wielded a whip or two in his life, he knew that to do so with the skill she was renowned for required strength and a certain athleticism.

Content to follow her for the moment, he managed to keep her within eyesight as they walked. But to where? He was terribly curious to see where she was going. A quarter of an hour later, he found she had led him to another brothel. How curious.

Amelia stood before Decadent Delights and stared at the door. It was equally as nice as The Market. But she knew the ladies inside were not treated quite as well. Word had gotten to her that one of the ladies of the house was also missing. Determined to find out what she could about her disappearance. She knocked on the door despite the early hour.

A man dressed in livery opened the door and greeted her. "Good morning, madam. How may I help you?"

Amelia hesitated and then decided to press on as she had intended. "My name is Mistress Lash. I've come from The Market, and I wish to speak with Abbess Cordelia about an urgent matter."

The man nodded and opened the door wider. "Please come in and have a seat in our front parlor. I shall speak with the Abbess and see if she's available."

"Thank you." Amelia followed him inside and sat down as directed. Taking in the more modest decor, she took in the simple room, done in soft green with silver and gold accents. As she waited, she continued to ponder the man that she had met only a few weeks ago. It seemed that he was still popping into her head at the most inopportune moments, such as now when she was on the hunt for her missing apprentice. Something about him stuck with her all these weeks. He still stirred her when most men had left her indifferent for years.

Before her mind wandered too far down that path, the door to the parlor opened, and a woman with soft brown hair and dark brown eyes dressed in a silk wrapper entered.

"Good morning, Mistress Lash. I'd apologize for my attire. But as you know, this is rather an early hour for us."

Amelia stood and nodded as the woman entered. "Of course, my apologies for coming by at this hour, but I felt the visit was warranted. You see, my apprentice has gone missing. And I understand that one of the girls from your house, a Lucy Ming, has also gone missing. Is that true?"

The woman nodded. "Indeed. She's been missing for almost a week now. I did attempt to report her at Scotland Yard, to no avail."

Amelia snorted. "I know exactly how that conversation went. As I just recently had it myself."

Abbess Cordelia sighed. "Yes, they don't seem to care very much what happens to us unless we're not here to service their needs."

Amelia nodded. "It does seem that way. Rather disheartening, all things considered. But I fully intend to look into this matter myself and see if I can't find the missing women."

Abbess Cordelia's brows rose. "Is that safe? I fear what you may find."

Amelia shrugged. "No one else is going to do it. And I'm unwilling to allow my apprentice to simply be gone. Her family needs her."

Abbess Cordelia nodded, her eyes soft with understanding. "Very well. You have my support and any information that I may come across."

"Excellent. Can you tell me when you last saw Lucy?"

"Yes, it was about a week ago, on a Monday afternoon. She stepped out before opening hours to collect some new undergarments that she had ordered. She went to pick them up, and she never returned. It was like she vanished."

"Do you know where she went to collect those items?"

"Yes, her modiste is in Bayswater, Mrs. Waterman's, I believe. After, she was going to have lunch at a tavern near there, the Cock and Kitty, the girls tell me."

Amelia nodded. "Yes. I am familiar with the establishment. Thank you very much. I shall be stopping by there to see if anyone knows anything. And I shall keep you apprised of any developments."

"I know we aren't always as supportive of each other when we work in different houses, but I do appreciate you following up on this."

"You're quite welcome."

Amelia headed to the next brothel that she was going to visit, where another girl had supposedly gone missing. Glad that it was a little later in the morning after her rather lengthy visit with Abbess Cordelia, she found herself before The Gilded Lily, which was run by Madam Covington. Repeating the same events as previously, she knocked on the door and was greeted by the butler, who then let her in and directed her to a front parlor. This one decorated in a soft blue with tan and black accents was nearly as nice as The Market's rooms and decor.

After a very brief interlude, Madam Covington joined her, fully dressed for the day. "Good morning, Mistress Lash. How can I be of service?"

Amelia smiled. "I believe I am the one who may be of service. I am in looking into the whereabouts of a number of missing women from our industry. My apprentice is among them, as is Lucy Ming from Decadent Delights. I was told that you also had a girl by the name of Ophelia, who has been missing."

Madam Covington sighed and shook her head. "Ophelia has been located. She was found holed up with one of her customers in a house over in Mayfair. It would seem she decided to take him up on his offer while failing to mention it to me. Of course, the gentleman in question has now been apprised of the fact that he owes me a price for claiming her as his mistress. But that aside, she is in fine fettle, and her whereabouts are known."

"Ah. Well, I suppose that's good news. I'm glad to hear that she's not possibly in danger, as the other ladies potentially are. Thank you for your time. I have a few more houses to visit before my rounds are finished." And with that, she headed off to her next stop.

At each of the three last stops that she made, she discovered that the women that were missing had all been located and their whereabouts accounted for by family visits or patrons who had secured them as their mistresses. By the time she was finished, it was too late to head over to Bayswater and see the modiste or the tavern before The Market opened for business. So, she decided to wait for the next day to make those visits. Heading upstairs, she figured she had just enough time for a short nap before she needed to be dressed and ready for her first customer.

Tired from all the walking she had done, she stripped down to just her chemise and crawled into the sheets. There, her mind once again wandered to Lucifer. Under the circumstances, she understood why he might have preferred the anonymity of his mask as she remembered the way she had touched him and the desires he'd shared during their various interludes.

Then she remembered the way he touched her and the things he had done to her after his needs had been seen to that first night. She ran her hands up her sides to cup her breasts through the thin cotton chemise, causing her nipples to harden and her pussy to ache. She moaned and knew that she was going to have to take care of her situation before she could sleep, let alone manage a client. Plucking at her nipples, she thought of how he had spread her thighs and dragged his tongue from her wet hole, all the way up over her clit and back. Over and over again. She remembered the sensation of his warm breath on her hot flesh and the way his broad shoulders forced her thighs wide to accommodate him.

Dipping her fingers between the lips of her labia, she found herself already wet and her clit sensitive to her touch. She worked her fingers in and out of her body and then brought them up to circle around the nub in a similar fashion as he'd done with his tongue. Sensation bolted through her as her need began to build. Her hips jerked with each stroke, and she continued to pluck one nipple and then the other with her free hand. All along, she worked her fingers in and out and then up and around her clit, spreading her moisture around the silky flesh with the other hand.

She was able to clearly picture Lucifer now—no mask required. She could easily imagine how his dark, glittering eyes would devour her every response as he licked and sucked on her throbbing cunny. The way his beard brushed against the tender flesh of her thighs, only to scrape over her sensitive nub as he sought to pluck every nerve she possessed in her body. Then her mind shifted to the image with such alacrity that she nearly cried out at the loss.

Again and again, she circled the nub, stroked around it, stroked over it, and then dipped back down until she remembered the feel of his cock as she sank down on him. The look of pure pleasure that crossed his face as she looked down at him had stolen her breath then, as it did now in her memory. A few strokes more as she pinched her nipples, and her body tensed and then exploded, letting her orgasm loose as she curled up off of the sheets and rode her own hand. As the wave passed, and she gently stroked over herself, easing the pressure with each successive stroke, she wondered what had happened to him. Wondered even if she'd ever see him again.

Chapter Nine

Lucifer had spent the previous morning trailing Amelia from one brothel to another, the entire escapade leaving him quite confused. When he'd lived in the brothel where his mother worked, he did not remember the ladies from other establishments paying social calls. In fact, it had been quite the opposite. The houses operated under the auspices of a sort of rivalry. Nothing too caustic, but they were all competing for the same clientele, and ultimately someone had to win, which meant others lost out on that business.

Unfortunately, since she'd visited inside each establishment, he'd had no opportunity to hear what was discussed. Somehow, he doubted it was typical chatter about ribbons and lace. Amelia had looked far too grim and determined with each progressive stop. Today he'd given up any pretense, even to himself, of trying to speak with her and had lurked outside The Market in hopes she might continue her activities in such a way that would allow him to discern what was happening. Very soon, he intended to have a conversation with her, but since information was his stock in trade, he far preferred to enter that discussion armed with some knowledge.

Today her travels had taken him to a different part of town where the slightly less fashionable shopped and sometimes ate, Bayswater. Despite the fact that Amelia was entering a tavern across the street, he was confident that she was not there for a simple repast. Stepping out into the busy street, he dodged a delivery wagon, and two men mounted on respectable examples of horseflesh. He caught a peak of her dark hair draped down her back in a most eye-catching fashion as the door of the tavern closed. He completed his journey across the road and popped into the tavern as well.

A glimpse of her bright blue paletot that matched the skirts of her walking dress drew his eye to her. She approached the proprietor and slid a coin across the bar. "I am looking for a woman," she said.

The man's face turned ruddy, making his bulbous nose turn a bright red as he looked disdainfully down at the money. "This ain't that kind of establishment."

Since he stood behind her, he had yet to see her face. However, judging by the way her shoulders drew back, he imagined her face had pinched in indignation. But then she laughed, a full-bellied sound that surprised him and delighted him all at once. "Of course, it isn't. The woman I'm seeking is said to have had lunch here a few days ago." She paused and cast a glance over her shoulder at the mix of customers. Some were better dressed than others, but none so well turned out as she was. Her gown appeared to be made of a heavy silk and was tailored expertly for her rather tempting curves. "She would have stood out from your typical clientele."

Completely caught up in her reason for being there, not just her attractiveness, he drew closer still to better hear the conversation.

"Her name is Lucy. She is—"

Realization dawned on the worn-down man. "There was a fancy piece in here a few days ago." His lips turned up in a sneer. "Bitch left without paying for her meal. Stiffed me; she did for a fine meal too."

Lucifer reached into his coat and pulled out three quid. He tossed it on the bar. "That should cover this Lucy's tab."

Amelia turned around and gasped in surprise. A softly uttered, "You!" Escaped her as she eyed him with dismay and more than a bit of suspicion. The moment stretched between them as she seemed to gather herself finally. "Mr. Lucifer, what are you doing here?" Her question came out as more of a demand than anything else.

He found himself transfixed by stormy gray eyes that now snapped with anger. Despite their actual color, he'd have described them as red-hot steel. They were anything but cold. "This is a public place, is it not?"

She eyed him up and down with a thoroughness that had his entire body tingling with anticipation. He'd only recently experienced such a sensation with her, which was what made it so intoxicating. "I suppose it is. But I'll have you know I'm quite capable of covering Lucy's tab, *my lord.*"

"I have no title, as you well know, Miss. Kettering." He pointed out reasonably.

"It seemed appropriate. It is clear you are one of those who believes they have a perfect right to interfere in other people's business. In my experience, only the titled feel so empowered to interfere where they are not wanted." She stopped and stared at him in a most peculiar fashion. "Unless you knew Lucy?" Her gaze narrowed.

Lucifer threw his hands up. "I'm afraid you are wrong on both counts, Miss Kettering. I am merely a man who thought to offer aid to a lady." He bowed slightly in deference to her.

She snorted. The woman actually snorted! Then she handed him back his money. "Your aid was neither requested nor was it required. Please feel free to be on your way." She turned back around to find the owner had moved on to other paying customers. In a whirl of blue silk, she whipped back around. "Now, do you see what you've done? I was just getting to the information I need to find my friend, and you distracted me, letting the barkeep slip away." She turned back around to get the man's attention once more. "Bloody men are insufferable."

Lucifer's ire was pricked, or perhaps it was his ego—it seemed a minor point to quibble over and not worth the effort, really. "Now, wait just a moment. All I did was try to help. I'm sure the Duke and Duchess of Shropshire would appreciate my intervention on your behalf."

She glared at him over her shoulder. "And you still have not answered my earlier question. What brings you to such an establishment?" Then she slowly turned back around, giving up on the barkeep. "In fact, what do you know of Lucy's whereabouts?"

He held up his hands. "I know nothing of this Lucy you are looking for. I was ac—" he realized he couldn't say he was following her. He wasn't ready to tell her that he knew she had been his lover. "I came in here to quench my thirst."

"And how do I know you aren't lying? Your gender, let alone those of you who engage in businesses such as yours, are not known for their veracity."

Lucifer couldn't explain it, but while the woman nettled him to no end, he found her ridiculously attractive. It made no sense, really, but his cock was growing uncomfortably hard, and more and more, he was imagining turning her over his knee and spanking that sass right out of her. How would the infamous Mistress Lash take to having her backside warmed? "You wound me with your words, madame. I admit there are those of my gender who would tell falsehoods as soon as look at you, but I do not typically count myself among them."

She appeared unconvinced, if her crossed arms and tapping toe were any indication. "Typically, you say, which suggests you might be lying to me as we speak."

Bloody hell, the woman was quick-witted. "I was passing by when I realized I was parched and in need of refreshment. I came here for an ale. Barkeep!" He waved the man over and put another coin on the bar. "An ale for me and whatever the lady would like."

Honestly, at that moment, if Miss Kettering's eyes could have spit daggers at him, he would surely be dead.

"The lady merely wishes to know if you saw the woman, Lucy, who is of Chinese heritage, leave with anyone?"

The barkeep plonked a tankard of ale down, swiped the coin, and shook his head. "It was too busy in here. I looked up, and she was gone without leaving a half-penny for my troubles."

The woman sighed but nodded as she tossed a few quid on the bar. "Thank you. That should cover Lucy's tab." Then she turned and brushed past Lucifer to depart without any semblance of good manners. But he was utterly unable to let her go, so he reached out and stopped her by wrapping an arm around her waist.

"Unhand me, you fiend," she demanded, though really as more of a hiss of annoyance than a cry for help.

"I find I have more to say to you, Miss Kettering." He couldn't help the corner of his mouth that curled up in a half-smile.

"What more could you possibly need to say to me?" She looked as shocked as he felt at having her in his arms.

"I..." His thoughts deserted him as her lush lips drew his attention.

"Yes?" Her question dripped with annoyance.

"Bloody hell." He muttered and then crashed his mouth down on hers. Having caught her by surprise, her mouth opened to him immediately. He swept in, exploring the sweet mintiness mixed with something more earthy. His cock swelled further as she melted into him, seeming to welcome his kiss for a moment. And then suddenly, she stiffened and retreated. Not an utter cad, he released her.

Crack!

She slapped him hard on his cheek. "How dare you take such liberties?" she seethed before storming out of the tavern. Stunned and a little bemused by his own actions, he stood there for a moment. Then it occurred to him.

Oh, he dared. To taste a woman with such fire and passion? He'd dare just about anything—even inserting himself into her business. And since she seemed to be looking for someone, this Lucy person, it seemed he would need to put his resources into play because he wanted far more than just a heady kiss.

Chapter Ten

Amelia stepped inside the inn and looked around. Peering into the shadows that clung to the edges of daylight, she hesitated. The establishment was a little dingy, a little more worn than the average coaching stop, definitely on the seedier side of London. Despite that, the tavern adjacent to the inn appeared busy, even at such an early hour. Resolved to follow through on a mysterious note she received only that morning, she eased deeper into the dim interior in search of the proprietor.

She'd been taking her morning tea, considering her next steps, when Phillipe had knocked on her door with a note addressed to her, though it was unsigned. Curious, she quickly opened the missive and read the contents. Two lines were scrawled across the page.

Go to the coaching inn on Woolsey Lane. There you'll find important information.

It was so cryptic; she considered ignoring the summons. But then realized she had no other leads to go on, and she could not afford to discount even the smallest tidbit. The trips to the modiste and to the Cock and Kitty had been fruitless. So, here she was, attempting to discern where this mysterious clue might be hidden.

The innkeeper bustled in, found her standing there, and greeted her with a smile. "What can I do for you, my lady?" He'd clearly fixated on her finely made clothing with an eagle eye. "I'm not sure precisely. I am searching for two women. One is a bit shorter than I am, with blonde hair and blue eyes. Her face is shaped like a heart. And the other girl is of Chinese descent with dark hair, dark eyes, and a slightly rounder face and pointed chin. Have you perhaps seen one or both of these ladies recently?"

His gaze narrowed. "This isn't that kind of establishment."

Amelia sighed and rolled her eyes. "I am well aware that this is not a brothel. Nonetheless, I'm seeking these two women who are *friends*. Have you perhaps seen them?"

The man turned a bit pink. "My apologies, miss, I did not realize—"

She ignored the downgrade from lady to miss and cut him off. "Of course, you didn't realize. Now, if you'll just answer my question, I shall be on my way."

He was just about to respond when the door behind her opened, letting in a blast of sunshine and fresh air that cut through the dim, musty interior of the entry. The innkeeper immediately stepped past her to greet the interloper. "My Lord, how may I be of service to you?"

The hairs on the back of her neck stirred as an all too familiar voice sounded behind her. "I am seeking a woman."

The innkeeper sighed. "Another one. Does nobody need a room?"

Amelia turned to find Lucifer standing there, as she'd already known he would be. When he spied her, he somehow looked completely surprised at finding her there. Ignoring the innkeeper, he stepped over to her. "Well now, imagine meeting you here."

She couldn't believe the man's audacity to play innocent. More and more, she was beginning to suspect that *he* might be the person she was looking for since he seemed to be at every location she looked.

The door of the inn opened again, and two men stepped inside, only to find Lucifer and Amelia blocking their entry.

Lucifer waved to an open table just inside the door of the taproom. "Shall we sit?"

She turned and eyed it for a moment and then nodded her assent. She'd come here with a purpose and had yet to find what she was looking for. Perhaps she might find a new line of inquiry by talking to Lucifer. She did not wish to do so, but there was no easy way for her to extricate herself from the situation without being outright rude. And while she was willing to say things to put the man off, she was unwilling to cross certain lines—yet. Though she had all but done so that night at Ros and Flint's party. She refused to dwell on that and comforted herself with the fact she hadn't given him the cut direct, and she'd apologized for how she'd treated him. Shuffling quickly out of the way, they took a seat at a table as Lucifer waved over the innkeeper. "Two ales, please."

The innkeeper huffed, "Finally," before he stalked off to retrieve their drinks. A few moments later, he came back, set the tankards on the table, and headed over to where the two new gentlemen had taken a seat. Amelia turned to find Lucifer settling back into his chair. Then he picked up the tankard of ale and took a swallow. Pointedly ignoring her beverage, Amelia looked at him and asked, "Why is it that

I keep running into you every place I've gone to search for Cat and Lucy?"

Lucifer set his drink down and looked at her with a question in his eyes. "Why are you the one searching for these women?"

She harrumphed and glared at him. "I certainly can't rely on anyone *else* to do it for me. Certainly, no *men* of my acquaintance. And you are avoiding my question."

Lucifer moaned, "You wound me. I know I am but a mere man."

She eyed him warily. "What brought you to this particular Inn and tavern? This is rather far outside of your London haunts, I should think."

"Well, as you obviously are aware, as an information merchant, I often come across tidbits of knowledge that might otherwise not be known to others. I was made aware of a scene that took place here the other night. I saw a young woman with blonde hair to have run out of the inn and into the tavern, screaming for help. However, it seems that because of the late hour, most of the patrons were more inebriated than not and took the moment to be a raucous good time between a man and woman. So, no one helped her when she was dragged back into the rooms."

Amelia gasped, her hand pressing to her breast. "That's awful. Blonde hair and blue eyes, she could have been Cat."

Lucifer shrugged. "She could have been anyone. It's hard to say without reliable witnesses. And by all accounts, no one in the taproom could be counted as a reliable witness."

She slanted a look at him. "And yet you seem to be aware of what happened."

He let one corner of his sensual mouth drift up. "Indeed. I said nobody in the taproom could be considered a reliable witness. I have other sources." At that point, he drained the last of his ale and waved the innkeeper over. "A refill if you please, sir." The innkeeper took the tankard, filled it, and returned it promptly. Lucifer reached out and grabbed his wrist as he pulled back from setting the tankard on the table. "And a moment of your time, if you don't mind."

The man huffed. "I'm a busy innkeeper. I do not have time for idle chitchat."

Lucifer let that brow rise again. "Oh, I wouldn't call this idle chitchat. I understand that there was a woman who was dragged from this taproom back into the inn two nights ago. Blonde hair and blue eyes. She was crying for help?"

The innkeeper stiffened and tried to pull away from Lucifer's grip. "I've no idea what you're talking about."

Lucifer threw a sovereign on the table. "Try again and make me believe you this time." The man eyed the gold coin but shook his head. Lucifer threw another one onto the table. "Don't test my patience or my generosity. Both are in short supply."

The man let his eyes close. And then he opened them again. "Aye, there was a woman here. She was dragged back into the rooms. And when I went to check on the occupants later, they'd already vacated. Without paying their bill, I might add."

"There seems to be a rash of people not paying their bills in London." Lucifer released the man's wrist, which left him free to snatch the gold coins off the table and stalk off.

Amelia had remained quiet during the entire exchange but now looked at Lucifer. "So, someone was here and possibly dragged away again."

He shrugged. "So it would seem. But, without anything conclusive, I'm not sure the knowledge does us any good." He leaned in, his gaze riveted to her lips, and suggested, "You know we could work together. Two heads would be better than one."

Amelia's fear pulsed through her veins, and she stood abruptly as a bit of sweat prickled her brow. "I think not, Mr. Lucifer. I'll do quite fine on my own."

He stood up and backed her into the corner. "Are you sure about that, Mistress Lash? I can think of more than one way that the two of us working together could benefit both of us."

She growled and tried to push him back. "Why, you overbearing prick! I have no interest in you, as a partner in finding my apprentice or as a lover. Stay. Away." She tried to move past him, but he blocked her.

"Oh, Mistress Lash, don't be so quick to dismiss me. As I recall, you enjoyed our first kiss every bit as much as I did. Not to mention all the naughty things we found to do at The Market."

Oh, God! He knew it was her. Knew she was his masked lover. But how? Madame would never betray a confidence. She couldn't fathom how he had figured it out. She would not acknowledge his comment. "I have no—" Then he cut her off with another kiss. Sealing his mouth over hers, slipping his tongue in to steal not only her words but her thoughts. And for a fanciful moment, she thought perhaps even part of her soul. But his kiss was short-lived, clearly meant to make a point. Because he turned and stalked out of the tavern entrance and back into the daylight.

Amelia stood there for a moment in the shadows, recovering from the shock of the desire that pulsed through her veins, thick and heavy. There was no question she wanted him physically, but there was even less question that she trusted him.

Chapter Eleven

Lucifer sat in his office and closed his eyes. It had been a long day and even longer night. The club was still in full swing, but he was done. He puffed on his cigar and closed his eyes for a moment. A knock on the door interrupted his moment of solitude.

Gordie poked his head in. "Apologies, Mr. Lucifer. But there is a Richard Mattingly here to see you."

Lucifer paused for a moment. "Mattingly? Does he have an appointment?"

Gordy nodded. "He says he does, sir."

Lucifer sighed. He really needed to get a better secretary. "Very well, show the man in."

Mr. Mattingly appeared through his doors a few moments later. The man was tall, though not too tall. And wore a very fine suit, as far as Lucifer could tell. His golden-brown hair, liberally peppered with gray, was neatly combed without a strand out of place. The man smiled as he approached. "Thank you for seeing me, Mr. Lucifer."

Lucifer stood and shook hands with him. "Not at all. I apologize for the late hour. But obviously, my secretary couldn't find a better time in my schedule."

"Not at all. I run a similar establishment back home. And so, I'm quite used to these hours."

"And where's home? Exactly. Clearly not from this side of the pond."

Mr. Mattingly nodded. "That's a keen ear you have. Yes, I'm from New York City."

"I see." Mr. Lucifer nodded. "Well, please have a seat. What can I do for you?"

Mr. Mattingly sat down and leaned back in his chair, steepling his fingers under his chin. "Mr. Lucifer, I can see that you are a well-established businessman. So, I won't dilly dally with my request. I'm here because I'd like to partner with another club here in England to have sister agreements. My establishment in New York City is one that is exclusive. I have clientele who travel and would like very much to have a similar establishment to frequent when in London on business."

Lucifer paused, a little confused by the man's request. "Mr. Mattingly, as you are no doubt aware, having clearly visited my club before approaching me. This establishment is not one based on exclusive membership. One need only have enough blunt to lay at the tables to enter my doors. Membership is a nominal barrier for my club."

Mr. Mattingly nodded. "Of course, but I think with a few strategic changes to your business format, we could be very well paired. One need only establish a stricter membership requirement to keep out the riffraff. And then, of course, my clientele would expect the access and use of a certain type of female companionship."

Lucifer set his cigar down and looked Mr. Mattingly square in the face. "I'm afraid, sir, that my business runs as it runs. I have no interest in having prostitutes available for my customers. That merely draws them away from the tables where they're spending their money. It doesn't make sense for my operation."

Mr. Mattingly shrugged. "I could quite easily argue differently by providing them the types of entertainment that they want under this roof. You could actually keep them here longer, removing the need for them to leave to go find other types of entertainment."

Lucifer shook his head. "Let me be more explicit. I don't pedal flesh."

Mr. Mattingly crooked his head and asked.

"And yet, you have hostesses downstairs. Are you suggesting to me that they do not offer sexual favors of any kind to your customers?"

Lucifer ground his teeth and sat up straighter. "That is precisely what I am telling you. My hostesses are merely here to make the men content with platonic companionship. They get them drinks, they root them on when they're winning, and console them when they've lost. And by console them, I mean a gentle pat on the shoulder as they escort them from the building. My ladies have not ever, nor will they ever, cater to a man's sexual needs. That is not the kind of establishment I operate."

Mr. Mattingly seemed as shocked by Lucifer's insistence as Lucifer was by his suggestion. "I see. Perhaps I misunderstood the nature of your business."

Lucifer nodded. "I think you must have. It's not that I think less of a woman who might need to engage in that type of business. But I refuse to be the type of man who makes money off of her back."

Mattingly stood and nodded. "Understood, Mr. Lucifer. Thank you for your time, and I apologize for disrupting your evening."

Lucifer stood, as well, as the man exited his office. When he opened the door, Gordy poked his head in. "Will that be all, Mr. Lucifer?"

"Yes, Gordie, I shouldn't need anything else tonight. Thank you."

Gordie nodded and closed the office door before Lucifer said anything else. Bone weary from following Amelia all over London, as well as running his normal business operations, Lucifer stood and walked to the door tucked just around the corner behind his desk. He walked in and closed it before he stripped off his evening attire. By the time he removed his coat, waistcoat, shirt, pants, and gotten down to his skin. He didn't have the energy to do more than drop into the bed. Lying there, he let his thoughts wander around all the discrete events of the day and even back to past days.

His mind slipped back to the masked woman from a few weeks ago—the other version of Amelia—who had so eagerly pleased him. Despite his exhaustion, his cock stirred to life. With a sigh, he knew he'd have to deal with it or pay the consequences. Reaching down, he wrapped his hand around his length at the base and stroked up his length. As he remembered his rather memorable sexual encounter with the very real Amelia Kettering, he couldn't decide what he liked best about her. It could be her dark eyes, lush round breasts, or perhaps it was her small waist that highlighted what he knew to be curvaceous hips. He moaned as he ran his hand up and down the length of his cock.

What he wouldn't give to wrap his hands around her hips as he sank into her sweet cunny from behind. As tart as her tongue was, he knew that pussy was very sweet. The image morphed again, and he imagined filling her saucy little mouth with his length. Fucking into her face over and over again as she took his cock down her throat.

It only took another stroke or two, and he was coming hard on his stomach. Reaching over to the chair near the bed, he grabbed a shirt and cleaned himself up before rolling over and passing out.

Chapter Twelve

Amelia slipped through the servants' entrance of the Grand Hotel on the backside of the graceful building. She was looking for a maid that went by the name of Jenny inside the bustling back corridors. She found a woman dressed in a maid's uniform and stopped her. "I'm looking for Jenny. Is she here today?"

The woman eyed her warily. "Jenny Who?"

Amelia racked her brain. "Jenny McGuire. Red hair, green eyes."

"Ah, the Irish, Jenny. She's here. Just around that corner in the pantry."

Amelia nodded. "Thank you."

As directed, in the pantry, she found a redheaded woman dressed in a neat, plain black dress with a white apron tied over the top. "Jenny?" She inquired as she poked her head in. The woman turned, surprised to find someone not dressed as an employee of the hotel looking for her.

"Perhaps. Who are you?" She asked in a soft Irish lilt.

"My name is Amelia Kettering. I was told by a mutual friend that you might be able to help me."

Her eyes widened. And she glanced around. "Not here. I'll speak to you in a moment. There's a cafe down the street. I can be there in half an hour."

Amelia nodded. "Very well. I'll wait for you there." She started to exit out the back. And Jenny stopped her.

"Oh, Miss, please. Not that way. I'm shocked you came in that way. Our manager is always hovering around that back entrance, watching to see who comes and goes. Come, follow me." And she slipped past her, out of the pantry, and past another set of doors before she pointed to a door that swung back and forth consistently as men and women dressed in the uniform of the hotel came and went. "That's the lobby. You'll be safer walking out that way."

Amelia nodded and slipped out behind one of the maids who was carrying a vase of hot-house flowers.

In the lobby, she looked around and tried to look as though she were a guest of the hotel, waiting for someone. She finally decided that she'd been there long enough to blend in and could leave without looking too obvious, so she headed toward the door. But, lo-and-behold, Mr. Lucifer appeared again. The man had an uncanny sense of location, so it seemed.

"Why, we meet again, Ms. Kettering."

She eyed him more warily than ever after their latest encounter at the inn. "Oh! I don't know why I'm surprised that you're here, but I am. What brings you to the Grand Hotel?" she asked, curious as to how he would explain this visit away.

He chuckled, a dark and rich sound that made the hairs on her body stand on end. "Me? I'm here for a meeting." He stepped closer to her, inappropriately close by anyone's standards. "What, pray tell, are you doing in such a high-flying establishment?"

She ground her teeth, annoyed that he might think that she could not afford to have business in such a place. Whether as a guest or as a patron of the restaurant. "I was here to meet with a friend. They weren't able to make it. I'm afraid I'll have to meet up with them later. And what kind of meeting are you here for, exactly? At such a fine establishment."

He grinned, and she couldn't help but find the man's smile made her heart race a little faster and her blood pulse a little thicker through her veins. "Why I'm here for a meeting with some of my peers."

She snorted. "Your peers. You mean other owners of gambling hells?"

"Well, of course." He laughed as though it was absurd that he might consider anyone else a peer. She was about to make yet another acerbic comment when four women approached them, or more correctly, him.

The tallest of the set eyed Amelia with her piercing, light green eyes before she looked at Lucifer and tapped him on the arm with her fan. "Don't keep us waiting, Lucifer. I expect you to be on time."

He smiled and nodded. "Always, Miss Martin, I wouldn't dream of keeping you lovely ladies waiting. I believe I saw Mr. Blackburn walk in just ahead of me."

Ranged behind the dark-haired woman with the light green eyes, Miss Martin, stood three more ladies. The shortest of the group had blonde hair piled on her head as if to compensate for her lack of height and balance out all her curves. The next woman only stood a little taller, but she was thinner and had more of the look of the day except for her fiery red hair and intense, all-seeing brown eyes. For a moment, Amelia swore the woman could see into her soul and find all her dark secrets. It was a disturbing thought. And finally, there was the next tallest woman, who was whipcord lean and looked as if she spent more time working in the warehouse than running a gambling hell. Her skin was sun-bronzed and weathered as though she spent a great deal of time outdoors, which did not make sense in London.

The dark-haired woman smiled and said, "Excellent. We'll see you upstairs." And then the gaggle departed. Leaving a bemused Amelia standing next to Lucifer. And she couldn't help but blurt. "Are you trying to tell me that those four ladies own a gambling hell?"

He nodded. "Indeed, they do. The Four Lilies is one of my stiffest competitors."

Amelia nodded. "I've heard of the establishment. I just had not realized that the name, The Four Lilies, was reflective of its owners."

"Indeed, the four have been fast friends for years and now run their business together. I really shouldn't keep them waiting. But I would like to suggest, once again, that I would very much like to aid you in your investigation. Two of us working on this, particularly with my resources, would be more fruitful."

"Why? Why do you wish to help me?"

"Because you intrigue me." He leaned closer so only she might hear him. "For some inexplicable reason, I can't stay away from you. And if that means helping you in your search because you won't let me in your bed, then it seems I'm willing to take what I can get of you."

Amelia sighed and rubbed her forehead. "Although it goes against all of my better judgment, perhaps you're right about the two of us working together. I'll agree to a trial run, but there are some rules. There will be no intimacy between us."

He seemed confused for a moment. "Intimacy?"

"Sex, Lucifer. I mean, there will be no sex between us."

"Ah." He shrugged. "Damned disappointing, but I suppose we'd probably do best to keep things amicable between us."

"Very well, then. We'll be partners. I'm off to meet with someone. My apologies. I do need to leave. When would you like to next meet?"

He hesitated a moment. "I'll send round an address and a time. I'm thinking around ten tomorrow morning?"

Amelia nodded. "Very well. I'll expect your note and see you then." As she walked down the street towards the café, she questioned if she was doing the smart thing. But when she thought about it more, she had to recognize that having Lucifer's information network at her disposal during her search would be far more valuable than constantly running into him and fighting with him. And at least now, he would keep his hands to himself. Although she wasn't sure how much she really wanted that either.

She slipped into the café and took a seat in the back at a small table in a corner. A few minutes later, Jenny appeared. She sat down and kept her bonnet and veil down so that it was difficult to see who she was. "Thank you for meeting me here. I'd prefer not to be seen sharing information about guests inside the hotel."

Amelia nodded. "Understood. My name is Miss Kettering. Abbess Cordelia suggested that you might have some information that would be pertinent to my search for Lucy and my apprentice."

Jenny nodded. "No one at the hotel, of course, knows about my past. You see, I knew Lucy when I was a maid at Abbess Cordelia's establishment. I saw her two nights ago being dragged in through the back entrance of the hotel. And up to one of the exclusive suites. I tried to signal to her to say hello. But her eyes looked glassy, and her hair was stringy and hanging in her face. I wasn't even sure it was her for a moment. When she finally looked up and saw me, her eyes widened. But then she was dragged away before I could say anything. I realized pretty quickly that the men were holding her against her will. I sent a note over to Abbess Cordelia in case there was something she could do to aid Lucy."

Amelia nodded. "I'm grateful that you did. Can you describe the men who were with her?"

Jenny shook her head. "They were tall. One was dark-haired. The other, blond, kind of scruffy looking. I didn't get a good look because they disappeared around the corner by the time I realized that Lucy needed help."

Amelia nodded again. "I understand. It must have all happened very fast."

Jenny nodded. "Indeed, it did. If that's all, I should go. I am expected home anytime now."

Amelia thanked her and rose as Jenny left. Sitting back down to sip the tea that she had ordered. She considered this new information. It seemed strange that they would move from such a rundown inn, as the one on Woolsey Lane, to something as posh as the Grand Hotel. There was most definitely a mystery here. And if she wanted to find Cat and Lucy, she was going to have to solve it.

Chapter Thirteen

Amelia stood on the curb in front of the Mayfair address Lucifer had sent. His short missive had arrived late the night before and been waiting for her in her room when she'd finished with her last client. Still a little puzzled by his choice of places to meet, she opened the note to confirm she stood in front of the correct location. She had assumed they would meet at his club, not someone's home. But *whose* home was it? That was the question that truly worried her.

Considering the mysterious meeting address, she was pleased that she'd worn one of her best walking dresses. Her royal blue silk with the ruffled hem always boosted her confidence. With a tug of her jacket by the front hem, she drew in a deep breath and prepared for whatever might happen next. Stepping up to the large double doors, painted a shiny forest green as though they had just recently been freshened up, she lifted the door knocker and firmly tapped it twice before letting it go. Moments passed, seconds punctuated by the beating of her heart. She swallowed, her mouth inordinately dry.

Was she nervous? About meeting with Lucifer? Or about the investigation they were pursuing with greater and greater urgency? Either? Neither? Both? It likely didn't matter under the circumstances. She would fend off any advances made by Lucifer, and she would find Cat. Anything less was unacceptable.

The door opened, and a man wearing black and silver livery with a snow-white shirt and cravat answered the door. "Good morning." He flicked his gaze over her person as though assessing how to address her. "Madame."

Amelia had been judged and found wanting by far greater men. She would not be cowed by an uppity butler. "Good morning. Mr. Lucifer is expecting my call." She presented her card made of thick cream paper with an elegant scrawl of her name across it that many ladies of the Ton would be jealous of.

The supercilious butler raised his brows at the obvious quality of her card and nodded. "Indeed, madame. He instructed me to expect you this morning. Please, come in."

And with that, the veritable bulldog stepped back, granting her admittance to the home. Inside the foyer, she took in the understated elegance of the white marble and black-and-white checkered floors. The space was immense by town standards. She shrugged off her cloak with the aid of a footman who materialized from nowhere and dematerialized with equal stealth.

With a nod, the butler turned and opened a door just off the foyer. "You may await Mr. Lucifer in the drawing room."

Amelia swept past the servant and into a room that fairly dazzled with its sunlit beauty. The pale blue walls with yellow accents seemed to amplify the morning sun that streamed in through the large bay window. Nothing about the home suggested that the owner was a man who ran a den of iniquity such as Lucifer's. She couldn't help but wonder once more whose home she was in. Unable to sit still, she strolled around the room, taking in the cheerful still life paintings and delicate porcelain figurines depicting various forms of wildlife.

"Do you appreciate the work of Kändler?" The familiar deep voice of the man she'd come to see startled her.

She turned around and tried to reconcile the room with the man that now dominated it. "They're quite lovely, but I am not familiar with the artist."

"He is a well-known artist I learned about not too long ago when someone offered me a figurine as repayment for a debt." He shrugged and motioned for her to take a seat. "Please, sit."

"Are we not waiting for someone else to join us?" She looked past him to the doorway.

He glanced over his shoulder. "Who were you expecting?"

"The owner of the house?" she suggested as more of a question.

Lucifer chuckled. "I am the owner of the house."

"Oh." Nonplussed, she tried to recover. "My apologies. I assumed you lived on the premises of your club, not unlike Madame de Pompadour."

"I do. I sleep there most nights, but I maintain this residence as well." He motioned once more to the settee that mirrored the one he stood beside.

Taking his lead, she sat down and arranged her skirts while she resisted the urge to ask the clearly unwelcome question: Why? Why did he maintain a separate residence that he did not frequently use? It seemed a rather costly outlay of money for no obvious benefit.

"I appreciate you joining me here. I had some other business I needed to attend to, and this was a convenient place to meet, as well as far more private than my club can sometimes be." He sat back, almost lounging like an apex predator. One who knows there is nothing in his vicinity that might be a threat.

She decided to focus on her reason for being there, which was not to ogle him. Taking a deep breath, she pressed ahead. "Of course." She paused for a moment, marshaling her thoughts. "I am very worried about the safety of my apprentice, Cat, and now Lucy. Someone has taken them, though I do not know why."

"I assume you tried to sort out what enemies they might have?" He asked the question she had been wracking her brain to try and answer with little success.

"I did attempt to discern if there might be any enemies, but Cat has none. And by all accounts, Lucy is also a sweet and generous person. Neither of them have any obvious possibilities." She licked her lips in a pointless attempt to moisten them.

He picked at some invisible thread or speck of dust on the arm of the chair he occupied. "What did you learn when you met with Jenny from the hotel?"

Amelia inhaled sharply. "How did you know I met with her?"

"You seem to keep forgetting that I am an information merchant as much as I am a gambling hell owner. I must point out that information is far more lucrative than chasing preening lords and ladies for their debts owed." He nearly grumbled the last part. "Now, tell me what you learned from her."

Annoyed, she smiled. "Didn't your source give you all the details?"

He merely stared at her intently as he waited.

She huffed. "Fine. Jenny shared that she saw Lucy in the hotel." After relaying the details Jenny was able to provide, she wrapped up with the question that was still plaguing her. "I don't understand why they would have moved from the inn where their activities would be remarked on less to a hotel where they would clearly stand out?"

"It is odd. Though I imagine if they have the financial backing required, silence can be bought at the hotel where discretion is key to their success. It was just bad luck that they happened to snatch the one woman who actually knew someone who worked at the hotel." He reached into his pocket and pulled out a folded sheet of paper. "I had some of my people poking around the hotel. It seems that the men vacated the premises shortly after they saw Jenny. They disappeared into the warehouse district near the docks. As it happens to be that I own a few of those warehouses, I can safely eliminate quite a few for us to inspect."

"You own a house, warehouses. Next, you'll tell me you are of a mind to settle down and take a wife. Start a family." The words were out of her mouth before she could stop them. Bloody hell! Why had she said that?

A smug smile tipped his too kissable lips up on one side. "Are you applying to fill the role?"

"Don't even suggest it in jest. I would never be with someone whose interests are so unsavory." She cringed at how priggish she sounded at that moment. But while she viewed the exchange of money for sex or other similar services to be an honest trade, she drew the line at preying on the weaknesses of others, such as taking money from those who could ill afford to lose it, or worse could not control their own impulses like—no. She refused to dredge up her past. She had put it firmly aside years ago.

His face hardened as if a mask had slammed down. "My, you certainly sound judgmental, considering most women working in the sex trade are not there by choice but because they have no choices left."

"Nevertheless, even at my lowest point, when I was near to starving and desperate, I was still able to make a choice. It may not have been a great choice to die or sell my body, but at least it was a choice. I've seen too many men caught up in the frenzy of gambling, either trying to compound their winnings or, worse, trying to repair their losses. Inevitably they have no choice. Some unseen thing, be it avarice or ego, has control over them, leaving them no ability to even choose not to place another bet. And the things... " Her voice drifted off as her father's death flashed before her eyes. She stood up, needing to escape the conversation, the room, and even the man. "I'm sorry, I should go."

Lucifer flowed out of his chair like water filling a lock to block her departure. He placed a hand on her arm to arrest her progress. "What were you going to say?"

"Nothing." Her cheeks felt cold even as tears pricked her eyes.

Lucifer reached out and tilted her chin up. He studied her features, his gaze a physical touch that had her shivering despite her upset. Then he shifted his finger from her chin to catch the single tear that had escaped to roll down her cheek. Damn it. She didn't want to cry in front of him. "Don't cry, Amelia."

"I'm not." She refused to acknowledge what they both knew to be true. Just as she refused to acknowledge how desperately she wanted to feel his arms around her, his lips on hers.

"I—" He seemed at a loss. "I don't like it when you cry." And then he hauled her into his arms and kissed her.

No, kiss was too tepid a description. He claimed her mouth. Claimed her lips and her tongue, swept in to establish his domain, his dominance. And heaven help her; she could feel her knees giving out as his arms held her up. Their tongues dueled, each of them taking turns as the aggressor, but she knew, in the end, she would lose because while she enjoyed being in charge, enjoyed giving people what they needed, he simply didn't know how not to be in control. It was simply not how he was made. And as she snaked her arms up around his neck and gave in to the kiss entirely, she feared, despite all the reasons she shouldn't want him, that there was no denying that there was something between them.

Dimly, she heard a door open and then a feminine gasp and squeal before the door slammed shut as they pulled apart. Amelia blinked, a little dazed from the intensity of the kiss, as she glanced owlishly around the room.

Lucifer chuckled. "I'm afraid one of my maids must have walked in on us."

"Well, I dare say she may be more scandalized than either of us." Amelia shook the last of her desire-induced haze off. "I really should go."

"I'll have my coach brought around. It can drop you wherever you are going." His offer was more of a statement than anything else.

There was little else to do but accept. "Thank you."

He stepped out of the room for a moment and then returned. "I am having my men check out the most likely warehouses. Once they've narrowed it down, I shall contact you."

Her head was spinning with the way he'd swept in and taken charge of everything. And despite her judgments about his business interests, he had just put the entire power of his resources at her disposal in a way that was both terrifying and breath-stealing.

Chapter Fourteen

It was morning, but with fog so thick you could have rolled it into balls and made a snowman, it might as well have been night. The darkness was probably for the best since she and Lucifer were creeping into a warehouse down near the docks. And not just any warehouse, one they thought Cat might have been held in recently, if not at that very moment. Though she supposed Lucifer wouldn't have allowed her to come along had he really thought they would be running into the thugs they were searching for.

She huffed out a frustrated breath.

"What's wrong?" His whisper sounded even more muffled in the cold, damp air.

"I just realized you already know what we are going to find in here." She straightened up from where she was crouched behind him as he looked around a corner to see if anyone was about.

"Not precisely." He glanced back at her over his shoulder, his face inscrutable.

Her gaze narrowed as she stared at him. "Oh really? So, you didn't have your men thoroughly check out this warehouse before you brought me along?"

He pressed his lips together in annoyance. "Well, of course, I had them take a look around. How else would I have known this might be a possible location?"

"Then why in the world are we sneaking around like someone might be here?" She huffed and then brushed past him and around the corner.

A hand suddenly latched onto her arm and hauled her back to where they'd been crouched. Lucifer pressed his body up against hers as he clamped a hand over her mouth.

Then the muffled sound of footsteps, followed quickly by voices, carried to them. "Hell, Harry, me bloody wife would chop off me bollocks if I tried to do that!"

"I thought the same thing, but I'm telling you, Ralph, Matilda can't keep her hands off me now. Every night she crawls into bed after the little ones are asleep and begs me to do it again." The one she assumed was Harry chuckled as their footsteps faded into the morning mist.

Lucifer slipped his hand from her mouth, and she couldn't keep her thoughts to herself. "I wonder just what Harry did to Matilda?"

He chuckled darkly after staring at her for a moment. "Too bad, you'll never know. Now, can you please keep your voice down and follow me? My men thought this was a likely place, but that it was clear the warehouse was no longer in use." He shook his head. "Regardless, there's no reason to alert anyone to our presence here."

Amelia nodded and whispered. "Fair point."

Then Lucifer leaned in as though he were going to kiss her. For a moment, indecision warred within her. She'd clearly told him no kissing and no sex. And he'd just as clearly ignored her dictates the day before. Why wouldn't he ignore it now? But did she want him to kiss her? Nope, she wasn't going to answer that. But she didn't have to because her body betrayed her as she swayed toward him, leaned into his almost kiss with every intent of crossing the distance. But then he withdrew.

Somehow, she managed to refrain from cursing as he looked at her with a knowing smirk. She flushed and then did as she always did. She stiffened her spine and pressed on about the business at hand. Her adopted country may think they had the whole stiff upper lip thing sewed up, but she knew no one could suck it up and get on with things better than her. She'd been doing it all her life. Hell, she'd been doing it to *save* her life!

He leaned around the corner again and then waved her forward. "I think it's clear."

Clear? She shook her head slightly as if that might knock things back in place. She needed to keep her head around this man. He was not to be trusted. Not with Cat's life, and certainly not with her heart. Without a word, she stepped around him and the corner to head toward the warehouse door. Before she could reach it, he had once again skirted around her and led the way. "Bloody well stay behind me, or it will be the last time I bring you with me."

"Don't make threats you can't follow through on. You're lucky I waited for you at all." She whisper-yelled at him.

"Hush, woman." Was his only reply as they slipped through the door. Inside, the warehouse was even darker than the fog-clogged morning.

He headed down one long row of crates that rose on either side of them like the edifices that often lined the narrow London alleys. She stayed close behind him for fear that she might never find her way out if they were separated. Not that he was any more familiar with the inside of the warehouse than she was. But he turned a corner and then another, and they found themselves in an open space. There they found three structures that wanted to be beds but looked more like the cots she remembered sleeping on that one time she'd convinced her father to take her hunting with him when she was ten. Oh, her mother had been furious when she discovered where they'd gone, not to mention the trousers Amelia had been wearing. It was the first time she'd donned men's pants, but it certainly hadn't been her last. Much to her mother's dismay.

They looked about to see if there might be any other clues, but there appeared to be little else to tell them who had slept there. Just the cots and some blankets. Then something caught her eye from the shadows. Creeping closer, she bent over to fish it out from behind one of the cots.

Lucifer wanted to groan as he watched Amelia bend over and present her delectably pert arse to him. His cock grew semi-hard at the sight, despite her coat and what he assumed were many layers of petticoats beneath. But now that he was actually looking, she wasn't wearing a bustle or skirts. She couldn't be for that perfect roundness to be displayed so well. What the hell was the woman wearing?

She stood up, ending his scrutiny of her rear assets, and held something aloft as she crowed in triumph. "Ah ha!"

"What have you found?" He asked, his curiosity pulling his focus back where it belonged.

She stepped closer to him and out of the deeper shadows. "A shoe."

A single shaft of sunlight seemed to have penetrated both the late morning fog and the grimy windows of the warehouse. Holding it up to that light, her breath caught as she got a better look at her prize. Her face blanched, draining of all color as she inspected the shoe.

Unexpected and unwanted, worry gnawed at his gut. "What's wrong?"

She seemed to recover herself enough to answer. "It's Cat's shoe."

"How can you be sure?" Lucifer looked at the pale blue shoe with a bow tying two straps across the mid-foot. It looked like many a woman's shoe he'd seen strewn across his floor.

Amelia looked up from the item and sighed sadly. "Because I bought it for her. The pair was a birthday gift to her a few weeks ago. She'd been so delighted with them, having never been given such an expensive gift. She cooed and sighed over them. And she wore them almost every day. I worried she would wear them out before she could afford to buy a second pair on her own."

"But don't many women's shoes look essentially the same? Surely there is more than one pair of blue ladies' shoes tied with a bow in all of London?" He found it hard to believe otherwise.

"Not with her initials sewn inside. My cobbler does it for all of my shoes, and so did the same for Cat's. When you live in a house full of women, having your initials embroidered on your belongings is an easy way to avoid conflicts over items that might be coveted by others." She shrugged. "It hasn't been an issue in many years, but it's a habit I find hard to break."

Lucifer nodded, well aware of the petty, and not so petty, disputes that could erupt between ladies residing in a house, even one as well run as The Market. "Well, then we can confirm that Cat has been here recently. That's a good thing in that it puts us closer to sorting out who has her."

She dropped the hand holding the shoe and looked up at him. "But who owns this warehouse? Unless we know that, it truly doesn't put us any closer. I suppose we could go to City Hall—"

"Phineas Golden is the owner of the warehouse." He frowned. Phineas could be unscrupulous at times and certainly was a man who looked out for himself first and foremost. But abducting women? That didn't strike him as something he would be involved in. This certainly required an immediate visit. "Come, we should go. I shall drop you home before I go to speak with Phineas."

Amelia's head snapped up. "I think not. I shall go with you. After all, I'd like to meet this man whose warehouse last housed my apprentice."

Lucifer groaned. "That is not a good idea, Amelia."

"And why not?"

He did not want to take her to meet Phineas. If she thought he was a rake, Phineas was a true Lothario. The man would seduce and sleep with anything in a skirt. He glanced down briefly. Well, at least she wasn't wearing one. A low growl escaped as he swung his gaze back over to her long coat that lay far too flat to have a proper lady's garment underneath it. "What in the bloody hell are you wearing?"

She glanced up, startled by the roar of his question. "What?"

He closed his eyes and tried to take a deep breath in the musty confines. "What do you have on under that bloody coat?"

She blinked. "My leather trousers."

Lucifer couldn't believe she'd actually left The Market wearing those. It was positively indecent! "Why would you go out in public wearing those?"

She rolled her eyes at him. "Pray tell me, what does a proper lady wear to go skulking about a warehouse investigating a missing person?"

"Not men's clothing, I'm certain." He ground out.

"Well, you're wrong. A proper lady doesn't skulk about warehouses at all. And as I long ago established. I'm. Not. A. Proper. Lady."

Lucifer snorted. There was no doubt in anyone's mind that she spoke the truth. "Be that as it may, you should at least make some effort to blend into society."

"It's a bloody good thing your opinion doesn't matter one bit. Now, can we cease this ridiculous argument and leave before someone finds us in here?"

He hated to admit she was correct. They really should go. But there was no way in hell he would be taking her to see Phineas. "Let's go," he rumbled and then turned to lead them back the way they'd come. They exited the warehouse and returned to his carriage without incident. As he climbed into the vehicle, he called to his driver, "The Market, posthaste."

He settled across from the woman who seemed to plague his days *and* his nights.

She looked furious. "I am not going to be dumped at The Market while you go off to inquire after this Phineas person's involvement in this."

Lucifer pinched the bridge of his nose and tried to stem the headache blooming over his eyes. "That may be, but you will absolutely put on a proper dress if you are going to insist on accompanying me. Phineas Golden is not a man to dangle bait in front of and expect him not to take it."

Amelia's face turned beetroot red. "Bait? Did you just call me bait?"

"Dressed like that, you most certainly are. And since Phineas makes me look positively harmless when it comes to seducing women, I suggest you march yourself upstairs and change your clothes when we arrive." He scowled at her, furious that he was even having to have such a conversation.

She shot daggers at him in return as she reached inside her coat. But whatever she had reached for, she never withdrew. She simply stared at him in silent fury.

When the carriage rolled to a stop, she stood and pushed open the carriage door to jump down on her own to the dismay of his coachman, whom he heard sputtering from atop the carriage. Then she swung around, her coat flaring wide to expose both her lush curves and the whip she had secured inside her coat. "I shall be fifteen minutes. If you are not still here when I return.... Well, let's just say I wouldn't recommend you make that choice." Then she whirled around and disappeared inside The Market. Lucifer couldn't contain the laughter that he was certain she heard as she stomped away.

Damnation, the woman was a firebrand. She had actually considered uncoiling her whip in the carriage; she was so angry. He couldn't contain his grin. She was not as immune to him as she liked to pretend. And undoubtedly, he was going to have to have her wear those trousers for him in a *much* more private setting. Good God, the woman was temptation in kid boots. And he was not one who could resist temptation on the best of days. But he wanted her as she'd been at his house in Mayfair and again earlier outside the warehouse, all eager, breathless woman. He liked the firebrand too. But in bed? He wanted the soft, pleasing woman he'd had glimpses of.

Chapter Fifteen

Lucifer would have preferred to have this meeting in neutral territory, but that was impossible with Amelia in tow and the urgent need to learn what they could. Without a doubt, if he'd tried to meet without her, she likely would have scheduled her own meeting with Phineas. And that would be a disaster of proportions he didn't want to contemplate. She would never be alone with Phineas Golden. Not that he didn't trust her, but because he didn't trust him.

A man—a butler, but not a butler at all—opened the door of the residential entry to Phineas' club. His townhouse resided just to the right of the Golden Swine. "Good day, Mr. Lucifer. What can we do for you this afternoon?"

"I need a word with Phineas."

"Very well. If you'd like to wait in the salon, I shall let him know you are here."

Lucifer nodded and stepped inside. As usual, he stopped and opened his coat, letting the man pat him down quickly and efficiently. Next, Amelia followed him in, but when she moved to step past the butler, she was stopped. "You too," was all he said.

Amelia looked at Lucifer in shock.

"You heard the man." Lucifer prompted her to get on with it, despite the overwhelming urge to punch the man in the face.

"Um, well…" She opened her coat, and the butler snorted and shot a glare at Lucifer as he plucked Amelia's whip from her coat.

Lucifer wanted to curse. He'd assumed she only had it with her because they'd gone to the warehouse. He did not expect that she would have it with her when they paid a call.

The butler patted her down as best he could with her full skirts in the way. After he was as assured as he could be that she hid no further weapons, he collected their coats. "I'll return your whip to you when you go." Then he led them to a salon. "Mr. Golden will join you momentarily."

Alone again, Amelia looked at him queerly. "That is the strangest-looking butler I have ever seen."

"That was not a butler. That is Phineas' bodyguard *cum* butler. That man would slip a stiletto between your ribs as soon as look at you if you said or did the wrong thing to Phineas. The whip was not well done of you." Lucifer hoped she took his message to heart. The only thing worse than Phineas taking a shine to Amelia would be for her to do something to draw his ire. And frankly, either outcome was possible where she was concerned.

"Had you given me some warning, I wouldn't have brought it." She lifted her brows.

"My apologies. I did not realize a whip was a standard accessory for the lady about town. I shall be sure to provide guidance in the future."

Then the salon door opened, and big, blond Phineas Golden walked in. Even he could acknowledge the man looked like he could have taken a place among the pantheon of the Greek gods.

"Lucifer! To what do I owe the pleasure of a personal visit to my home?" Phineas grinned as they shook hands.

"Expediency outweighed my better judgment," Lucifer drawled.

Phineas darted a glance at him, but then Amelia moved across the room and drew his attention. "As I live and breathe, please tell me you have delivered this dark angel to my door as a gift."

Amelia's brows lowered at his suggestion. "Mistress Lash, Mr. Golden. And may I add, I am no man's property to gift to anyone."

Phineas laughed and grinned over at Lucifer. "Oh my, she is a feisty one!" Then he turned back to her. "Mistress Lash? Do you mean *the* Mistress Lash?"

"Indeed, sir." Amelia smiled slyly. "If your man would return my whip to me, I'd be happy to prove my identity to you."

Phineas chuckled again. "My God, you are fucking delightful. What are you doing with a stuffed shirt like Lucifer?"

Lucifer grunted and stepped between them. "We're here because we have questions about your warehouse at the corner of Port and White Streets."

"The one you asked to borrow?" Phineas' brows drew together as his head cocked to the side slightly.

"Lucifer?" Amelia looked at him with confusion, hurt, and anger.

"What the hell are you talking about?" Lucifer demanded rather than asked.

"What do you mean? You sent a note around to ask if you could use my warehouse. I thought it was deuced strange, but you sent payment in cash with the request. I figured you had your reasons." Phineas looked unconcerned.

"So, you let someone—who you thought was me—use your warehouse without knowing why or what they might be keeping there for a few days?" Lucifer wanted to punch his sometime friend.

"So it seems. What did you keep there that has you so overwrought?"

"It wasn't me." Lucifer ground out, frustrated by Phineas' blithe obtuseness and Amelia's accusatory glare.

"Yes, yes. As you say, it was someone else. But what was kept there?" Phineas flapped a hand around as though it was a small point.

Amelia made a strangled noise in her throat. "My bloody apprentice!"

"What? You mean a woman was held there?" Phineas sounded as appalled as Lucifer felt.

"Not just one, at least two. Possibly more." This whole conversation was exhausting between Phineas' thickness and Amelia's killing glares.

"Who in the bloody hell did I rent my warehouse to?" Phineas glanced back and forth between himself and Amelia.

"We don't know. But we shall find out. We have to if we are going to find Am—Mistress Lash's apprentice." He nearly slipped, but in truth, neither he nor Amelia had wanted to tell Phineas her real name.

Phineas looked at Amelia, and his gaze drank her in. "I should very much like to put all my considerable resources at your disposal to aid you in solving this mystery."

Lucifer was quite certain that Phineas would like to put more than his resources at her disposal. "That won't be necessary. I am more than able to assist her sufficiently in this endeavor."

The man offered her a dazzling smile. "Are you certain I can't interest you in my help?"

She blinked and then shook her head before darting a glance at Lucifer as if considering Phineas' offer. "No, I think I have all the help I require, but thank you."

Relief swept through him that all was not lost with her.

"Yes, well, we should be on our way." Lucifer reached around Phineas and took Amelia's hand. With a slight tug, he drew her around the other man and tucked her hand into his arm. "Thank you for your time, and apologies for the interruption."

"No, not at all. Feel free to bring the lovely Mistress Lash to visit me anytime. Or better yet, Mistress, bring yourself and leave your guard dog at home." Phineas grinned beatifically.

Lucifer growled and walked faster toward the door. But then he stopped. "Can you send the note you received around? I'd like to see if I recognize the handwriting."

"Of course," Phineas answered before he followed them out of the salon and then peeled off to go upstairs.

As they departed the residence, Phineas' butler stood waiting with their coats and Amelia's whip. As they stepped outside, the street was quite busy since it was now edging into late afternoon. Men and women were bustling along a street that had a mix of residences and businesses. Lucifer ushered Amelia through the throng and toward his carriage that stood waiting at the curb. But, as they neared the vehicle, she stopped dead in her tracks as her face blanched for the second time that day. Instantly on alert, he looked around but failed to see anything obvious that might have alarmed her. "Amelia? Are you well?"

She didn't respond. She simply stood there with a vacant stare and what he could only describe as fear in her eyes.

"Amelia!" He called her name louder and jostled her shoulder a bit.

She blinked and looked up at him as though surprised to see him standing there.

"Are you well?"

She licked her lips and seemed to gather herself together. "Of course. Why do you ask?"

People bumped them occasionally as they passed, but he remained where he was. "Why do I ask? Because you froze and then did not respond to me when I called your name."

"Oh," she breathed and then offered a small smile. "My apologies. I must have gotten lost in my thoughts for a moment."

People were getting more irritated as they had to peel around them. "Let's get in the carriage." He nudged her forward, and they climbed in as he directed his driver back to The Market. Once they settled on the bench together, he angled toward her, still concerned about what had occurred. "What thoughts had you so lost you couldn't hear me?"

"Nothing important." She took a breath and then frowned at him. "Who exactly would have known that Phineas—Mr. Golden—would even allow you to rent one of his warehouses?"

"I'm not precisely sure. But I do intend to find out. Now, do not attempt to switch the topic under discussion. What upset you so on the sidewalk?"

She looked at him for a moment, seemed to be considering how she might respond, and then, to his dismay, leaned in and planted her lips on his. He meant to resist, to pull her away and demand an actual answer. But the feel of her body pressed against his, the way the flare of her hips fit to his palms, and the heady taste of her lips had him growling and wanting more. Much, much more. He was just about to pick her up and settle her in his lap when the carriage rocked to a halt. The next thing he knew, Amelia was out of his arms and out of the carriage. "Thank you, Lucifer! We'll talk soon."

And then she fled into The Market, leaving him alone with a cockstand that he was certain would not abate anytime soon. They'd talk soon? Bloody right, they would. And likely sooner than she planned.

Chapter Sixteen

Amelia had the uncomfortable sensation that someone was watching her. It was making her skin crawl even as she walked down a bustling Bond Street. She stopped for possibly the tenth time to look about and see if she saw him. It had to be Lucifer following her. She'd been avoiding him for days. He'd tried coming to The Market in the late afternoon, but she had been out trying to find Cat on her own. Not that her effort resulted in anything useful. Then he'd tried to appear during peak hours at The Market. She had easily dodged him across the crowded salons, ultimately hiding in the maid's quarters downstairs.

Why? Because she had absolutely no desire to explain what had occurred on the street outside of Mr. Golden's residence. Partly because she still wasn't certain she had actually heard the voice she had thought she heard. How could she? The man it belonged to was across the Atlantic Ocean in America. Or he was supposed to be. And the rest of the reason she didn't want to explain what happened to Lucifer? It would only lead him to ask more questions about her past, which simply would not do. She needed her past to remain where she had safely tucked it.

Shaking her head, she pressed on with her errands. Despite her apprentice having gone missing, she still had errands to take care of and a business to run. She was picking up some necessities on her way to a customer's home for a private appointment. She stepped into the shop, letting the bell tinkle merrily as the door closed behind her.

"Good afternoon, Mistress Lash." The shop owner, a tall, rather burly man, greeted her.

"Good afternoon, Mr. Grampton. I need to pick up more of that leather conditioner you carry."

He nodded. "I've got some right here. Just got a fresh batch in."

"Excellent." She had hoped he would have a new batch. He'd been out the last time she'd stopped by.

After she paid him and collected her purchase, she stepped outside of the shop. A man bumped into her, causing her to turn to her right, and then suddenly, an arm clamped around her waist as a hand covered her mouth. In a panic, she dropped her purchase as she scrabbled at the hand over her mouth. She knew she couldn't escape the band around her waist. He lifted her up, making her think her assailant was taller than her, which freed her feet to kick as best she could. Unfortunately, that wasn't much since her blasted skirts hampered both her movements and any impact she may have made. Her heart was pounding in her chest, both from fear and the fact she was not able to draw a full breath with her mouth covered. Then she saw the carriage sitting at the curb with a door open and a man waiting to receive her.

She managed to bite the hand covering her mouth and screamed with the last bit of air she had left in her lungs. People seemed to take note of her distress, but that was when she was ripped free of her captor's arms. A dark avenging angel slammed a fist into the face of the man who she assumed had been holding her. He dropped to his knees but quickly staggered back to his feet. Having gotten back up, he lunged at her savior, who she could now see was Lucifer—she knew he'd been following her! Lucifer and the man squared off as the surrounding people surged back, giving them space. Furious at her attack, Amelia reached into her satchel that was strapped around her body and pulled out her whip. Uncoiling the length of leather, she stepped into the space and let the fall fly. The man who had attacked her cried out as her lash landed across his shoulders. There were gasps all around her, mostly from women, but a few men were quite shocked as well.

The man's coat parted, exposing his dingy shirt beneath. He turned, partially unsure who was the bigger threat. Her or Lucifer. In the end, he decided retreat was the better move and leapt toward the still waiting carriage before the door snapped shut and the vehicle raced away. With no target left, she coiled her whip and tucked it away as Lucifer straightened up and stepped toward her. "What the bloody hell do you think you are doing?"

Confused by his anger at her, she looked at him for a moment. "What do you mean? I was running an errand when I was attacked."

"I'm well aware of that. Why did you engage him when I had the situation under control?" Lucifer loomed over her and now had his hands on her shoulders.

"I didn't see that it was under control. I saw that a man who was equal to your size was ready to fight you. I have a skill that, under the circumstances, seemed to be rather useful." She snapped as she attempted to jerk her shoulders free from his grasp.

She was unsuccessful.

"Do not ever put yourself in such danger again! Do you understand me?" He nearly yelled as the crowd around them shifted uncomfortably.

"No. I shall do as I see fit should such a situation arise again. I am not a helpless woman. I have a skill that makes me rather dangerous, in case you weren't sure." She looked down at his hands. "Now kindly unhand me."

Out of the corner of her eye, she saw a carriage pull up and Lucifer's coachman jump down.

"No." He glared at her. "Not unless you will get in the carriage so I can take you somewhere safe."

She looked at him, then at the carriage. "I have an appointment I must keep."

"Woman, you were just attacked. Do not be stubborn about this. Let me—"

"I shall be perfectly safe with my customer. We can discuss this later, after I do my job." She glared at him, willed him to understand. She had to work to survive even as she looked for Cat. She needed to shove what had just happened into a tiny little box and go about her day. She refused to allow anyone to intimidate her ever again.

"No." His implacable reply was quickly followed by him bending over and planting a shoulder in her stomach before he stood back up. Three strides had him dumping her in the carriage and onto a bench. "If you will not take care of yourself, then I shall see to it for you." He jumped inside and snapped the door closed. "Home, Mr. Brown."

The carriage dipped as the coachman climbed up, and then the vehicle jerked and pulled away.

Fuming, Amelia sat and stared out of the window, watching London slip past.

Lucifer's gut still churned as he watched Amelia intently studying anything but him. He wanted to shake her, to rattle some sense into her hard head. He was well aware of her renowned skill with a whip, but that did not make her indestructible. He also knew she had been and still was avoiding him, but he wasn't certain why. That was a question he planned to get to the bottom of shortly.

They arrived at his Mayfair home in short order. It appeared Amelia had lost some of her fight by then since she regally dismounted from the vehicle, sailed up the steps of his home, and through the open door under her own steam. By the time he caught up to her, she had stalled in the foyer, unsure which way to go. "We can finish this discussion in my study."

He stalked past her and down the hall to his study. She came just behind him and then stood stiffly next to a chair in front of his desk. He tried to calm his mind and allow the adrenaline coursing through his veins to dissipate, but he was finding it difficult. "Please, come and sit here by the fire."

"I'm fine where I am." She had crossed her arms under her breasts, which only served to plump them up. Fortunately, she wore a modest dress with a high neckline that wrapped her delicate throat in lace. The navy blue silk made her eyes look dark and stormy. Or perhaps that was her temper? He couldn't be sure.

He crossed to where she stood, and that was when he noticed that she was visibly shaking. On a muttered curse, he hauled her into his arms and held her as she drew in a deep, shuddering breath. "You're safe."

She sighed and melted against him, her arms wrapping around his waist. "Thanks to you."

The feel of her pressed against him, even with all of her skirts in the way, was everything he knew it would be. Bloody hell, she was his. She belonged to him—with him. Why didn't she understand this? He drew back from her slightly and looked down at her. "You've been avoiding me. Why?"

Her lashes lowered, hiding the worry and fear in her eyes. "I told you when we started on this partnership that there could be no intimacy between us. No kissing. No sex. And yet, at every turn, I find your lips on mine."

He grinned unrepentantly. "I dare say you rather like it."

She shook her head, but no denial passed her lips.

"Liar." He growled as he leaned down and captured her lips in another kiss. Her hands slipped to his chest, and she pressed away from him. But he refused to allow her to lie to herself, let alone him, so he tightened the band of his arms and drew her closer to him. At the same time, he delved past her lips to sweep into the recesses of her mouth where she seemed to always taste of whiskey and something that was distinctly Amelia. As their tongues tangled, a low moan escaped her, and her hands slid up his chest until her arms snaked around his neck.

She met him stroke for stroke and taste for taste as she shifted closer to him. His cock grew thick and hard until it pressed against his trousers. He wanted to free his length and drive into her there in his study. It had been weeks since he'd last been with her, and the company of his own palm was simply not enough to replace her warmth, the tight clasp of her cunny around his cock, or the sweet taste of her desire on his lips.

With a growl, he broke their kiss and dropped to his knees. Lifting her skirts, he helped her prop her leg on the chair next to them, and then he found the opening in her drawers as she held her skirts back. "Lucifer, we shouldn't—" Her denial was swallowed by a breathy moan as he slid his tongue along her slit from her opening to her clit. She was already soaked with the sweetness he remembered and still craved.

He drew back and looked up at her. "I'll stop if you insist."

"Bloody hell, it's too late for that! Put that tongue back to work," she snapped, causing him to chuckle.

But he did as he was told and drove his tongue deep inside her before sweeping out to tease her nub. Her hands sank into his hair as his beard brushed her thighs. Her legs trembled with the effort required to hold her up, so he shifted until he was directly under her and could then reach up and brace her with his hands on her delectable arse. Continuing to feast on her, he worked over her clit and back inside her to fuck her with his tongue until she was grinding herself on his face in sheer abandon.

"Oh, God! Don't stop Lucifer! I'm so close." She cried out as her hips thrust into his face over and over. And then her entire body stiffened up as though she was about to tip over a precipice. He flicked his tongue over her clit once, twice. And then a third time, and she finally careened over the edge. "Yes!" She screamed loud enough that he was sure Parliament could have heard her. Nevertheless, he continued to work her clit even as her legs seemed to give out, and she slumped over him. As her body spasmed and more of her delicious juices flowed onto his tongue, he took her weight. Slowly he eased her back to the present, all the while continuing to stoke her desires to carry them over. He needed to sink into her, to feel her wrapped around him once more.

She dropped her leg from the chair and stood up under her own power, allowing him to rise to his feet. With the exception of the dampness around his mouth and the dreamy look in her eyes, it would be hard to tell she had just orgasmed for him. Her skirts fell back into place, her bodice remained primly buttoned up the front, and not a hair on her head dared to be out of place. He desperately wanted to destroy her serene façade, to muss her hair and dishevel her clothes as he fucked her hard. He darted a glance at his desk and decided there was no reason to wait. Kissing her once again, he eased her over toward the desk and then pressed her bottom against it. Pulling back, he looked down at her and tried to compose himself. His attempt was an utter failure.

He gave in to the need to kiss her further, even as he began to unbutton her bodice. He kissed her as though she were his very source of life. It certainly felt that way at the moment. Finally, after a few agonizing moments, he managed to get her bodice opened and reached into her corset to lift her breasts free. On a groan, he stooped down and sucked one nipple into his mouth to tease and nibble as he pinched her other nipple between his thumb and forefinger. She gasped and arched into his ministrations, as lost in the pleasure as he was. He switched to her other breast and reveled in the way she arched into him, pressing her flesh into his mouth. "More Lucifer. I need more."

More? He'd be happy to oblige.

Chapter Seventeen

Had she demanded more of him? She blinked as he redoubled his efforts and sucked even harder on her nipple. The sensation shot from her breast to her pussy and then straight to her feet, where her toes curled in her black kid boots. Yes, she wanted more, but bloody hell, it wasn't his mouth she wanted more of. She needed his cock inside her, forthwith!

She drew a breath, sank her hands in his hair once more, and this time pulled his head back until he was forced to leave off her nipple. She looked down at him, locking gazes until she was certain she had his full attention. "Fuck me, Lucifer."

His lids lowered slightly, his eyes filled with dangerous heat. "Are you sure that is what you want? I need to hear you say it again, Amelia."

"Fuck me, Lucifer. I need your cock in me. Filling me. Now." She infused her Mistress' voice into her demand to ensure he knew she wanted this. It was, of course, an utterly stupid thing for her to do, but once he'd started kissing her again, she knew she would break. Knew she would fall like a house of cards in a soft breeze.

"As the lady commands." He straightened up and then grabbed her by her shoulders and spun her around. "Bend over and grab the other edge of the desk."

She did as directed, eager to have him slide deep inside her again. She heard paper crinkle behind her, and then he lifted her skirts, letting the cool air of the room rush over her skin. Her pantalets were hanging by a thread thanks to his earlier attentions with his mouth, but apparently, he felt they were still in the way. He quickly shredded the linen undergarment and let each side slide down her legs. She whimpered, either with need or excitement. She couldn't be sure which. But whereas she normally preferred to be in control of her sexual encounters, she found herself perfectly content to allow him to lead. He'd always seen to her needs before his own, and she had no need to think he would do otherwise now.

He nudged her feet wider apart with his foot. "Spread your legs nice and wide. I want to see your pretty pussy before I fill it with my cock."

She groaned and did as he said. She must be quite the sight bent over his desk with her skirts up around her waist, ass bare, and her breasts smashed against the hard surface. He used his cock to spread her juices around before sliding along her slit and over her clit. She arched her hips back, trying to get more contact with him. Was he going to make her beg? She would. Right now, she would get down and grovel if only he would slide his hard cock inside her.

"Your cunny is soaked. So fucking wet." He ran a finger through her folds and then dragged it up between her cheeks to circle over her anus. "And this sweet spot is calling me. I want to see your ass stretched tight around me."

Again, she moaned. She tried not to speak, but the words slipped past her lips as her need took over. "Yes. Anything you want, just fuck me. Please!"

He growled and then pushed his cock into her pussy. She'd missed the feel of him sliding into her, stretching her. He finally seated himself all the way inside with his hips pressed to her backside. Then he pulled out to his tip and sank in again. A strangled noise escaped her somewhere between a moan and a groan. No one had ever filled her so perfectly. So thoroughly.

She gripped the desk, the edge cutting into her fingers a bit as her hands started to cramp. But she refused to let go, to move lest he become distracted from fucking her. He pumped into her over and over, hitting all the right spots to send sparks sizzling along her limbs. "Harder!"

Lucifer grunted and redoubled his efforts, thrusting into her again and again. Then he reached down and strummed her clit with his finger. Lights danced behind her eyes as her body exploded for the second time. "Lucifer! Yes," she yelled as her hips bucked backwards to meet his thrusts. He continued to stroke her little bundle of nerves, driving her through her climax and into another one, like riding the cresting waves of the sea. She rolled through a third orgasm as he continued to work in and out of her body. Slumped across his desk and boneless, she couldn't do anything more than lie there and receive him as he finally stiffened and then groaned as he came.

He pitched forward, covering her body with his and crushing her skirts into what she was sure would be an irreparable mess. She couldn't have cared less about that fact as she took his weight. As his cock wilted inside her, she felt him slide out. Then she heard the sound of his French Letter hitting the trash. She stood up and looked at him, trying to gauge what to say. How to behave after violating all her own rules in such a spectacular fashion.

He smoothed out her skirts as she closed up her bodice. He looked up from where he was bent over. "Are you well?"

She drew a deep breath. "I am. I still don't know if this is wise, but I can see that we are foolish to believe we might be capable of working together and not indulging whatever this spark is between us."

"Indeed. I must say I never had any intention of abiding by those silly rules. I wanted you when I didn't know who you were, and I still want you now that I do. You make me crazed with lust, and I refuse to ignore it." He crossed his arms over his chest. "But what we must discuss is why you were attacked today."

She sat down in the chair she had propped her foot on earlier and considered. She couldn't tell him about her past, but the truth was, the attack was more likely related to their investigation. Add to that, she wasn't even certain what she heard the other day, so it had probably been her imagination. Really, there was nothing to tell him. "I assume it is related to our search for Cat. Perhaps we are getting too close to our villain?"

He nodded. "I suppose it could be that simple. But I am certain there is something you are not telling me." He hesitated and then let out a breath. "I don't suppose you are of a mind to tell me what happened the other day out front?"

Her cheeks heated as she shook her head. "It was nothing. I thought I saw someone I know. But obviously, I was confused, because they are supposed to be elsewhere at the moment." There, she had not lied at all.

"Mmmm." He did not look convinced by her story.

Lucifer stared at her with his dark-eyed gaze, and it felt as though he could see inside of her. See all the secrets, all the lies, all the fear she'd carried around for the last twenty years.

"Most women who had been attacked on the street as you were today would have gone into hysterics. But not you." He reached out and tipped her chin up. "You were very self-aware as it all unfolded. Even now, in the privacy of my study, you seem relatively unfazed by what occurred."

She let her gaze dip downward despite his holding her face tipped up. "When one has experienced the worst life has to throw at you, everything that comes after is merely a shadow of what you've survived."

"You should not have had to survive such things. Did your parents not protect you?"

He stared at her, the weight of it heavy on her as she continued to look down. "They did what they could until they couldn't." She drew a shuddering breath and switched subjects away from her dark secrets. She shifted her gaze up to his implacable features. "Did you ever receive the correspondence Mr. Golden promised to send over?"

"I did. It contained nothing of import." He searched her face as though still trying to discover her truths.

"How disappointing. I'd hoped it might reveal some further avenue of investigation." Her chest grew tight as worry for Cat reasserted itself.

"Even if it had, considering what happened today, your time as an investigator has come to an end." His tone brooked no argument.

She pushed his hand off her chin and rose. "You have no authority over me. I shall investigate for as long as I need to."

"You will not. I insist you step aside and allow me to finish what you have started. It is no longer safe for you to continue." He crossed his arms over his rather impressive chest.

As physically attractive as she found him, his current stance on the subject of her investigation severely tarnished his appeal. "If you believe for one moment that you have any say in this matter, then you are as delusional as someone with late-stage syphilitic insanity."

He loomed over her despite her ungainly height for a woman. "You will not put yourself in further danger. End. Of. Discussion."

Anger thrummed through her veins as she stared up at him. "You. Have. No. Say. In. This." She punctuated each word with a poke of her finger, causing him to back up just enough she could sweep past him. "I shall speak with you later when you have calmed down."

He grunted. "I'm perfectly calm, and this will not change. You are finished searching for Cat. I shall find her for you."

"Good day, Lucifer." She started to walk out of his study but stopped when he called out.

"Amelia! Do not make me do something we shall both regret. I can and will stop you even if I must tie you to my bed to do it," he growled out behind her.

Incensed, she looked back over her shoulder and growled. "Just you try it, Lucifer. Just you try it."

And then she stormed out of his study and out of his house.

Chapter Eighteen

Lucifer needed to separate Amelia from the details of the investigation. The question was, how? How did he get her to let him handle it? Why did he even want to? Why did her missing apprentice matter to him? He groaned as he rolled over in his bed and sat up. It mattered because *she* mattered. Bloody fucking hell! How had that happened? How had he allowed her to worm her way inside him?

He stood from his empty bed, naked and annoyed. He fucking cared about her, about making her happy. Grabbing his robe, he slipped it on and stalked into his office. Regardless of the whys, he still had to figure out the how. How was he going to keep her away from the search for Cat so he could find the woman and still keep Amelia safe?

First, he needed to speak with Madame du Pompadour and see if she could intervene with Amelia and convince her to stay out of the search. If not, then he would scoop her up and keep her at his home. Even if he had to lock her up or tie her down. Second, he needed to figure out who sent the note to Phineas. The scrawl was familiar, but not so much so he could put his finger on who. Lastly, he wanted to go back and chat with Jenny at The Grand Hotel to see if there was anything else she could remember. There was some critical piece they were missing here. He just couldn't see what it was.

He swung the door to his office opened and bellowed, "Gordie! Breakfast!"

A moment later, the man came trundling into his office bearing a tray loaded down with breakfast. "No need to be yelling, Mr. Lucifer. I've got your breakfast right here." He set it down on a table off to the side of his desk.

"Apologies, Gordie, I seem to be out of sorts this morning." Lucifer felt his cheeks heating slightly with contrition.

His right-hand man straightened up. "That'd be because there hasn't been any cunny in your bed in too many weeks. Seems to me you should set that fact to rights."

Had any other person said such a thing to him, Lucifer would likely have struck them down where they stood. But Gordie had been with him since the beginning. He knew Lucifer when they'd both been scrawny boys scrabbling out their existence in the gutters of Seven Dials. "Shut your mouth lest I shut it for you."

Gordie grunted and kept moving out of the office. "Don't be surly just because you know I'm right."

The door closed, and Lucifer was blissfully alone again. All the better to stew in his own frustration. Gordie didn't know the first thing about where he'd had his cock of late. He may not have had Amelia in his bed, but he'd had her nonetheless. And it did nothing to take the edge off his temper. In fact, it had made him even more irritable since the headstrong woman wouldn't do as she was told. Well, except for when he was buried balls deep inside her. Then she was putty in his hands and would do whatever he told her. But, as soon as he slipped free of her body, he lost all control over the strong-willed woman.

He sighed and addressed his breakfast. He'd visit The Market shortly and see if he could get that part sorted out.

Lucifer looked at the woman who ran The Market from across her desk. Her blue eyes drilled into him. "And why should I intervene in this matter? Amelia is a grown woman and quite capable of making her own decisions."

Lucifer stiffened. "As I have already explained to you, if she continues to pursue this line of inquiry, she is putting herself in danger. She was attacked yesterday on Bond Street in front of a crowd of people. If someone is willing to do that, then she is not safe anywhere."

Madame harrumphed. "Of all my girls, she is the most capable of taking care of herself. You yourself said she used her whip to great effect to fend the assailant off of you."

Bloody hell! "That was after I ripped the man off her. He was about to toss her in a carriage and spirit her away!"

"I'm certain she would have turned things around if given an opportunity. And while I do understand your concern, please understand she is not my child or even a servant. I simply cannot control her comings and goings." Madame almost looked apologetic, but not quite.

Lucifer sat there a moment, considering his options. He could simply assign one of his men to watch her around the clock, but if she suspected he was doing that, then she would undoubtedly do her best to slip him when she chose to. That would leave her exposed. If he tied her to his bed, he couldn't very well just leave her. She would find a way to get loose unless he locked her away. And that would absolutely infuriate her. He sighed. Needs must. "I apologize in advance for the disruption to your business."

"Whatever do you mean?" Madame's eyes narrowed.

"Thank you for your time." Lucifer stood and exited her office. Gordie sat in the main salon waiting for him as he'd requested. He jerked his head, and Gordie immediately fell into step with him.

"Lucifer, what are you going to do?" Madame asked as she watched him march to the front of the house.

"What I must." Then he and Gordie walked upstairs. On the third floor, a maid hustled along the hallway but stopped short when she saw him and Gordie striding toward her. "Where is Mistress Lash's room?"

The girl squeaked as she jumped at his abrupt demand. "Here now, you two can't be up here. Customers must stay downstairs."

"Which door?" He growled rather than asked.

The girl paled but shook her head.

"I shall open every door up here if I must." He glared at the girl, who finally lifted a trembling finger and pointed at a door just to his left. Then she spun about and sprinted the way she'd come, heading toward what he assumed was the servants' stairs. She'd be alerting Madame and house security, no doubt.

He reached over and turned the knob on the door. It didn't budge. Stepping back, he lifted his foot and slammed it against the door near the knob. The wood splintered but didn't fully give. A second slam of his boot and the door swung open to reveal a gloriously furious Amelia. She stood in her morning robe with her black hair cascading about her shoulders and breasts. "Lucifer!"

"You're coming with me. Now," he barked at her as he stepped into her room. Everything was done in a rich mix of red, blue, and green.

"I most certainly am not. And you will pay to have my door repaired." She glared at him.

"You are, and I shall." He crossed to where she stood and latched on to her arm. "You can go with me willingly, or I can toss you over my shoulder and haul you out of here."

She snorted. "I'm no waif for you to carry about like so much baggage. But I shall not go willingly. Now stop this foolishness."

Clearly, she had forgotten that he'd done that very thing the day before and his warning. He bent over, planted his shoulder in her stomach, and straightened up.

Amelia screeched as she pounded on his back. "Put me down, you overbearing son of a bitch!"

"I gave you fair warning." Lucifer cleared her splintered doorway and headed down the stairs. Gordie led the way, prepared to deal with any resistance they may encounter. They reached the foyer as Madame appeared flanked by her biggest footmen. They still came up short of Gordie's height by easily five inches, though one of them was nearly as broad as his man. "If you will excuse me, Madame. I am going to keep her safe, even if she refuses to cooperate."

"Put me down! This is outrageous, even for you!" She continued to beat her fists on his back.

"Gordie, the door." Lucifer shifted her weight higher up on his shoulder and secured her with one hand gripping her arse and the other the backs of her knees.

With the door quickly opened, he marched out of The Market, down the front steps, and then dumped his cargo in his carriage. He climbed in behind her before she could get herself righted and make a lunge for the other door. Once Gordie joined them, she settled down, realizing there were two of them to contain her if need be.

"I hope you understand I am doing this for your own good." He offered as he settled back on his bench.

She just glared at him.

"It's not safe for you to be out there poking around. I told you your investigation must end, and I meant it." He crossed his arms over his chest. He would not allow her to be injured or worse. "I've put all my resources on this issue. I promise I shall find Cat for you."

She refused to speak to him still, just sat there fuming and glaring as the carriage rumbled over the cobblestone streets. It was mid-morning, so most of Mayfair was still abed and would hardly notice if a woman was carried kicking and screaming from his carriage to his house. The vehicle pulled to a stop.

"Are you going to walk into the house, or shall I carry you again?" He asked and waited as he subtly adjusted his throbbing erection. Having his hand planted on her backside while hauling her about had stirred his darker instincts. In truth, a part of him hoped she'd force him to carry her in. Though he wasn't certain he would be able to resist taking her straight to his bed should that occur.

"I'll walk inside. I'd rather you didn't touch me at the moment." She spoke through clenched teeth with her hands fisted at her sides.

Lucifer tilted his head as he tamped down his disappointment. "Very well."

Gordie opened the door and jumped down from the carriage. He then lowered the steps and held out a hand to assist Amelia. She, however, lifted the hem of her robe and swept from the carriage and up to his house for the second time in as many days. Lucifer pinched the bridge of his nose. This was not going well.

Inside the house, Amelia stood in the foyer once again. Her back was stiff, her hands fisted at her sides. "Show me to my cell," she spoke so loudly all of Mayfair might have heard her.

Lucifer was horny, angry, and frustrated by the sheer obstinance of the woman. His butler had appeared when the carriage pulled up. "Peters, please see Ms. Kettering to the room we prepared for her. Gordie will escort you to ensure our *guest* does not cause any trouble."

"Very good, Mr. Lucifer." He turned to Amelia. "This way Miss."

Amelia strode behind him, followed by Gordie.

Lucifer turned and headed to his study. Fearing this would be the outcome, he had his paperwork sent over from the club so he could remain nearby should he be needed. He was shuffling through the invoices when something caught his eye on an old invoice. But a knock sounded on his door before Gordie walked in. "She's settled in the room, and Brig and Huntly are sitting outside her room. Gentry and Larkin are in the garden, ensuring she doesn't do anything foolish."

"Thank you. If you could return to The Market and collect some clothing for her as well as any ladies' things," Lucifer waved his hand around vaguely, "she may require. I'm sure Madame or one of the ladies will be able to assist you."

Gordie nodded and quickly departed.

Lucifer returned to the invoices he'd been looking at and reached down to adjust his cockstand. It would subside shortly, he was certain. He scanned the pages and wished he could fire his old manager all over again. He'd caught the man skimming off the books by over-ordering supplies from his partners, who then paid him a large percentage of the overpayment. He would then falsify the inventory counts. It wasn't until a number of employees had complained about the shortages that anyone had figured out what was happening. Lucifer fired the man and had punctuated that news with a beating by Gordie. The same message had been delivered to the man's partners, along with termination of their supply agreements. He didn't do business with cheats and liars.

He had yet to replace the man, which was why he was reviewing the invoices against inventory to be sure they had received everything they had paid for and that there weren't any further issues to address. It had been three months without issue, and he was fairly certain the thieves had been rooted out. Now, he needed to hire a new manager.

As he stared at the notes in the margins of some of the old invoices, which he was using for comparison, the handwriting jumped out at him. He quickly shuffled the invoices aside and dug about for the note Phineas had sent over. He found it tucked in a drawer and unfolded it, laying it out next to the invoices. He saw the similarities immediately. His former manager had sent the note to Phineas. But the question was, where was he now?

Chapter Nineteen

Night had fallen as Amelia stewed, locked in an elegant suite on the second floor of Lucifer's Mayfair home. She'd considered shimmying out the window but had quickly noted the two guards located in the garden. She assumed there was at least one more outside of her door, not that she'd confirmed that since said door was locked.

A tray had been delivered around mid-day, but she'd been too angry to eat a thing. She'd sent the tray away untouched. A decision she was beginning to regret. Her stomach rumbled loudly as a knock sounded at the door. She rolled her eyes at such an idiotic courtesy. She was a prisoner. "By all means, do come in."

The sound of the lock clicking preceded the door opening. A footman entered carrying a trunk, followed by a maid with a cart. Behind both of them stood Lucifer. He allowed them to deliver their burdens, and then he stepped inside as the door locked once again. She eyed the trunk, a little worried about what it might indicate. Was it for her? Was he planning to make her disappear? She'd seen a man she'd known all her life do unspeakable things. She'd only known Lucifer a few months by comparison. Why wouldn't he be capable of disposing of her? Especially if he was the very man she'd been hunting.

Her gut twisted. He had appeared everywhere she'd searched for Cat. It had become farcical even. But she'd lain with him. Had given him free access to her body, and he'd never done anything to confirm he was the man she'd been searching for. So, the trunk introduced more questions than it answered. And it certainly didn't match with what appeared to be a dinner service for two. She was so confused!

Lucifer motioned toward the trunk. "I had Gordie go back to your room and collect some of your things to make your stay more comfortable."

"My things?" She didn't understand. That trunk had her clothing and things inside it?

"Yes, your things. Clothing, toiletries, etcetera." He walked over to the cart and lifted one of the lids off the plates. "I also had dinner brought up for both of us. I understand you refused to eat earlier today. I expect you to eat tonight. I shall not tolerate you starving yourself in some misguided protest over your stay with me."

"Misguided protest!" Her ire surfaced in a flash, as though it was simmering water that had merely needed to have the flame turned up to begin to boil. "I am a free woman. A rational, intelligent woman capable of making my own decisions! Should I choose to starve myself in protest, I would hardly call it misguided. It might even be self-preservation since, for all I know, you've doused my food with drugs... or even poison."

He seemed to choke and then growl at her last declaration, but she refused to be cowed, even as her cheeks heated at such outlandish accusations. "Did you just accuse me of poisoning you?" He looked incredulous. "Are you in your right mind, woman? Why in the bloody hell would I poison you?"

His face grew thunderous as he loomed over her, closing the distance between them.

"Answer me!" He bellowed, clearly furious at her suggestion.

"I don't know! Why would you imprison me?" She yelled back, just as distraught at her suggestion and at the idea that it might be true.

"To protect you! To keep you safe when you won't do so yourself. I'd never drug you, let alone poison you!" He shook her a little as he yelled at her further.

She gulped past the knot in her throat. "How am I supposed to know that?"

He growled again and then crushed his lips to hers. Her hands pressed against his chest, trying to push him away. She turned her head and whimpered. "I can't."

Reaching up, he used a finger to turn her face back to his. "You can. You can, and you want this as much as I do."

"Damn you!" She cried as she slipped her arms around his neck and pulled him down for a kiss. Their tongues tangled, twining as he plucked at the ties of her robe. He peeled the sides open and slipped his hands up to cup her breasts. She arched as her nipples pebbled, and her cunny throbbed with desire. The man was a weakness. He made her want things she had no business wanting.

He kissed his way down her throat to her breasts, where he suckled one through her linen chemise. The suction of his mouth, the heat, and the texture of the fabric all colluded to bring her to her knees. Or she would have been, had the bed not miraculously appeared behind her. When had he walked them closer to it? How had he known she would need that support? Did it matter?

She moaned and pressed up into his mouth as he shifted from one nipple to the other. Lost to the sensations, she melted into the mattress and let him have his way. When he finally pulled off her sensitive peaks, she looked up at him, her eyelids heavy with desire. He looked just as affected as she was, except that he was still fully clothed. She sat up and reached for his trousers. "Please."

He looked down at her, his eyes a black blaze of desire. "Please what?"

"Please, don't stop." She needed him. Needed to feel him inside her.

"No. Say it. Say what you want. I shall not be accused of taking what was not freely given." He crossed his arms and waited.

She slipped her robe off, slid back on the bed so she could spread her legs, and stroked her fingers over her soaked pussy. "Please, I need your cock inside me."

His eyes widened, and then he fell on her like a ravenous man. He spread her thighs wide and rubbed his beard along her inner thighs, up one side and down the other. "Fuck, look at that sweet, wet cunny."

Then he licked up her slit and swirled over her clit. Sensation rippled along her body, from her core to her fingertips and toes. Her hips bucked, and she reached down and sank her fingers into his hair. Then she ground up against his face, loving the scruffiness of his beard as he worked her clit over. She moaned and laid back, keeping a hand on his head. "That's it, Lucifer. Yes."

He added two fingers, sliding them deep inside her heat and curling them up to stroke that spot deep inside her. Her body shook, and she cried out. "Yes! Oh God, yes!" As her pussy clenched on his fingers, her hips rocked, and she fisted the bedspread in her other hand. All the while, she pulled his hair, keeping him where she wanted him as she ground against his face. When she finally floated back down, he looked up the length of her body, a wicked, smug grin on his shiny lips.

Then he stood up and shucked his clothing before she could form a coherent thought. Afterward, he crawled on the bed and came between her thighs. He reached down and grabbed the neck of her chemise with both hands. Then he shredded the sheer cotton right down the middle. Since she had no drawers on to start with, she lay completely exposed to him. And despite still being angry about what he'd done, she could not deny the man made her blood thrum. "Yes, fuck me."

He grunted and slid deep inside her with one firm thrust of his cock. She loved the way he filled her up, needed him like she hadn't just had him the day before. With one of his hands planted by her head, he withdrew and slid back inside her. He worked his cock in and out of her, finding a steady rhythm that teased her body right to that edge but never let her slip over into bliss.

Instead, he kept them both dangling on the edge for what seemed like forever. Then he stopped altogether. She wrapped her legs around him and tried to force him to fill her, but he simply smiled at her and shook his head. "No."

She looked up at him, startled. "What is this? Some new form of punishment?"

"No, I want to fuck your arse." He ground the words out as his body shook. Clearly, it was costing him to not slide back inside her.

"Now?" Her voice came out in a much higher pitch than she had intended.

He shook his head. "No, not now. But soon. I want to sink into your tight arse and feel the heat of you there."

She wasn't sure what to say. She'd never allowed a man to do that to her. Had never really considered it.

"I want to see your tight little ring stretched wide to take me as I sink into the soft globes of your bum. Maybe even spank them until they glow red while I do it." His voice was thick, almost slurred with his desire.

She tried to lift her hips to push him back inside her aching cunny. "Can we discuss this later? After you make me scream your name again?"

Indecision warred with determination on his face. "Not until you say yes. Tell me I can take your arse."

She rolled her lips inward as she tried to decide, but thinking was so hard when the tip of his cock was teasing her entry, hinting at all of the delicious fullness she'd had only moments before. "I- I- I've never let anyone do that." She finally got out.

"Fuck, woman! It's mine. I'll take it if I have to, but I want you to give it to me. Say yes." He ground out as his upper body trembled with his restraint.

Could she? God, yes. She'd take him wherever, however, he wanted if he would just sink back inside her. "Yes. You can do whatever you want to me. I'm yours." She cursed as he slammed deep inside of her. Had she said that last part out loud? But then he was stroking into her again and strumming her clit with one hand. She raced up the precipice and was quickly flung over the edge as he pumped into her over and over. She screamed his name as her body seemed to shatter into a thousand pieces.

She slowly came down as he held still, waiting for her to come back to him. "So fucking beautiful." Then he pumped into her, slamming his hips against her pelvis as he leaned down and sucked on one of her nipples. He quickly let go and groaned, then pumped once. Twice. A third time, and then he shouted her name as he shot his load deep inside her. He sank down on top of her and panted in her ear as they both recovered. Finally, he lifted up and slid out of her. That was when she felt his seed on her thighs.

"Bloody hell!" He looked down in horror. "I forgot to wear a letter."

She looked up at his concerned face and laid a palm against his cheek. "I know how to take care of this. If your man packed all my things, then I should have what I need."

"I should have been more careful. I'm always careful. I won't sire a bastard like my father did." He cursed again as he climbed off the bed.

She sat up, unselfconscious about her nudity. "If I were pregnant, would you acknowledge your babe?"

He looked offended that she would ask. "Of course!"

"Would you help me care for the child and see to its welfare?"

"What kind of monster do you think I am?" He turned his back on her, soft curses slipping from his lips.

"Then you are not like your father. You are a good man, Lucifer." And she gasped. She felt like such a bitch at that moment. Earlier, she had allowed her ridiculous fear and anger to get the best of her. Had allowed it to let her believe he would kill her and shut her in a trunk. But she knew this man. Knew he was a good person inside, no matter what circumstances had made him do to survive.

He grunted. "I am not a good man. Do not allow yourself to be so easily fooled. I've done things. Hurt people. I am not a good man. But you're right; I am not my father."

She scooted forward on the bed. "I disagree. And I apologize if I suggested otherwise earlier. I was hurt and angry. But I know you would never hurt me."

Climbing off the mattress, she stepped up behind him and circled her arms around his waist. "But we do need to discuss you locking me away."

"I need to keep you safe." He croaked the words out, though she wasn't sure if it was because he was upset or just parched from their vigorous activities.

She stroked his stomach and felt his muscles ripple with each touch. "What if I promise to let you have someone follow me everywhere I go, with or without you? If I promise not to sneak away?"

He turned in her arms and looked down at her. "And you'll stay here under my roof until this is over?"

Deep down, she wanted to suggest such a thing would ruin her reputation, but then she realized that didn't matter. It did not matter because she wasn't a society miss and because this man only cared that she was safe. Not that she was pure, or even appeared to be. "Yes. I'll stay here as long as I can share your bed. I won't stay in this room alone."

He grinned. "My room is through that door there." He pointed to the other locked door in the room.

She looked at the door and then back at him. "I should have known these rooms were too nice to be mere guest rooms."

Her heart skipped a beat as he leaned down and kissed her again. She was in way too deep with this man. She only hoped it wouldn't end badly when the time came.

Chapter Twenty

Lucifer gritted his teeth as yet another drunk stumbled into him and Amelia. How in the hell had she convinced him to bring her to The Devil's Den? He reached over and wrapped an arm around her waist, drawing her closer to his body. He leaned in so he could speak into her ear. "Please let me take you back to my house and return here to ask our questions."

She slid a glance at him, her nose tipping up in sheer obstinance. "No. I shall do this with or without you."

He cursed silently in his head and reconsidered his original plan to lock her in his house. But despite the unsavory environment of the gambling hell nestled on the edges of Seven Dials, he knew he couldn't do that. He should, but he couldn't. He frowned. Another slovenly drunk staggered toward them, but this one had a more lascivious glint in his eye. As he stumbled toward Amelia, Lucifer shoved her behind him and reached out to slam a fist directly into the man's face. The fool never saw it coming. As he collapsed in a heap on the ground, Amelia gasped, but Lucifer kept urging her past the man.

"Lucifer! That was unnecessary!" She kept glancing over her shoulder as he moved them toward the man he'd been looking for since they arrived.

"That was very necessary. If only for my peace of mind," he growled. The man they'd come to this establishment to speak to stood off in a corner doing largely what he'd done while running Lucifer's club. Nothing. He recognized the activity, or lack thereof. "Mr. Lewiston, a word if you please."

The man in question straightened up and paled as he realized who had spoken to him. That knowledge satisfied the savage streak that ran through Lucifer. He didn't tolerate cheats, liars, or thieves. Lewiston had turned out to be all three. "Lucifer."

"That's Mr. Lucifer to you." Lucifer opened the note they'd been sent by Phineas and showed it to the gangly man. "Who had you deliver this note to Phineas Golden?" He swore his former employee's knees were knocking.

The man blinked slowly. "I'm afraid I don't recognize that letter."

Lucifer growled and leaned in. "Try again. I matched your handwriting to some old invoices with your notes on them."

The man paled but remained mute.

"Do not make me ask again." Lucifer glared at the man.

"I-I—"

"Lewiston!" A pair of aspiring dandies sauntered over and ignored that Lucifer was currently speaking with the man. They circled around him, slapping him on the back and behaving as though they were long-lost friends. "Where've you been, old chap!"

"Excuse me. I was speaking to Lewiston, here." Lucifer ground out through gritted teeth.

The two men looked at him in surprise, as though they hadn't seen him when they brushed right past him. "Were you?" The one on the left asked.

"Listen here, old man. We were just saying hello to our old friend here." The other one said as he patted Lucifer on the shoulder.

Lucifer grabbed the offending hand and bent it backwards until the man dropped to his knees as he cried out. "Do not put your hands on me, you glorified peacock."

"Stop that! Here now, let him go!" The other one started dancing around, squawking.

Lucifer looked up to tell the man to shut up but realized as he did that Lewiston had slipped away. "Which way did Lewiston go?" He barked to no one in particular as he released the peacock's hand.

Amelia glanced around as they both tried to find their quarry once more. Meanwhile, the man on the ground was huddled over his hand, crying as though it might never work again. His friend grew more indignant and pushed Lucifer's shoulder. "You can't just go about breaking people's hands!"

"I did no such thing. Now move if you don't wish to join him on the floor." Lucifer growled and spun around. Across the room, he spotted the green jacket Lewiston had been wearing slip between two men and then disappear. "Fuck!"

"Lucifer, we should try to catch him." Amelia urged as she started after the man. Ignoring the ridiculous dandies, they bolted through the thickening crowd. Where he'd last seen the man was a door. A locked door.

"Bloody hell!" He wanted to kick the door in but knew it would be pointless… and possibly not needed. "We should go."

Amelia looked shocked. "But he went through that door. We should go after him."

"It's locked, Amelia. Besides, you didn't think I waltzed in here with just you at my side?" Lucifer snorted and then tucked her hand under his arm. They strolled out and found his carriage awaiting them.

As he helped Amelia climb in, she stopped abruptly and gasped. "It seems you were prepared for the man to try and slip you," she drawled as she delicately stepped over the trussed-up form of Mr. Lewiston.

"Once a snake, always a snake." Lucifer grinned at her, but really it was more of a baring of teeth. "Now, I shall drop you by my home, and then I shall go have a private chat with our guest. Somewhere we won't be interrupted a second time."

Amelia crossed her arms and got that stubborn glint in her eye. "You know I'll not agree to that. I'm coming with you."

He sighed and pinched the bridge of his nose. "I do wish you'd simply do as you're told once in a great while."

"And I wish you'd stop believing that you have the right to tell me what to do." She glared at him.

He reached up and slid the window open to speak to his driver. "Straight to the club."

"Very good, sir." The muffled reply was cut off as he closed the slider.

Twenty minutes later, they were in the warehouse behind his club. Mostly he stored supplies, gaming tables, and whatnot back there. But on occasion, he used it to speak with certain people who needed more convincing than the average.

With Lewiston tied to a chair and unable to slip away again, Lucifer felt confident he could get to the bottom of things. Amelia, of course, stood off to the side to watch the proceedings. He looked at his former employee and slipped the gag off his mouth.

"Mr. Lucifer... I swear. I don't know anything." the man stammered out as soon as he could.

"As I said earlier, I know it's your handwriting. Do not pretend you didn't write the note." Lucifer crossed his arms and waited.

Lewiston's eyes darted around the room as though looking for someone who might rescue him. When his gaze landed on Amelia, he focused on her. "Pleas Miss. I don't know anything. I swear I don't."

Amelia glared at the man, and Lucifer chuckled. "Don't look to her. If she had her way, you'd be strung up right now, feeling the bite of her whip. She's rather invested in finding who sent the note since they have taken someone she cares about."

The man nodded. "I wrote it. But I did it for an old mate."

"Who?" Lucifer demanded.

Lewiston sat there, eyes wide and darting around wildly as he seemed to consider his options.

Amelia sighed. "Just break a finger or call Gordie in. Do something. This dithering is tedious."

His gaze snapped to her as his jaw hinged open in shock.

Lucifer shrugged one shoulder. "I warned you she was not the weak spot in the room. And I do tend to agree with her. This whole conversation has grown tiresome." He walked over to the office door and opened it. With a simple nod, Gordie joined them in the warehouse. "Our friend here needs assistance with loosening his tongue."

Gordie reached down to where the man's hands were tied to the chair and grabbed his index finger on his right hand.

"Please, Mr. Lucifer. I-I-I can't!" Tears leaked from his eyes as he watched Gordie.

The snap of bone breaking was drowned out by the man's screams. After long moments of moaning, the sound died down.

"Once again, who asked you about the warehouse?" Lucifer stared. He needed the name, and he needed it now.

Lewiston shook his head, mumbling to himself as he rocked as much as his bindings allowed.

"Again, Gordie."

"No!" Lewiston cried out, ending his litany. "It was Garvey. Manfred Garvey." Lewiston looked panicked.

"And this Garvey, was this his plot? Or someone else's?"

The man's eyes widened and then focused back on him. "I swear I don't know. He just asked me for a warehouse!"

"Then why did you send the note as though it was from me?" He wanted to know why he'd been effectively incriminated by this Garvey. "Did Garvey ask you to do it?"

"I can't say more. He'll kill me!"

Lucifer's body went rigid. "As will I if you don't answer my questions. I'd be doing London a favor if I did."

The man let out a strangled groan. "Please, Mr. Lucifer."

"Again, Gordie."

"Fuck!" The man's upper lip quivered. "He just asked me to find him a warehouse. He thought I still worked for you and had access to them. I figured I could send a note to Golden as though it was from you, and neither of you would be the wiser."

The man slumped over, his breathing ragged as his bindings took his body weight.

Frustration rode Lucifer as he looked at the wrung-out lump of man. He'd clearly told them all he knew, except for one last thing. "Where can I find Manfred Garvey?"

"A taproom in Seven Dials. The Crown and Sow. Please, no more." The man whimpered.

"Very well. It seems that is all you know. Now listen carefully, Mr. Lewiston." Lucifer waited until Gordie grabbed the man by his hair and forced his head up. "I am not going to kill you. Instead, I'll give you an opportunity. Leave London tonight. Do not let the sun rise on your worthless hide, and never show your face in this city again. Should I hear of your presence, it will be the last of you. Am I clear?"

"Yes! Thank you, Mr. Lucifer!" Lewiston answered quickly.

"Do not cross me on this. I shall not let you go a third time." Lucifer stared at him for a long moment and then turned his back. "Shall we head upstairs, Amelia?"

She nodded and took his arm as they left the warehouse through another door that let them into his club. He was glad this night's work was done, though he knew Gordie would send someone to look for this Garvey fellow. That went without saying.

Amelia held onto Lucifer's arm as they entered his club, her heart finally slowing after what had occurred in the warehouse. It was hard to believe that he had been instrumental in garnering this new clue. Could she have discovered any of what they'd learned without his help? Highly unlikely. And even had she somehow managed to track down Mr. Golden or even Mr. Lewiston, she certainly would not have had the resources to secure Mr. Lewiston's cooperation as adeptly as Lucifer had. No. She had to admit that despite all of her life experience, which told her men were not trustworthy, this man seemed to defy the norm. He was rather high-handed at times, overly bossy, and much too sure of himself. But the one thing he had not proven to be was untrustworthy.

At least, up to now.

The crowd at Lucifer's was quite thick, people milling about as they decided which games to play. Most of the tables had both active gamblers and spectators, though there was room for others to join in yet. It seemed the evening was really on the cusp of being in full swing. All around her, men and women, though mostly men, were talking and laughing. The cacophony of sound swallowed them whole as they moved through the throng.

Lucifer leaned over so she could hear him. "Why don't we head upstairs where it is much less noisy and certainly more private?"

She nodded, finding the growing crowd more than she cared for. She often avoided The Market's main salon at peak times because the number of people that crammed in there could be overwhelming. This appeared to be even worse from her perspective. Though she was certain Lucifer was pleased, as the number of bodies indicated a fair amount of soon-to-be realized income.

They pressed through the crush and were nearly through the masses when a voice caught her ear. Her feet stopped as though the vines in the carpet pattern had come to life and wrapped themselves around her ankles, anchoring her to where she stood. Lucifer tugged on her arm, but she remained rooted to the ground as she strained to hear that voice once more.

American accents tended to standout amidst both the more cultured English accents as well as the harsher, less cultured ones. She looked at the faces she could see in her proximity, searching for a familiar one. But everywhere she looked, she saw strangers. Her heart pounded in her chest, and her palms grew sweaty as her breathing became shallow. Had she laced her corset too tight? She could barely draw a breath.

Lucifer pulled closer to her again and curved an arm about her shoulders. "Are you well?"

Was she? Was she well? No. No, she didn't think she was, because if Richard Mattingly was in London, then her very life could be at risk in a far greater capacity than Lucifer even realized. She blinked and tried to draw a steadying breath. "No. I think the crowd…"

He seemed to take her response as a call to action and quickly drew her the last few steps through the bodies and up the stairs. As they walked along the gallery that looked over the crowded gambling hell, she couldn't help but continue to search for a face to match the voice she'd heard. She refused to believe she'd been hearing things. It was far too real to be her mind playing tricks on her. It was also the second time she'd thought she'd heard it.

If she was right and he was in London—the question was, why? Why was he there? Had he somehow discovered her whereabouts? Her identity? Had he somehow pieced together the missing American heiress and a notorious harlot from London? Was he there to finish what he'd started twenty years before?

Chapter Twenty-One

Two days later, Amelia was disappointed to learn that Lucifer's men had been unsuccessful in finding Garvey. The man was eluding them, whether by design or sheer luck. She needed him to be found, but she was once again trapped in Lucifer's home in Mayfair, with no way to escape his ever-vigilant staff. She paced the length of the front salon with the lovely bay windows. Lucifer was out, either at his club or investigating without her. Obviously, he'd said he would be at his club taking care of a few things that had cropped up, but she worried that he was attempting to protect her again.

After her moment of panic the other night, she was certain Lucifer would press her more about what was wrong. But he'd thankfully taken her allusion to the crowd being an issue at face value. Of course, he may also have assumed she'd been overwhelmed by what had occurred in the warehouse. At the time, it had seemed that he understood the depths of her need to find Cat, to rescue her. But later, as he'd peeled her clothing off her in his room behind his office, he'd seemed more concerned. Had even been reluctant to touch her until she'd gotten some color back in her cheeks. That and she'd demanded he fuck her. That had been the thing to turn the trick.

Still pacing, she was at a loss about what to do next. Restless and frustrated at seemingly just sitting there with no plan of action, she was beyond grateful when the butler knocked and then entered, bearing a silver salver. "A Message has arrived for you, Miss Ketting."

She ceased her endless walking and approached the man who seemed to be her salvation. "Thank you, Peterson." She took the note from where it lay and waited for the man to make his exit. Alone, she pulled on the flap of paper and opened the envelope. Inside, there was another short note scrawled in unfamiliar handwriting. She was growing weary of being manipulated in such a manner, with a second mysterious note now appearing.

Don't miss the boat, or you will miss your last chance to save your friend. Dock 44 at 2 p.m.

She glanced at the watch pinned to her breast and cursed. It was already half-past one. She threw the door of the salon open and burst into the foyer. "Peterson! I need a hack."

He appeared from wherever it was that butlers lurk. "I can have the carriage brought around shortly."

"No time! I'll just be a moment, if you could hail a cab for me."

She flew upstairs to grab her cloak and whip before bounding out the front door a few moments later. Peterson looked far too placid for her taste, but then he was not the one that had received such a note. Nonetheless, the man had a cab waiting for her at the curb. She clamored into the cab and called out instructions to the driver. "Dock 44 and hurry!"

She'd already lost five minutes grabbing her cloak and whip, but she would not leave unarmed, as it were. The docks were no place for a woman alone, and, well she knew it. But she couldn't wait for Lucifer to return home, let alone have the time to send him a note. She needed to save Cat.

As usual, London traffic was monstrous, and she cursed every few minutes as she watched the clock tick. What might normally be a ten-minute ride had stretched to nearly double that, leaving her minutes to find the ship. She cursed and reached into her pocket for the note she'd received. She came up empty-handed. "Bloody hell!" She must have dropped it in her haste to leave Lucifer's house. But then, as she thought about the words on the page, she realized they'd given her no ship name. Just the dock number and a time. It was nearly two o'clock, and she had no time to waste. She threw open the cab door and barreled out as she called up to the driver, "I shan't be but a moment. A sovereign for your patience!"

She could hear the man cursing behind her, but she figured he'd wait based on her promise of coin. She rushed down the dock and was dismayed to see there were no less than five ships docked. A frustrated growl escaped her, and then she began yelling as loud as she could. She called Cat's name over and over as she ran down the length of the dock.

As she neared the last ship, a hand latched on to her arm. "Here now, miss; maybe I can help you?" The man's thick Cockney accent fairly swallowed the words, but she understood enough to know he wasn't likely to be of much assistance.

She pulled her arm free. "No, thank you. I'll find who I need on my own."

The man shrugged and let her go. She started back the way she came when two men appeared ahead of her. Shoulder to shoulder, they blocked her path, taking up the entire available space left from crates stacked along the dock's edge. It was one of many choke points she had slipped through on her way down the dock. The problem was, these men did not look friendly and proved such as they stopped where they stood. She had no path forward.

Not hesitating, she reached into her cloak and pulled her whip free as she flipped the sides of the garment back over her shoulders and out of the way. "Gentleman, I highly suggest you clear a hole."

The man on the left smiled and shook his head. The other laughed openly. "Careful, you don't hurt yourself now, miss. We were told to bring you along unharmed."

She huffed but relished that, as was to be expected, most men underestimated a woman's ability to defend herself. The one on the right moved forward and lunged for her. She snapped her whip forward and clipped his right cheek. "I suggest you rethink your actions. I've merely given you a taste of what is to come if you pursue me."

The man growled. "Bitch!"

And then he pressed forward again. She sliced across his shirt and side stepped him as he stumbled toward her. She put the crates to her back and now had the bleeding man on her left and the other man on her right. Again, the man she'd struck came at her, but this time, his friend joined him. With two quick snaps of her whip, she managed to clip both their faces, causing more damage than the first nick she'd given the one. They both cursed and fell back, but she'd neither gained ground nor lost it. They were drawing the attention of the men on the surrounding ships, though none that took the form of assistance. She decided it was time to end this little interlude. She took the offensive.

In a move neither man anticipated, she snaked her whip out and wrapped it around the man on her right's ankle. With a heave that she was sure would have thrown her back out, she unbalanced the man enough that he took two steps forward and toppled over. She freed her whip and started to dart past him when two things happened at once. The man that had felt the bite of her whip multiple times lunged toward her again. Meanwhile, the man on the ground reached out and grabbed her ankle.

Unexpectedly, the worker she'd encountered earlier slammed his fists down on the lunging man's back, causing him to drop to the dock in a heap. Distracted by this, the man holding her ankle released her when she jerked her foot forward, allowing her to sprint away. She was nearly clear of the dock when she chanced a glance back to ensure no one pursued her. Thankfully no one had, but then she slammed into a hard chest that smelled all too familiar.

"Amelia!" Lucifer's growl rumbled from his chest as his arms closed around her. "What the devil were you thinking coming here alone?"

She glanced behind her once more. "Do you have men with you?"

"Just Gordie." He didn't need to motion to the hulking man behind him.

She peeked over his shoulder and spotted him immediately. "Please, there is a man down there who helped me escape an ambush. He would be the one not bloodied by my whip and likely fighting two rather large men."

Lucifer sighed. "Go."

Gordie thudded past them and disappeared into the melee of men on the dock, most of whom were simply putting in a hard day's work.

Lucifer then bundled her closer with one arm and picked her up with the other beneath her knees. She should object to such manhandling, but she wouldn't. She realized she'd been rather terrified, now that the moment had passed, and she was able to admit such without fear of repercussion. "Thank you."

She wasn't certain he'd heard her as he climbed into his carriage with her in tow. But he grunted and said, "I'm not certain what you are thanking me for since you'd already rescued yourself."

A smile she couldn't control slipped over her lips. "But you came for me."

He nodded. "Of course I did."

Bloody hell! How could she think I wouldn't? He'd follow her to the ends of the earth if she required it of him. Of course, she didn't need to know that. His heart still pounded in his chest from receiving the alarming note from Peterson that Amelia had darted out of the house and was on her way to Dock 44. He'd found the note she'd dropped in the front salon and had sent it along as well.

Lucifer took one look and realized it had been a lure. For whatever reason, they now seemed to want to capture Amelia as well as Cat and Lucy. But he hadn't discerned why yet. It seemed strange to consider that even in this day and age, women could still go missing, and no one seemed to be concerned. Of course, they weren't ladies of the Ton, so why would there be a hue and cry? He repressed the growl that wanted to erupt.

"Oh no! My hackney. I still owe him for carrying me here, and I promised him a sovereign for waiting."

"Yes, I've already taken care of that. Found him on our way in, and he was more than happy to confirm he'd brought you here once he was assured I would cover your fare."

"Thank you. I dashed out of the house without a farthing, I'm afraid."

She still sat in his lap and in his arms, which might be the only reason he was able to remain calm about the entire situation. "That is the least of your transgressions today."

She wrinkled her nose at that and then apparently decided it was a conversation best left for later. "Should you go and check on Gordie?"

"He'll be along momentarily. No need to worry." Lucifer knew his man could take any situation in hand. His hope was that he managed to retrieve some information about who had been after Amelia. "Did the men say anything to you about why they wanted you?"

She shook her head. "No. Though one did say that they had been instructed to bring me in unharmed. I think the chap was worried I would hurt myself with my whip."

Lucifer certainly knew there was little chance of that. "Was that before or after he felt the sting of your lash?"

"Oh, before." She grinned unrepentantly. "After, he was too worried about where I might strike next to say much."

Lucifer shook his head slowly back and forth. She was a handful to begin with, headstrong and independent. The need to curtail her activities as a result of this little escapade would only make that penchant worse. "Amelia, this is now the second time someone has tried to grab you. I don't know how this is related to looking for Cat, but your involvement ends now."

She sat up and grew still in his lap. "You are neither my father nor my husband. You have no authority to make such a decree. I've already told you—I won't stand for it."

His fear and anger surged within his chest. "And I am telling you that I won't allow you to put yourself in harm's way again. You will cease to be involved in this investigation at once. I won't allow it."

She glared at him, her grey eyes hard and angry. "You and what army, may I ask? I don't think you have the ability to fulfill your promise to help me *and* keep me locked up in your home."

"You are correct. I cannot do both alone," he conceded.

She relaxed back in his arms, seemingly sure in her victory. "Then this discussion is moot."

For the moment. He allowed her to relax and be pliant in his arms once again. She'd find out soon enough just what army he possessed that would keep her in check. He grinned as they waited for Gordie to join them.

Chapter Twenty-Two

Lucifer waited for his reinforcements in his study. He'd known he needed all of his men to both run his businesses and search for Cat. So that left only one person—or group of people—he could turn to. Peterson knocked on his door and then opened it to admit the very men he'd been waiting for. "His Grace, the Duke of Shropshire, the Earl of Stonemere—"

"Yes, yes, Peterson. I know who is here," Lucifer cut him off, or he'd spend the next five minutes announcing each and every one of their bloody titles.

While his butler looked somewhat scandalized, he allowed the men—the Lustful Lords, as they were known—to file into his study. He'd met them all at one time or another, though he only really knew his half-brother Flint, Linc, and Arthur. He'd spent the most time with them. He stood and welcomed them. "Thank you all for coming. I appreciate you all answering my brother's request for aid on my behalf. Please, sit."

Linc grinned. "We came for you as well. It's not often a man can say the notorious Lucifer needs your help."

Lucifer grunted. "Yes, well, it seems I could use some assistance with corralling someone of the female variety. She's rather adept at getting into trouble, and I need her to remain safely out of said trouble while I solve this pesky little mystery for her."

"Who are we corralling?" Flint asked from the couch he'd sat on.

Lucifer cleared his throat. "Miss Amelia Ketting."

"Who?" Wolf asked while casting a confused glance around the room. He was not alone.

"Mistress Lash." Lucifer clarified as Flint began to grin.

More than one pair of eyebrows rose at his announcement. Stonemere tilted his head to the side. "Who are we protecting her from?"

"That's the bloody problem. I don't know. I should think it is whoever has taken her apprentice as well as another wh—woman who works in a brothel. But since I do not know who has taken them, I do not know who is after Amelia. And she has not made me aware of any other potential threats against her." Lucifer pinched the bridge of his nose. "Though I suppose it could be any one of hundreds of men who have availed themselves of her services and not be related to the missing women at all. It just seems too much of a coincidence for it not to be related."

"Well, keeping her safe does become more difficult if we don't know the source of the threat." Wolf pressed his lips together. "And nothing else in her past that might be connected?"

"To be honest, I hadn't asked beyond the general queries about who it might be. I can ask her again when she joins us. I wanted to discuss a plan to see to her safety before announcing it to her. I don't expect it will be well received."

The men all grinned.

"Such plans never are." Wolf nodded.

After a half-hour of discussing how they would arrange things, Lucifer asked Peterson to fetch Amelia.

"To be clear, she is staying here. With you. Without the benefit of a chaperone." Flint looked concerned.

Lucifer rolled his eyes. "Don't be so bloody stuffy, your grace. Neither of us is bound by the same strictures you lot suffer under. Besides, even if we were, both of our reputations are so deep in the gutter we'd be considered irredeemable. So, no need to fret."

Flint slanted a look at him that suggested he did not agree with Lucifer's assessment, but the door of the study opened, and Amelia sailed through it before stopping short at the gathering of men. "Oh, I beg your pardon, Lucifer. Peterson said you wished to speak with me. I did not realize you had guests." She turned to leave.

"He was correct. Please stay." Lucifer waved her over. "I believe you have met everyone present before." He snaked his arm around her waist as she neared him and pulled her closer to his side.

She nodded. "Yes. Good day, your grace, my lords." She attempted to curtsy.

"No need to be so formal, Amelia. After all, this is the army that is going to protect you while I finish our little investigation." He waited for the ire to surface... one heartbeat, then a second. And... there it was.

She ripped away from his side and turned to face him. "I thought we had agreed that was a moot point."

"We had. At that moment, I had no army to point to. Now,"—he swept his arm in an arc to indicate the seven men gathered in his study—"I do."

She glared at him. "Lucifer, I told you I would not be kept from investigating this with you based on two little incidents with ruffians. Did you expect to knock on their bloody door and to ask nicely for them to return my apprentice to us?"

"Not at all, but I do not expect you to be harmed in the process. Though we do have a question for you. Are you certain there isn't anyone else who might wish to harm you? No customers or other people from your past?"

He watched her blanch before she forced out an uncomfortable laugh. "Of course not. It must be related to the investigation. Perhaps a sign we are getting closer to discovering who has taken them." She paused and crossed her arms for a moment. Then she stepped into his body and placed a hand on his arm. "Please, Lucifer. Don't do this. I've never been a shrinking violet, and I'll not start now."

Lucifer hardened his heart to her appeal. "I'm sorry, Amelia, but I must keep you safe. One of these men will be with you at all times. You are not to leave the house without discussing it with me. Am I clear?"

She stepped back and glared at him. "As I've already said, you are not my father or my husband. You have no say."

Someone in the room coughed and sputtered as someone else slapped them on the back. Neither he nor she turned to see who it was. "If a wedding is all that is hindering your compliance, I can see to that in a trice."

"You can't force me to wed you either." She somehow came across sounding determined and confident versus petulant and mulish. Though her chin tipped up and her eyes had that stubborn glare he was becoming familiar with.

He wasn't sure where she got such conviction, such self-assuredness, but it was definitively one of the things he found most sexy about her... most of the time. At the moment, it was becoming something of a problem. "I absolutely can. I know any number of priests who would willingly perform the ceremony regardless of your level of compliance. I have more than enough blunt to grease those wheels. However, I would much rather you comply with my request on this issue. My other choice is to tie you down and leave you naked in my bed." He darted a glance around the room. "Or perhaps merely scantily clad."

A series of chuckles burbled around the room.

"I refuse to be a prisoner."

"I'm sure we can find a way to make your confinement bearable." Lucifer was growing tired of the endless argument.

She gasped. "You are mistaken if you think I am going to grace your bed as anything other than a prisoner."

He sighed. "I meant, I feel certain your friend the Duchess would be willing and able to visit along with some of the other wives of the Lustful Lords that you have met. They can help keep your mind off your lack of freedom."

"Oh," she said softly as her body relaxed and her gaze dropped to his chest. Then her head whipped up, and her eyes grew wide. "I don't see how that would be safe for them."

Flint cleared his throat. "I assure you, we—" he glanced around the room at the men he called friends. "We shall all help to ensure both you and any of our wives who visit you are safe here. There isn't a man among us who wouldn't lay down his life to protect you."

She stared at Flint and then turned to look at Lucifer. Her brow crinkled, and she shook her head. "I don't understand. Why would you"—she looked at Lucifer, then the others—"any of you be willing to protect me?"

Flint coughed and looked at him. Lucifer's collar grew tight as her question hung in the air, unanswered. He tucked a finger between the fabric and his skin and tugged gently as he dragged it between them. How did he explain that to her? He wasn't sure why he felt so compelled. Didn't know what to tell her. As for his brother and his friends, he had assumed it was the desire to have a man such as himself indebted to them. But as they all ranged around the room, some sitting, some standing, they looked at him as though it should be obvious why they were there. But, though he didn't really understand why either, he wasn't about to look a gift horse in the mouth.

Lucifer looked at Flint, feeling a little at a loss. He let his eyes widen in hopes his brother might take the hint and come up with some appropriate response. After all, the man was a bloody duke. Didn't he know how to handle such delicate matters as difficult questions? *Bloody hell!* "I..."

Flint chuckled and shook his head. "What my brother is struggling to say is that it is simply what we do as gentlemen. We protect those who are weaker than ourselves."

"But I am no lady." She still seemed baffled by the offer.

"Perhaps not by title, but you are still both a generous woman who came to my aid when I needed it most and someone I consider a friend. Add to that, you are my brother's woman, and it makes sense to all of us that you are now one of us." Flint shrugged a shoulder.

She blinked slowly. "I'm sorry, you must think me dim-witted. But when precisely did I become your brother's woman?"

Flint grinned. "Not at all. I suspect neither of you has truly come to terms with it yet, but it's quite clear to all of us that you two belong together. It makes no difference how long it takes you two to figure it all out. You are still his, and he is yours. Based on that alone, we would come to your aid." Lucifer's brother pulled his pocket watch out, opened the gold lid, looked at the time, and then snapped it closed before tucking it back into his pocket. "Now, I dare say if I do not return home soon, my duchess will become quite cross with me. Lucifer, do you need one of us to stay immediately? Or can we make arrangements for someone to be here tomorrow morning?"

"Tomorrow morning will suffice." He ignored an open-mouthed and dumbfounded Amelia.

"Excellent. I shall come by obscenely early and bring Ros along. We can have breakfast, and then you can be on your way while we keep Amelia company."

"Now, just a minute, I never agreed—" Amelia broke in.

Lucifer nodded to Flint. As the group filed out of the room, he stepped into Amelia and took hold of her shoulders once again. "Do cease fighting me on this. The decision has been made, and there is nothing you can do about it."

"The hell I can't!" She growled and jerked away from him, but his grip was stronger than expected.

"Amelia, I shall tie you to my bed tonight if you refuse to cooperate," his reply rumbled from his chest. "Please don't force my hand on this. Don't run."

She pressed her lips together, making her mouth a hard slash as she yanked against his hold.

Lucifer sighed. "Very well."

Then he bent over, planted his shoulder in her stomach, and hoisted her over his shoulder. Immediately, her fists pummeled his back, which set her weight off balance. In order to hold on to her, he had to slap a hand on her backside, though with all the crinolines bunched around her hips, it was hard to be sure where her backside began. He grabbed her flailing legs and crushed her skirts with his other free arm before she accidentally—or perhaps intentionally—kicked him in his bollocks.

"Put me down! Put me down this instant, you bloody nodcock!" She yelled as he strode from his study and down the hall. "I swear I shall have my revenge, Lucifer. I'll whip you within an inch of your life!"

He laughed heartily as he took the stairs up to his room. "First, you would have to tie me down, and unlike my dear brother Flint, I shall not be so easily trapped."

She growled again, though she finally seemed to lose some of her steam and ceased beating on his back. He wouldn't be surprised if he found a few bruises later. She was not a weak woman, no matter what his brother had suggested earlier. Once he arrived at his room, he was grateful to find the door ajar. He nudged it open with his toe and strode inside.

Halfway across the room—nearly to the bed—he noticed his valet standing in the closet door, staring at him with his mouth agape. "Excellent timing, Jenkins. If you could bring me two of my cravats, I would be greatly obliged." He managed to yell louder than the ongoing tirade that streamed from his captive's mouth.

The man stood there, still in some shock at seeing his employer striding about with a woman tossed over his shoulder. Not surprising, since he normally kept his bits of muslin entertained at his club. Nonetheless, he needed the man to move it along. "Now, Jenkins," he barked, causing the man to jump and quickly dash into the closet to fetch the cravats he requested.

By the time he tossed Amelia onto the bed, his manservant appeared next to him with the strips of cloth. Without a word, he held them out. Lucifer climbed on the bed and straddled Amelia before she could catch her breath and resume either yelling or fighting. Then he grabbed one strip, pulled her wrists together, and wrapped the strip around her wrists. Once he tied it off with a knot, he then looped the second strip around the bindings and between her wrists before tying it around two of the spindles on his headboard.

Finished, he nodded to Jenkins. "That will be all. And, until I tell you otherwise, you will need to refrain from entering this room unless I am with you."

Jenkin's eyes grew impossibly wider, but the stalwart man merely bowed and said, "Very good, sir." Then he departed as quickly as his two feet would carry him.

Lucifer looked at a furious Amelia, who had ceased her tirade and was quietly trying to slip her wrists from her bindings. "I know how to tie a knot so that you'll not escape. If I thought you would cooperate, I would certainly untie you. But we both know, at this point, that any agreeableness on your part would be pure subterfuge. So, I am sorry to say that as much as I appreciate your gown, it is going to have to come off, and that will not happen in a fashion that will keep it in a wearable state." He reached down and drew the knife he kept tucked in his boot. Holding it up, he allowed her to get a good look at the razor-sharp blade. "I shall, of course, replace the gown with one of equal or better value once all of this is over."

He then reached up and grabbed the neckline of the dress and hooked his blade inside it. With a slow and careful motion, he dragged the knife down along the front of her bodice. Being a two-piece garment, he knew he could spare the skirt such treatment. But he was finding the whole exercise surprisingly erotic and opted to finish off the business. So, he repeated the motion with her skirt and split that all the way down. Then he sliced the waist of all the crinolines and underskirts until the entire collection could be dragged easily down her legs. She lay tied to his bed in her corset, chemise, and old-style drawers. He really wished fashion hadn't seen fit to modernize ladies' pantalets. The old-style undergarments allowed so much access versus the current closed style. Well, at least some women appreciated the charms of the old ways.

Lastly, he worked on unhooking her corset down her front and then sliding the restrictive garment out from under her. That left her in just her chemise and drawers. Naked would be better, but with the way his cock now ached and her nipples had pebbled to hard little nubs, having her utterly naked might be testing the bounds of his self-control. Because while her chest had flushed and her nipples hardened as her breathing grew labored, she still had murder in her eyes. And no amount of tied-up sex was going to smooth that over. He was fairly positive that it might only make her desire to flay him alive worse. He reached down and rubbed his aching cock through his trousers, which drew her gaze and had her licking her lips.

"Well, despite the delectable temptation you present, I shall honor my earlier promise to you. You are not tied to my bed so that I can avail myself of your many..."—he sighed wistfully—"... many charms. I shall bring a tray up for dinner after a while. We shall dine together here. I bid you to rest as much as you can, despite your current circumstances."

She said nothing as he stood there awkwardly for a moment. Finally, he shrugged and turned to leave.

"Don't do this, Lucifer. Don't make me hate you." Her voice was soft, entreating, but still carried across the room to where he stopped.

He looked back, regret choking him. "I only wish to keep you safe. And if I have to make you hate me to do that, so be it."

Chapter Twenty-Three

The early morning light peeked through the drawn drapes of her current prison. Well, it was Lucifer's room, but a prison nonetheless. She lay in the bed, still tied to the headboard, though he'd given her a bit more play in the cravat looped through the spindles so she could lie down with her arms over her head. It wasn't particularly comfortable, but she hadn't really given him a choice. He'd sat with her and ate dinner while feeding her from a shared plate. He was careful to cut small pieces so she could easily chew them, and he ensured she had more than enough to eat. Had it been the Dark Ages, she was certain it would have been viewed as a particularly chivalrous display, well, except for the bindings.

And then later, when he'd prepared for bed, he tried once more to gain her cooperation. Again, she had refused to give him any assurances that she would be there come sunrise. She licked dry lips and tried to swallow past the lump in her throat. Everything about what he'd done reminded her that men were not to be trusted. And yet, she knew the idea was wrong. That *he* could be trusted. That *she* had forced the issue. But she believed it was her duty to find her apprentice. She was the one that had convinced Cat to train under her. She had potentially exposed her to the kind of clientele that might have taken her. She was responsible. She *felt* responsible.

Of course—responsibility be damned—she was absolutely useless tied to his bed. She sighed. Perhaps she should agree to his terms. Give up the physical search and help him find Cat by using her brains and her network. He was not wrong in that someone had attempted to take her, if not kill her. And she had grown more and more worried about who that might be. Fear slithered through her thoughts like a poisonous snake lurking in a garden.

Lucifer rolled over and slowly blinked his eyes open. "You're still here."

"You left me little choice," she responded evenly.

He shrugged. "Had you been more cooperative, last night could have unfolded very differently." He glanced up at her, hands still raised over her head. "I don't suppose you slept very well trussed up like that."

"No, not particularly. Though, as you suggested, I'm not sure I gave you very many other options." She watched him carefully in the low light that had slipped into the room.

"You didn't." He watched her cautiously. "If I release you for a little while, do you think you can resist the impulse to bolt from my home?"

"I expect I shall be capable of controlling the urge to run," she agreed. "I'm sorry I drove you to tie me up, though I am not sorry for wanting to find Cat."

He reached up and cupped her face. "I never wanted you to quit wanting to find her. I simply need you to stay safe so I can do what needs to be done."

Her heart pounded in her chest as her eyes closed, shielding her thoughts from him. "I haven't found men to be the most reliable people in my life."

"I'm not men. I'm one man. I'm the one man who will not let you down." His thumb stroked her cheek over and over.

She looked up into his eyes. "Trusting others is not something I do well. I'm sure I'll get it wrong again in the near future, but I'm willing to try."

He nodded. "Then let's get you loose so the feeling returns to your arms. I expect Flint and Ros will arrive shortly if it's as late as I suspect it is."

Amelia rubbed her arms once more, still working to get all the kinks out from sleeping with them stretched over her head. She was dressed in a pink day gown with deep red velvet ribbon trimming the edges and another at her waist. It was a bit missish, but felt more appropriate in a Mayfair salon than most of her other gowns. Lucifer had left only an hour earlier, and despite the ladies who had gathered in the front salon, she found herself worried about where he was and what he was doing.

Ros touched her shoulder, drawing her back to the present. "Amelia, you remember Ladies Stonemere, Brougham, and Wolfington."

"Of course." Amelia curtsied. "My ladies. It is lovely to see you all again."

"I took the liberty of inviting Lady Carlisle, Lady Stonemere's sister, and I believe you know Lady Heartfield." Ros motioned to the last two ladies in the group.

Amelia's eyes widened slightly. "Madame—"

"Just Marie, please, Amelia." The woman she'd known for years as Madame Marchander swept in and hugged her. "It is wonderful to see you again, though I wish it was under better circumstances."

"Agreed. I had no idea you were acquainted with Ros—Her Grace." She allowed her gaze to flick back and forth between the two women.

"Marie has been quite the boon to all of us in this circle. Positively a fount of wisdom when it comes to sexual congress and our particular group of men." Theo grinned at the blonde woman who had been Amelia's employer for years.

Amelia laughed. "I can easily imagine. She was always a sage soul, even when she was starting out as Madame at The Market." Amelia waved the group toward the couches. "Please sit, ladies. I shall ring for tea if you all would care for something despite the early hour."

They all nodded in agreement. Amelia pulled the cord hanging in the corner and joined them on the couches. "You know, I am Mistress Lash because of Marie."

"Oh, do tell!" Ros clapped her hands together. "I should love to hear how you became who you are."

Amelia hesitated, cursing her addled thoughts and wayward tongue. How she became Mistress Lash struck too close to the secrets she needed to keep... well, secret. She supposed she could focus on her leap of faith into being an apprentice rather than how she came to be at The Market at all. "Yes, I was a maid at The Market, and Mistress Beatrix was ready to retire, but she needed to train someone to replace her at The Market. Marie was aware of her desire and approached me about being her apprentice."

"Indeed, I'd noticed Amelia. Even as a lowly housemaid, she commanded the attention of not only the other maids, but many of my customers as well. I had told more than one man she was unavailable at the time, as she was a bit too young yet. Though I suppose she was still older than myself when I started in the business." Marie shrugged. "Well, she had quickly worked her way up from a new maid to running the second-floor girls in little more than six months. I was certain she would learn what Beatrix needed to teach her so she could retire. And she did not disappoint. She quickly learned all she could from Beatrix and then took what had been a niche service we provided and grew it into a thriving part of The Market's business. She made Mistress Lash into the woman other women wanted to be and men wanted to be whipped by. She may have been my greatest accomplishment at The Market."

Amelia's cheeks heated at the glowing words from her former mentor. Yes, Beatrix showed her how to wield a whip. But Marie had shown her how to be an icon. Embarrassed, she was grateful when Lucifer's maid knocked and entered the salon. She requested tea for her guests and then turned back to fall into the ladies' conversation.

"My little ones are absolute angels," Theo gushed, causing Lady Carlisle to laugh.

"Angels! You are too much, Theo. Your little hellions are constantly dragging my baby into trouble." Lizzy looked at her sister pointedly, even as her mirth faded.

"Pshaw! Your little boy is as headstrong and mischievous as your husband likely was. I'd say he is the ringleader when those three are together." Theo retorted semi-indignantly before chuckling. "Perhaps we shall learn who the real troublemaker is once Emily's offspring joins the brood?"

Emily grinned. "Oh, I daresay any child of mine will take over as lead troublemaker. They'll simply need a few years to be mobile and able to speak. But boy or girl, they will be running the show before long."

Everyone laughed as the tea service was delivered. Amelia was grateful for the distraction the ladies provided, both from her concern about Cat and now her worry about Lucifer. It seemed their investigation had grown increasingly dangerous. The clock had just struck four when Lucifer finally returned.

"Good afternoon, ladies." He bowed to the room in general.

"Lucifer," Amelia stood, her hands clasped. "Any word?"

He shook his head. "I'm afraid there was little new discovered today."

Disappointment speared through her chest. *Damn.*

Theo rose and wrapped an arm around her shoulders. "I'm sure they will find her soon. Do not lose hope."

Amelia nodded and pressed a hand over Theo's on her shoulder. "Yes, you're right. Thank you."

Ros stepped forward. "Perhaps we should go. You've entertained us most of the day. I'm sure you could use a break. I'll try to come by tomorrow for a little while to sit with you."

"Thank you." Amelia hugged her friend, grateful for her and all the women who had sat with her.

Each woman stepped forward and said their goodbyes while promising to come by one day to sit with her. Something deep within her shifted at the support and love she received from this odd group of women. It was not unlike a family, and that was not something she'd truly had in over twenty years.

As the women departed, Lucifer stood across the room from her. Once the last woman exited, he stepped forward. "Amelia, it may take a little more time, but I promise you my men are continuing to search."

She turned away from him to look out the bay window at the bustling street. Not as a rejection of him, but to hide her disappointment. She knew he was trying, but the lack of any new news was upsetting, and it felt unfair to lay that at his feet.

"Please, do not be distraught...."

His voice carried on, though she no longer heard a word he said as her gaze landed on a frighteningly familiar face in the crowd. Her throat closed as she tried to force air in and out of her lungs. Her corset suddenly felt overly tight, and a chill swept over her body. The man's dark blue eyes locked on her as he leaned against the light post on the sidewalk. A small, knowing smile curved his lips before he tipped his hat to her in greeting.

Her heart abruptly lurched in her chest as though it might burst free and scamper away to hide. She spun around to face Lucifer as she willed her knees to hold strong. They could not give out. Not until she could get near a chair... or perhaps the settee. Something that might take her weight. She managed to take a stiff, uncoordinated step forward as she reached out, flailing her hand as though she'd lost the ability to see.

"Amelia? Are you well?" Lucifer appeared at her side, having materialized from thin air.

"No... yes... I'm not sure," she stammered as his warm hand wrapped around the one she had shoved out before her.

She glanced up to find his brow creased with worry. "You look deathly pale. Come, sit."

He seemed to wrap himself around her back as he supported her weight and helped her over to the settee. If not for his support, she was certain her knees would have failed her, and she would have collapsed into a heap on the floor. Somehow, the specter from her nightmares had stepped from her dreams right onto one of London's famed cobblestone streets. Richard Mattingly was here, and somehow, he had found her. What the hell was she going to do?

Chapter Twenty-Four

If Lucifer wasn't sitting in his own front parlor, he would have sworn an elephant had planted itself square on his chest. Amelia had turned as white as a sheet, and though she now sat next to him, she had not uttered a word of explanation. With her hands clasped in her lap to control their obvious trembling, her gaze darted about the room. He didn't know what had caused it, but he knew fear when he saw it.

"Amelia, tell me what is wrong."

He reached over and tried to rest his hand over hers in her lap, but he was knocked away as she stood up abruptly. "Wrong?" She strode across the room toward the fireplace as she wrapped her arms around herself. "What could be wrong?" She laughed awkwardly as she held her hands out to the small fire.

Lucifer watched her carefully. He'd not been mistaken—he had seen the fear. Hell, he could practically smell it rolling off her. He rose to his feet. "I am asking you that question. I realize you are upset at the lack of progress, but I promise you, my men are still searching."

She turned to face him, her cheeks holding more color than a moment before. But was that because of the heat of the fire or because whatever had disturbed her had passed? Damn it; he couldn't be sure.

She stepped toward him. "There is nothing wrong. A momentary chill took over me as I neared the window. It must be quite cool outside."

What was she going on about? "It is unseasonably warm today, though England is never actually warm in the spring. But I take exception to the notion that this house might be drafty. Now cease this ridiculousness and tell me what the hell upset you." He managed to refrain from actually yelling at her, though it was a near thing. No other woman could set his temper off so easily as the lovely Amelia.

She smiled at him as though he were a lunatic. "I am certain you've had a long and difficult day, Lucifer. But you must refrain from yelling at people. It is unsettling for everyone involved."

Who the hell was this specter of placid womanhood? The Amelia he knew and loved was of the fire-breathing sort, a woman as likely to snake her whip in your direction as look at you. "Do you know what is *unsettling*, Amelia? It is *unsettling* to watch a woman turn pale as death one moment, only to pretend it never happened the next. That, my dear, is *unsettling*." His hands fisted at his sides as he tried to control the urge to strangle her.

She stepped into his body and pressed hers against him as she slipped her hands up his chest, over his shoulders, and around his neck. "Do not be so cross. I've missed you terribly all day."

His eyes nearly popped out of his head as she pouted prettily and pressed her breasts against him. He left his hands at his sides, refusing to give in to her ploy, though his cock had begun to take notice of her proximity. Taking a deep breath, he attempted to take a step back, but her arms remained hooked around his neck. Giving in, he reached up and removed her arms so he could place some much-needed distance between them. "Considering the number of ladies I saw decamp from this very room not long ago, I feel confident that while my absence may have been noted, you by no means missed me terribly. I am not that gullible, sweetheart."

She put her hands on her hips and huffed. "Fine. I did miss you, but perhaps I laid things on a bit thick."

Lucifer tried to keep his smile in check. Ah! There was the woman he knew. "Yes, well, you still haven't answered my original question. What upset you?"

She stepped into him once more, wrapped her arms around his neck, and looked him square in the eyes. "Did you lock the door when you came in?"

He glanced at the door and back at her. "No, I had no reason to expect I would need to."

"Very well, we'll simply have to risk it." She shrugged as much as she could.

He wanted to sigh gustily. She was back to not making sense. "What will we have to risk?"

"This..." and then she kissed him. Not a gentle press of her lips. No, Amelia slipped past his lips to claim his tongue with a ball-tightening, cock-hardening sweep. Their tongues tangled and dueled. Breathing became optional as lust surged through him, obliterating all rational thoughts. Finally, desperate to breathe, he drew back and allowed the oxygen to return to his brain. With it came the ability to think past his aching groin. "You are intentionally distracting me."

She nodded. "I am. Is it working?"

He growled a yes and then claimed her mouth. The kiss turned molten as his hands began to roam to the back of her gown. Working the laces loose, he continued to kiss her, noting that he'd finally found something useful for her tongue instead of lying to him. It was, by far, a more satisfying outcome from his perspective.

With her laces loosened, he tugged at her bodice, drawing it down. He was about to reach into her corset to free one of her breasts when a horse's whinny pierced the veil of desire that had enveloped them. He looked up and realized they were standing framed in the window of his front parlor, where people were busily passing by. With a curse, he hauled her bodice back up and then took her by the hand to lead her from the room.

Behind him, he heard her confusion. "Lucifer, where are you taking me?"

"Somewhere private where there aren't people on the street passing by nor the threat of servants walking in unbidden." He started up the stairs but found she couldn't keep up with all her skirts tangling about her ankles. Ridiculous women's fashions! He stopped and tossed her over his shoulder before taking the stairs two at a time.

Hanging over his shoulder, an exasperated voice said, "Really, Lucifer? Over your shoulder again?"

"When you stop wearing such impractical clothing that you cannot keep up with me, I won't need to throw you over my shoulder." He continued up the stairs and into his bedroom.

There, he set her down and locked his bloody door because he would not be interrupted. He may not be able to make her tell him what had scared her, but he could make her feel good. And at the moment, he'd damn well take that small bit of control over continuing to feel like a man tossed about on stormy seas. As he turned around to reach for her, she flew into his arms.

The satisfaction of having her do as he wished spurred something in him. Something dark and possessive that he'd been fighting since he first saw her. He kissed her—claimed her, really. Pushed his tongue into her mouth and seized whatever ground she would cede to him. As he tasted and explored, she melted into him on a soft moan. Finally, forced to pull back to breathe, he looked down at her, their gazes locked as their chests heaved in unison. "You're mine. You're mine to protect, mine to care for. Whatever it is that is upsetting you; I shall make it right if you only tell me."

She nodded and then captured the hard slash of his mouth. Strangely, her kiss was more of a surrender than a claiming by her. She seemed to want to give him control, give up her control to him. Greedily, he took it as he worked her bodice off her shoulders again and down her arms without ending their kiss. Then he reached behind her and began working her skirts free. All the while, he kissed and nibbled at her lips until the bulk of her skirts and crinolines puddled at her feet. Then he shifted his kisses down the column of her throat, licking and tasting every dip and hollow as he moved down toward her breasts. He untied the strings of her corset and then unhooked the perpetual row of hooks in the front until her dusky-tipped nipples were exposed.

As the corset joined her skirts at her feet, he continued his path to her breasts. Taking one tip in his mouth, he pulled and sucked as he pinched and rolled the other tip between his fingers. She slid her hands up his shoulders and higher still until they found his hair. There, her hands fisted to ensure he did not move. Despite the pull on his scalp, he shifted to the other nipple and sucked the nub as he had the other. He loved the way her body bowed into him, her back arched as though she wanted more. More of his mouth. More of him.

A shiver coursed through her body, though he wasn't sure if it was from the cold or his attentions. Determined to be sure it was the latter, he lifted her from the puddle of her skirts and stepped closer to the fire and a wingback chair that sat nearby. Setting her down, he untied her pantalets, leaving her gloriously naked. The fire burnished her ivory skin as he stared at her. "So, fucking beautiful."

He couldn't believe she was there with him. As many lovely women as he'd spent time with, this was a woman he could never have imagined all those years ago as a street rat. The house, his club, all of that he had pictured. But never a woman so lovely as her. Never one that made him want to move heaven and earth to see her smile.

He slipped off his coat and let it drop on the floor. "Sit."

She did as he commanded, perching on the edge of the chair.

"Spread your legs for me. Let me see how wet you are." His voice sounded gravelly, even to him. His control stretched thin. He dropped to his knees and nudged her thighs wider with his shoulders. He reached up and drew a finger down her slick pussy, gathering her juices on the tip. Then he brought his finger to his lips and tasted her desire. On a growl, he surged forward and drove his tongue between her lips to gather her essence straight from the source.

"Yes!" she cried out as he drew his tongue over her slit again and again. Her hands clamped on his head once more as she pressed her quim into his ministrations. "Your tongue...so..."

Her hips squirmed, so he wrapped his hands around her thighs and pressed his hands over her hipbones to try to keep her still. He was only marginally successful, but it was enough. He drank her in, pushed his tongue deep inside her, and fucked her like he planned to do with his cock. There was something very erotic about being fully clothed as he licked her pussy while she was completely naked. He lifted up for a moment and gazed up at her. "Play with your tits, Amelia. Pinch your nipples as I make you come."

She moaned low and deep but did as he commanded. Satisfied she was following directions, he returned to tasting the sweet-tart desire of her quim. He sucked one of her outer lips into his mouth, loving the way she moaned and bucked. Then he repeated that on the other side. "Please, Lucifer. Stop teasing me."

The sound of her begging made his already rigid cock pulse with wanting. He wanted to fill her. Wanted to be buried so deep inside her she couldn't deny they were one. Redoubling his efforts, he swept his tongue over her clit and then back down to swirl around it. She cried out encouragement in a throaty, sexy tone that spurred him on. A few more swipes of his tongue, and she exploded for him. Quickly, he reached down and slid two fingers inside her to pump in and out as she ground herself against his face.

Slowly she began to float down as he eased his fingers from her body and gentled the swipes of his tongue until she lay there, replete and boneless. "Amelia, lift your lids and look at me."

Again, she did as he asked, though barely. But once he had her attention, he slid his fingers into his mouth and licked them clean as he relished every last drop of her taste. He then wiped the sleeve of his shirt over his beard and began to strip down as she whimpered and ran a hand down her body in response. "I need you inside me."

"And you'll have me soon. I promise I'm going to fuck you until you can't forget who owns you—body, mind, and soul." He growled as he shed the last vestiges of civility and stood naked before her. The primitive need to possess her, to claim her as his, was so intense he shook with it. But he never questioned it.

Climbing on the bed where she lay, he came over her and found her pebbled nipples plump and swollen from earlier. Leaning down, he licked and bit each one in turn until she was moaning and desperate for his touch once more. She was so fucking responsive for a woman who could be so obstinate. He marveled at how her body hummed for him.

Long past ready for more, he leaned up and rolled her over. There, he smoothed his hands down her backside and squeezed the globes of her arse. Then he helped her rise to her hands and knees. "That's it. Put that derriere high in the air for me." He leaned over and bit each cheek. "God, you have a beautiful arse." Then he straightened up and notched his cock at the opening of her pussy. He pushed forward and found her slicker than ever, between her orgasm and her renewed excitement. She moaned and pressed back into him, impaling herself on his cock. "Fuck, you are so wet, sweetheart. So hot and tight around me." He groaned and slid all the way to the root inside of her. Then he pulled out and slid back inside. Over and over, he repeated the motion as he picked up speed, varied his angle slightly, and put some power into his hips. He wanted her to remember this tomorrow morning as she went about her day.

As he looked down at the round swells of her arse and the tight bud of her rear entry, he couldn't resist pushing her harder. Filling her completely. So, he reached down and gathered her moisture from her pussy and his cock, and then brought two fingers up to her sphincter. He rubbed over the tight ring, pressing to see how she'd react. She moaned and bucked wildly until the tip of one finger slipped inside. She shook and cried out. "Oh God, yes!"

He could tell she was close, so he pressed in deeper, all the while keeping his pace shuttling in and out of her pussy. The heat of her engulfing both his cock and his finger had him near to blowing, but he pushed on. Pushed deeper. Fucked her harder. And she fucking loved it!

His balls tightened, drew up into him a bit as he sank deep into her backside. He pulled the digit out and added a second finger after gathering more of her juices as they dripped from where they were joined. He was close, but he was determined to bring her with him. He slid the two fingers past the tight ring of muscle and then spread them as he pounded her with his hips. Filled her pussy all the way to the base and then withdrew. She cried out in an incoherent string of words, but what he heard was "More." So, he worked his fingers and his hips until he realized she needed one last thing. "Stroke your clit, sweetheart. Push yourself over that edge."

She reached up at his urging and did as he'd suggested. And it sounded like a suggestion, because he'd lost the focus he needed to make it a command. He was so close to losing control. He needed her to come. Needed it *now*. He could feel her fingers rubbing over her clit, and then she stiffened and wailed so loudly he was certain Buckingham Palace could hear her. "Yes! Lucifer! Yes!"

As her sheath clenched down on his cock, he kept working her arse and fucking her pussy, trying desperately to hang on. For a moment, he considered pulling out and plunging into her arse, fucking her there until he came. But he realized he'd never make it. He was too far gone as the tingling sensation in his balls coalesced and spread out through his body and along his spine. Pulling his fingers from her rear, he gripped her hips and hung on as he came. Working his hips, he dragged his length in and out of her until further movement was impossible. His cock was so sensitive the slightest brush would trigger an aftershock that incapacitated him. So, he sank over her body, covered her back with his chest, and let them tip to the side. Together they lay there for a bit, still joined, each quiet.

Finally, his cock softened and slid from her despite his wishes to stay. But still, he held her, listening to her steady breathing as he basked in the glow of what they'd shared. If this was what love felt like, then he wanted more of it. More of it with her. The revelation of what he was feeling nearly had him blurting out the words, but sanity prevailed, and he managed to check his tongue. It wouldn't do to terrify the woman with spontaneous announcements of his feelings.

But he would tell her. Or better yet, he'd show her. He was always far more comfortable with action than words.

Chapter Twenty-Five

Amelia lay naked with Lucifer. The euphoria of their joining still lingered and made her feel safe with him. Rolling over so she could see him as she spoke, she knew she needed to begin to unravel some of her secrets for this man who would give her everything he had. She was already doing so in ways that she'd never expected. "Lucifer, I need to tell you something. It's about my past."

His eyes widened, but he merely nodded. "There is nothing you can't tell me."

She licked her lips, nervous as she prepared to bare herself to him. Primal instinct screamed out not to speak, but she knew she could trust him. Knew in her head and her heart that he would protect her and her secret. "I'm not—"

A knock on the door sounded. She looked in the direction of the offending sound.

"You're not what?" He urged her, ignoring the knock.

She took a deep breath. "I'm not—"

A knock sounded again, more insistent. "Mr. Lucifer, I apologize for the intrusion. But an urgent note has arrived."

His eyes closed. "Bloody fucking hell!"

The soft curse came as he rolled from the bed, leaving her swamped by cold air and a sense of clinging to a cliff. Pushing the silly notions aside, she sat up and pulled the sheet to her breast as he opened the door.

He turned the lock and opened the bedroom door without a stitch of clothing on. "What is so bloody important?"

Amelia repressed the insane urge to chuckle as she took in the firm roundness of his ass and the muscles that defined his thighs. He was a man who did not sit about leisurely. No, he was active and took care of his body, much to her delight. One moment she was about to bare her soul to him, and the next, she was appreciating the view he offered. She knew a life with this man would certainly be interesting, at the least.

He closed the door with a barely restrained thud and tore the note open. He looked up from the page. "My investigator has found a ship's manifest that is leaving tomorrow for America. The passenger list is small, and six more bodies were added without the benefit of full names. They are merely identified as an initial and then the last name Doe, which does not suggest they are real names."

Amelia climbed from the bed and wrapped her robe around her as she went to where Lucifer stood. "Who are the passengers?"

A frustrated growl escaped the very naked man standing next to her. "Three women and three men who all seem to share the same last name. They appear, at a surface level, to be married."

"But the undisclosed six seem likely candidates. Perhaps two or three men and three or four women? I can't imagine that Lucy and Cat are the only women they have taken." Amelia began to pace the room. "We have to find them."

"Well, we obviously have the name of the ship and the dock where it sits. I suggest we make a visit to the captain. With the ship about to leave port, I suspect we should be able to find him somewhere near the ship. Meanwhile, I shall have my men continue to look for a warehouse near the docks. This ship, The Sea Rose, must have cargo stored somewhere."

"Agreed. We could also approach the captain as another married couple seeking passage to America. Take his measure before asking our more pointed questions." Hope crowded her chest and made her feel as though she might split apart at the seams like a poorly made dress.

Lucifer looked hesitant. "I could simply approach him on my own. There is no need to have you involved."

"A woman's presence will probably make the man less suspicious. Less concerned about your inquiry. After all, what man in his right mind would bring a woman along to investigate?" She grinned.

His mouth formed a slash in his face as he slanted her a sideways glance. "Indeed, what man would bring a woman along for such an endeavor?"

Her gaze narrowed. "I am no milksop female who faints at the first sign of trouble. But once again, to our advantage, this captain will not know that either. Now, let me see about what to wear for this trip. We must hurry."

An hour later, they were strolling down the busy dock where The Sea Rose was supposed to be moored. At the very end, after passing more than a few other ships, they finally found the vessel. To Amelia's dismay, it was crawling with men, obviously preparing for a long voyage. Huge crates were being hoisted from dockside wagons and lowered into a giant opening in the deck of the ship to what she assumed was a cargo hold. Other men scrambled up the gangplank toting smaller crates on their shoulders that still seemed to be huge.

There was a sturdy-looking man, thick and packed with muscle, much in the way Lucifer's man Gordie was, directing everything. It struck her as strange that he might be the captain of this ship, but then, no one suspected she might wield a whip as well as she did either. She mentally shrugged as Lucifer seemed to come to the same conclusion and led them in that direction. "Excuse me, I'm looking for the captain of The Sea Rose."

The man turned to yell at two men who had dropped a crate before responding to Lucifer's inquiry. "The captain is up at the tavern having his bloody breakfast."

Amelia rolled her lips into her mouth to control the smile that wanted to appear at the obvious disdain the man had for his captain. This was clearly a man who was no stranger to backbreaking labor under precarious circumstances and knew all too well that it might be the only thing keeping him fed, clothed, and with a roof over his head, so to speak. She suspected the captain was not a man carved of such experience. "Which tavern might that be? I believe we passed no less than three on our way here."

The man looked at her as though he'd seen her for the first time when she spoke. "The only one serving food at this hour, the Land and Sea." He frowned mightily and then turned to call out to the men working the hoist. "Watch it! That rich niminy-piminy will pitch a fit if you break any of his blasted treasures."

Lucifer turned to her with an eyebrow raised, though he said nothing.

When the man turned back to find them still standing there, he almost seemed surprised. "Did you need something else?"

Lucifer smiled as though pained. "What is your captain's name? I was only given the name of the ship."

Amelia waited, wondering if he might not even be the man they were looking for—the thief of women.

"Walter Bright's his name." And on that last bit of information, he stormed over to a group of men struggling under the weight of a crate.

With a name for the man they sought, they turned and headed toward the Land and Sea tavern. It was not sitting at the top of the dock, as one might think. Instead, it was four docks down, closer to where the passenger vessels seemed to congregate since there was far less activity bustling around the ships. Though what kinds of ships could afford to take mostly passengers was beyond her. If she were a ship's captain, she would choose cargo over hauling people every day and twice on Sunday. Cargo couldn't ask for things, couldn't complain, and certainly couldn't tell lies. People were capable of all three. She glanced up at Lucifer and realized she'd at least let one man onboard her ship.

The tavern in question had a steady stream of men coming and going. They quickly stepped inside, and Amelia found herself the focus of many a pair of eyes. Other than the rather slovenly and harried barmaid, she was the only female in the immediate room. Nearly every table was filled with men who all seemed to have work-worn shirts and pants on. A few wore some kind of jacket to stave off the morning chill. She was about to stop the girl scurrying around when Lucifer took her arm and started towing her toward a well-dressed man sitting in the corner. Though well-dressed was relative to the company he kept at the moment.

He wore a simple dark coat, obviously not one tailored to fit him, a dingy white shirt, and he had a woven straw hat sitting on the table next to him. She suspected that hat was how he kept his weathered skin from being burnt to a crisp, like many of the men in the room. "Excuse me, you wouldn't happen to be Mr. Walter Bright, would you?"

The man looked at them, puffed up his chest, and snorted. "That's Captain Walter Bright."

Lucifer's lips twitched up for a brief second on one side. "Of course, but you are him?"

"I am." The man eyed them warily.

"Excellent." Lucifer intoned in the most pompous of voices. "My wife and I need passage to America rather urgently. I was told your ship leaves tomorrow."

"It does. But I ain't got room for more passengers. Some fancy bloke bought up all my remaining cabins, though he only has a few people with him." The man picked up his previously abandoned fork and shoved a piece of sausage into his mouth.

"So, he bought the cabins but has no traveling companions with him?" Lucifer darted a glance at her. "Sir, we are quite desperate. My wife's sister is gravely ill, and we must get there to see her. Might this man be interested in selling one of his cabins to us?"

Bright sat there chewing noisily, which was quite a feat considering the cacophony of voices and tankards engulfing them. "I doubt it. But even if he might, he paid me to keep my mouth shut about his name and who he's traveling with. So, I can't tell you his name to ask him." The man shrugged and speared a few potatoes before shoving them in his mouth.

Amelia allowed her disappointment to show as one would expect, considering their "plight." Lucifer sighed. "I see. Well, thank you for your time, Captain."

The man waved them off and continued addressing his breakfast. They slipped out of the tavern and huddled near the wall of the building to keep out of the flow of humanity. The stench of sweat and unwashed bodies mixed with the briny sea air to make a rather wretched smell. Despite that, Amelia needed a moment to regroup as they decided what to do next. "How do we find out who it is?"

"From the looks of how that ship sat in the water, they had only started to load the cargo. The rest must be in a warehouse around here. Let's check with the customs office to see where The Sea Rose keeps her cargo."

They walked back down the wharf and took a right on a fairly wide avenue that led away from the docks and all the activity. There was a rather large red brick edifice ahead on the left. It was imposing enough to catch the eye but still proximally located to its nexus of business. The customs office was fairly bristling with men of all shapes and sizes, though they all had a similar goal. To either get their product into the country or out of it by ship. She followed Lucifer around the melee and through a side door marked employees only. She started to suggest they try the lobby like everyone else when a man approached them.

"Hello there, Lucifer, I haven't seen you here in a while." The average man—he was of average height, with light brown hair, brown eyes, and a rather plain countenance—smiled. "What can I do for you?"

Lucifer grinned. "Hello, Peter. I suppose my shipping interests mostly take care of themselves these days. I'm more focused on my club. You really should come down for an evening of entertainment."

"I don't expect Molly would appreciate that none. Especially now that we have a little one at home." The plain-faced man beamed with a pride that lit up his face.

"Congratulations!" Amelia couldn't help but smile back at him.

"Oh! Hello, miss. Thank you." It seemed she had been the one unremarked until that moment.

"Yes, my felicitations on the good news." Lucifer clapped the man on his shoulder. "You two should have told me."

"You've done enough for us already. But the boy is going to be as big a handful as we once were, I suspect."

Lucifer chuckled. "I wish you well in taming that one, then."

Peter grinned back, and then a man approached them, dropped some papers on his desk, and dispelled the congenial moment.

"Yes, well, I came by to see if you could tell me where the Sea Rose is warehousing her cargo. I am looking for some friends, and I suspect they may be around there since they are sailing on the ship tomorrow."

Peter looked at them blankly for a moment and then smiled. "Oh, they're warehousing on Finch Street at Sparrow Lane."

"Excellent! Thank you, Peter. And really, if you and the Mrs. need anything at all, don't hesitate to ask." Lucifer shook Peter's hand.

"As I've said, you did enough for us, getting me this job and helping us find housing." Peter pumped Lucifer's hand and then let go. "Well, I should get back to work. It was good to see you!"

"Yes, it was. Thank you again." Lucifer waved, and they turned to slip out the door they'd come in.

Outside, Amelia turned to him, brimming with curiosity. "How in the world do you know him?"

"He ran in my gang as a kid for a few years. Then he had the opportunity to get into a good orphanage where he got educated."

Amelia wrinkled her nose in thought. "Why didn't you join him at that orphanage?"

"I never much went in for authority figures. It was easier to stay free and see to my own needs. But Peter certainly helped. He would sneak out at night and come teach the rest of us what he learned during the day. He's a good egg. Never forgot the ones who stayed behind."

She nodded, piecing together some of who the man she knew as Lucifer really was. "And despite all of that, he made it sound like you got him his job and a home."

"Bah, I had one of the customs officials over a barrel about some debts at the club. It was easy enough to wipe his slate clean in exchange for him hiring Peter." He shrugged. "He really got the better end of that deal since Peter is such a bloody outstanding employee."

"And the housing?" She pressed, eager to know more.

"Oh, when he and Molly got hitched, I made sure he had an opportunity to let a nice flat for them. He'd been having a terrible time since he'd only just started working at the customs office."

She looked at him, narrowed her gaze, and studied him. He seemed uncomfortable. "You bought the tenement, didn't you?"

He glanced around and then grabbed her hand and started off down a side street. "I don't know what you are talking about. I made sure he had a place to rent. That's all."

He walked briskly down the street, making her nearly run to keep up. "Slow down, Lucifer!"

As though he only then realized he was practically running, he slowed his pace so she could keep up. Slipping a hand under his arm, she patted him with her free hand. "We don't have to talk about the big heart you hide in that chest of yours. I'll keep it to myself." She laughed, causing him to shoot her a quelling glance.

She bit her lip and tried to cease smiling but found it rather difficult since the man seemed distinctly ill at ease with his own philanthropy. Then they were on Finch Street, and he slowed their pace. "The warehouse should be up here on the right." He hesitated a moment. "I don't suppose you'd willingly go back to my house and let me handle this?"

"Absolutely not. I have my whip and can be quite useful."

He sighed. "Very well. Come along then."

And so, they eased down the lane toward the warehouse they'd been searching for. Keeping to the shadows created by the tall buildings and narrow lanes, they crept closer to the warehouse until they could see who was coming and going.

Much to Amelia's relief, she did not see any familiar faces, but that didn't mean these men weren't dangerous.

Two men walked away from the warehouse, talking. In a moment of panic that they would be caught snooping, Amelia flattened her back against the building they were hovering near, hiked up one side of her skirt to expose a leg, and pulled Lucifer in for a kiss. The men continued chatting, not even noticing the pair.

"I'm telling you, I know what I saw in there." The shorter of the two said.

"Charlie, you'd be smart not to know a bloody thing. Those blokes don't look like the type to take others meddling in their business lightly."

"But they've got women locked up in there. It ain't right, Hal."

"That may be, but it ain't none of our business. Not if we want to keep being employed. And I, for one, like having a full belly and place to rest my head."

The pair kept walking as they talked. Clearly, Hal was of a mind to stay out of things, not that she could blame him entirely. Food and shelter were strong motivators, though it made her a little angry that they would just leave the helpless women there. Well, maybe that Charlie fellow would have said something. She took that glimmer of humanity and latched on since, in the end, it wouldn't matter. She was going to take care of things. Well, she and Lucifer. She looked up at him, which caused her breath to catch once she saw the smoldering desire burning in his eyes.

Then, suddenly the need was banked, and his dark gaze took on a brittle hardness. "Let's go. We've heard enough. I need to gather my men so we can raid the warehouse before they move the women to the ship."

"I can wait here and keep an eye out to be sure they don't leave." She suggested, worried now that she'd lose Cat once more just when she'd found her.

Lucifer's face grew hard, his muscles all clenched under her fingers resting on his chest. "The hell you will. You are coming with me so I can protect you, and then you are staying at my house while I take care of things."

She was so close. "Oh no, that is not even remotely a possibility. I shall be coming with you. I'm a familiar face to Cat, which will help keep the women calm and cooperative."

He growled deep in his chest, a low rumbling that might have been exciting if it was for other reasons.

"We'll discuss this on our way. We're wasting time here." With that, he turned and stalked off, but not before grabbing her hand and towing her behind him like a wayward child.

She wanted to stomp her foot and yell at him, but she wanted to rescue Cat more. And she knew he was right. They were wasting time.

Chapter Twenty-Six

Darkness had fallen, which truly served their purposes far better than the light of day. The carriage rolled to a stop, and Lucifer looked at the indomitable woman across from him. She still hadn't revealed her secrets, but he felt sure she'd been about to earlier that afternoon. Of course, fate had intervened and delivered actionable news, so they'd leapt from their bed—or at least he hoped it would be theirs before this entire affair was done—and gone to look for the missing women. Shaking off his wandering thoughts, he worked on staying focused. They still did not know who they were dealing with. And that caused a bit of churning in his belly, though it was no worse than the first few times he'd nabbed a loaf of bread so he and Gordie could eat when they were kids.

"Amelia, I need you to remain with the carriages until I signal Hadley; do you understand me?" He'd resorted to asking for fear if he demanded, as was his usual fashion, she would only dig in her heels and fight him. Time was of the essence.

Her glare was fiery and mutinous, but then her face softened ever so slightly. Nothing so reassuring as a smile appeared, but she didn't hiss at him. "I shall do my best." She gripped her hands in her lap and seemed to worry one knuckle after another.

"Am—" he began.

But one hand popped free of her mindless movements as she held a palm up. "Ah!" She cut him off. "I shall do my best to do as you have asked. I'll not make a promise I can't keep. Now, go find Cat and the others before we lose them forever."

He nodded solemnly and moved to exit the carriage. On an impulse he could neither have predicted nor explained, he reached over and took her shoulders in his hands and pulled her forward into a brief hard kiss on the lips. He pulled away and grinned. "For luck!"

Then he bounded out of the carriage and pressed through the grouping of his men. Many of them were tired from searching all day, but the knowledge that their objective was in sight rallied them. They were a rough lot, several of them the kind of men he'd likely been destined to become, except that for some reason, he'd had a grand vision of what his life might be like. Of fancy fabrics, glittering chandeliers, and enough money to know he'd never be cold or hungry for the rest of his life. He'd refused to accept that all he would achieve was surviving hand to mouth.

He looked into the faces of the men he employed. He looked into an eerie kind of reflection of what his life might have been but for the grace of ambition and sheer determination. Instead, he paid his men handsomely, and, as a result, they were all here to fight for him. With him. "You all know what your jobs are. We have no idea who or what we are dealing with, so stay alert and do not trust anyone you come across. I'd prefer if we kept any killing to a minimum, but do what you must to ensure both the retrieval of these women and your own continued well-being."

The group all nodded even as a few muttered, "Got it, boss," or the like. "Gordie, you take your men around the back. Harold and Jimmy, you take your groups through the two side entrances. I'll take the front with my men. We'll meet in the middle and squeeze them between us. Good luck!"

The men scattered. As everyone took their positions and they waited for the appointed time, he tried to keep his wandering thoughts from worrying about Amelia. Had she stayed where he left her? Done as he'd asked? He wouldn't know until after, but he hoped so. The last thing he needed was to have to worry about her appearing in the midst of things. He hoped Hadley could keep her from entering the building, at the very least.

Then he glanced at his pocket watch, and time suddenly exploded forward like a steaming locomotive at full speed. He and his men descended on the front entrance of the warehouse. He left two men standing guard by the doors to keep anyone from coming or going until he was ready. Then they opened the doors. It was eerily quiet inside except for a few voices that could be heard in the distance. It seemed that most of the excess men they'd seen earlier were either gone for the night or down at the ship. He guessed it was the latter, so any hue and cry could be answered faster than he'd prefer. Best not to allow that to occur.

Barreling deeper into the rows of tall shelves that made the warehouse a rabbit warren, he split his men up and sent three around one way while he and two others took the other. There wasn't a great deal of light in the building, but he could see a soft glow ahead. Moving swiftly, he suddenly heard a loud curse and then a crash. Some of his men had been discovered. The ruckus rose as he sped past the crates and barrels packed with products for people to buy. Then he heard screams of the feminine variety that gave him hope and spurred him on. He found the source of the glow and a brutal brawl in progress. Eight men were fighting his men to keep them away from the women. Two others had the women huddled against a wall as they tried to guard against anyone slipping in to take them. More men appeared from somewhere deep in the bowels of the warehouse, and Lucifer knew it was going to be a struggle.

He snorted and leapt toward one of the men guarding the women. He slammed his fist into the face of the big man he'd charged. The behemoth simply blinked and shook his head. Then he swung at Lucifer. He managed to duck, avoiding the man's meaty fist connecting with his face. Then Lucifer slammed a jab into his opponent's gut and caught him with an uppercut to the chin that sent the thug reeling. He stumbled back into a barrel that was being used as a table. The lantern that sat on top and contributed to the glow in the middle of the warehouse tipped over and landed on the wood floor. The fuel leaked out, giving the flame a path to freedom. The floor caught on fire quickly between the age of the wood and who knew what in the way of chemicals that had soaked into it over the years.

"Fuck! Fire!" He warned anyone who would listen. But it was the high-pitched screams of the women that alerted most of the men still fighting that there was a greater danger. Then a man grabbed Lucifer's shoulder, spun him around, and slammed a fist into his face. He stumbled a step or two and shook his head before he turned and rushed the man.

This one was more of a match size-wise, so he decided to wrestle him to the ground versus exchanging blows with him. The smoke grew thick as they rolled on the floor. The bastard was not a novice fighter. He'd clearly been in a few brawls in his time. But with time running out and the fire growing bigger as it found more and more fuel to burn, Lucifer knew he had to end the struggle.

Using all his strength, he rolled the man and got on top of him. Then he managed to slam his head against the hardwood floor. Dazed, the man ceased to struggle, allowing Lucifer to get one more good punch in, and the man was down for the count. Standing up, he took in his torn and filthy shirt before he coughed and nearly went down from breathing in the smoke. He looked around and saw that his men had prevailed in the fight. "Round up the men and take them outside. We'll figure out what to do with them shortly."

He turned to the women. One, in particular, stood strong and fierce with three others cowering behind her. "Who are you?" She demanded more than asked.

"I assume you are Cat. I am here on behalf of Mistress Lash." He offered a small salute. "As the building seems to be engulfed in flames, would you ladies mind continuing introductions outside in the alley?"

The blonde woman eyed him warily. "How do I know I can trust you?"

"You don't, but if I don't bring you outside shortly, I'm quite certain Amelia will barrel in here brandishing her whip at anyone who should be in her way."

At that, Cat smiled, and the fierceness slipped away to be replaced by relief and exhaustion. "Thank God! We're saved, ladies. I told you my mistress wouldn't just forget about me."

Then, in a far corner of the warehouse, something exploded.

Amelia cried out as the warehouse exploded on one side. It was not the side the men were streaming out of, but nonetheless, her heart seized in fear. Was Lucifer still in there? What of Cat? She hadn't seen a woman exit yet. She was out of the carriage and halfway to the inferno when Hadley grabbed her from behind. "Miss, I can't let you go in there."

She struggled against him, desperate to try to save Lucifer and Cat. "Let me go!" She tried to pry his arms from around her, to no avail.

"I'm sorry, miss. Lucifer's instructions were very clear. He'll kill me if anything happens to you." The man's voice was firm, despite the vision before them.

Amelia drew a deep breath and tried to calm herself. Flames reached up to the sky like fingers stretching out. The glow cast a wicked light on a dark and foggy night, creating strange shadows that danced in the sky. And the heat—despite being far enough away not to be immediately noticed—she could feel the heat pouring off the building. None of it spoke to the man she loved walking out of that building alive. Regret crushed her. Regret for not telling him how she felt. And for not sharing her complete self with him. She'd been about to tell him everything when they'd been interrupted, and now it was too late. No! She refused to accept that. She would not give up so readily. She straightened up in Hadley's arms. "If you do not release me when this is over, I shall string you up and flay the very skin off your back until you slowly and painfully die."

The man hesitated two heartbeats and then let go with a muttered curse. "You're scarier than he is," he whispered as he stepped back.

Amelia didn't bother to look back as she raced forward, glad she'd changed her clothes when they'd gone home to regroup. Her trousers were far more practical than the socially acceptable skirts she'd had on earlier. She ran toward the untouched side of the building, where she found the men milling about as though unsure what to do next. "Has anyone alerted the fire brigade?" She had to yell to be heard over the roar of the flames.

A few men looked at her in confusion, then Gordie appeared and responded. "Aye, we sent Jimmy to bring them along."

"Very good. Now, you all need to find buckets and water and start dumping it on those flames and the buildings nearest it, or this fire is going to spread." At first, she didn't think the men would listen, but Gordie nodded. "Right you are. Let's go, men!"

Once they were moving, she looked at the building and saw the smoke pouring out, along with a few stragglers. She was just about to head inside when a woman stumbled out. Hope leapt into Amelia's throat, only to choke her once she realized it wasn't Cat or Lucy. She rushed over to the woman. "Are you okay?"

She looked up, startled. "Who—I don't—" she coughed roughly. "I think so."

"Good." Amelia turned and yelled again. "Hadley! Where are you?"

"Right here, Miss." He appeared from just behind her, where she assumed he'd been hovering.

"Help this woman over to one of the carriages." She looked back to the brown-haired, soot-smeared woman. "Were there any others in there?"

"There were, but I lost them in the smoke. I hope the others are all right." She looked back at the building, worried. "Cat and Lucy kept us all calm. Kept telling us someone would come. And then they did!"

Amelia's heart pounded. "Go with Hadley. I'll just fetch the others. You're safe now."

The woman nodded and followed her guard to the carriage. Within moments, he was back at her side. Her gaze snapped around. "You should be with that woman."

"You're the one I was ordered to protect. If you're going into that building, so am I. Walter will protect her for now." Hadley glared at her as if daring her to nay say him.

"Very well." Then she headed toward the building. Just then, a cheer rose up amongst the men from around the corner. The fire was still ablaze, so she knew it wasn't that it was out. For a moment, she thought it might be that the fire brigade had arrived, but that did not appear to be true. She heard no clanging of bells to announce their arrival. Instead, she saw a huddle of four people come around the corner of the building, covered in soot from head to toe. She blinked as they came closer to where she stood, and then she recognized Lucifer.

Without making a conscious decision, she flew into his arms. He was alive! He had only one arm to spare her since the other had been wrapped around a woman he was helping, but he did his best to hug her back. She planted kisses all over his sooty face. "I thought you were dead, you blasted man. How could you do that to me? If I wasn't so glad to see you, I would wring your neck!" she said between kisses.

He laughed and kissed her soundly on the lips. "I'm alive. But not for long if you keep this up."

She stepped back and looked at the women watching their display and gasped. "Cat! We found you!"

Her apprentice grinned, a slash of teeth in her soot-darkened face. "I knew you'd come looking for me. I told the girls you wouldn't just accept that I disappeared."

Amelia hugged her apprentice, grateful the hunt was over. "I couldn't! Besides, I promised your mother I'd find you."

"Is she all right? How's my brother?"

"Everyone is fine, but certainly worried. I stopped by to check on them when this all started and left them funds to survive while I looked for you." She squeezed her apprentice and friend again. Then she looked over Cat's shoulder at Lucy. "Abbess Cordelia will be glad to know you are safe as well. She was quite worried about you too, Lucy."

The woman looked up with dark eyes full of surprise. "She was?"

"Indeed. When I spoke with her, she offered me whatever I needed to help find the two of you." Amelia smiled. "Now, let's get you all into a carriage and someplace where you can clean up and recover from this ordeal."

They all nodded as she and Hadley helped them over to the coach. Amelia was so grateful to have another chance to tell Lucifer everything, she had to fight the urge to blurt it all out in the carriage once they were alone. Rather, she opted to press herself against him and hold on for a little while until he recovered. After he bathed, she decided, she would tell him everything.

Chapter Twenty-Seven

Lucifer looked at the clock as he dressed after a wonderfully hot bath. The water had turned black from all the soot, and it still hurt to breathe a bit, but he figured that was to be expected after all the smoke. It reminded him of the night he and Gordie had smoked an entire box of cigars they'd nicked off a man with a bump-and-run ploy. He suffered a bit of nausea, and his chest hurt, but not so much that he was concerned. When they'd left the warehouse, his men were working side by side with the fire brigade to contain the blaze and hopefully prevent it from spreading. There hadn't been much they could do to save the building, but it seemed everyone had gotten out.

Amelia was down the hall with Cat and the other ladies they'd rescued, making sure they all had what they required for the moment. He knew she would be back soon, chock full of questions for him. So, he sat down to sip a whiskey and wait. A knock at his door sounded, and then Gordie was there. "Lucifer, glad to see you are well."

His man looked as filthy as he'd been not long before and as tired as he currently felt. "I'm glad to see you are, too. Is the fire out, then?"

"Yes. Though the owner is none too happy about the loss." Gordie passed on.

Lucifer snorted. "I imagine not, but then he should be more careful about who he allows to use his facilities."

Gordie grunted in agreement. "I also wanted to let you know we managed to hold on to one of the men from the warehouse. I thought you might fancy asking him a few questions."

He grinned, not so pleasantly. "Indeed, I would. Where is he now?"

"Downstairs in the cellar. I didn't figure to drag you all the way over to the club to see to the business." Gordie shoved his hands in his pockets and waited.

"Very good. I'll be down in a few moments. I believe I shall collect Amelia for our chat with the man." Lucifer stood up, suddenly rejuvenated, and followed his man out of his room.

Down in his cellar, a man sat tied to a kitchen chair, his head tipped forward so his chin rested on his chest. Like they all had been at some point that night, the man was so covered in soot it was hard to tell what color his hair was. Amelia stood shoulder to shoulder with Lucifer, practically vibrating with all her questions. "Is he conscious, Gordie?"

"No reason for him not to be, except to avoid answering questions. I suppose I can get a bucket of cold water from the well to throw on him and wake him up." Gordie started to turn to do just that when the man's head popped up.

"No need. I'm awake." The man shot a baleful glare in Gordie's direction.

"You were one of the men holding the women in the warehouse." Lucifer stared at him.

"I don't—" He was clearly prepared to deny his activities.

Lucifer held up a hand to stay the man as he cut him off. "I was stating facts, not asking a question. Where did you find the women you took?"

"I'm not telling you Peelers nothing," the man spat and continued to glare at them.

Lucifer laughed heartily. "Not a Peeler. You'd be lucky if I was. Unfortunately, you fell into my hands. So, I suggest you start answering questions before I start breaking bones."

The man flinched but remained silent.

Lucifer sighed, walked over to him, grabbed his hand, and then wrapped his fingers around a single digit of the man's hand. "Please feel free to speak at any point."

The man glared at him mutinously, as though he invited the pain. With a sharp jerk of his hand, a loud snapping sound bounced around the small cellar, followed by the man's cry of pain. Lucifer was far too aware of how much it hurt to have your fingers snapped, having done so to one of his in the warehouse once. Of course, that had been an accident and unexpected. How much worse was it when you knew it was coming?

He took a step back from the moaning man. "Now, where did you find the women?"

The man still refused to speak.

"Look, we can do this all night. Me slowly breaking each of your ten fingers. You refusing to talk. Then I would have to move on to bigger bones, some ribs, maybe an arm. In the end, you will tell me what I wish to know. The sooner you talk, the sooner we can call a doctor to set that finger. I'm not a monster, but I am determined to get the answers I require."

The man finally gave in to good sense. "We were told to find whores, given the addresses of some of the fancy houses, and provided descriptions of the types of women to nab."

"What do you mean, descriptions?" Amelia asked.

"What they should look like. Yellow hair, black hair, that Oriental one." He looked at her like she was an idiot.

"You mean the woman of Chinese descent? You were specifically told to find a woman who looked like that?" Amelia looked as nauseous as Lucifer felt hearing what the man said. *Dear God! But for a different description, it could have been Amelia that was taken, and then what? Who would have noticed? Who would have searched for her?*

"Aye. It was easy money, and most of them were easy enough to find. She was the hardest to find and to take. Bitch nearly got away a couple times." The man offered, cutting into Lucifer's spiraling thoughts.

"Who provided you the list? Who hired you?" This was the critical question. The one that could allow the entire episode to come to an end.

The man hesitated again as if considering if he should answer.

"I can return to breaking things if I need to," Lucifer offered as if it didn't matter to him one way or another.

The man turned white in the glow of the lantern they used to light the room. "Mr. Frank Lucifer hired me."

A strangled sound came from Amelia, and Gordie stepped forward on a low growl. Lucifer simply laughed, though he darted a worried glance over at Amelia. "That's a foolish lie to tell."

"It ain't no lie. The man said very clearly, he was Frank Lucifer." The man glanced from him to Gordie—who was growling louder now—to Amelia, who'd spun away to give them all her back.

Drawing in a deep breath through his nose as he pinched the bridge of it—a mistake considering the odors the man had brought along with him from the fire—he grappled for patience. "Since *I* am Frank Lucifer, I can assure you I did not hire you. Nor did I place an order for a group of women as though buying horses at Tattersalls."

The man looked as shocked as he had felt hearing his own name. "You don't look nothing like the bloke that hired us. How can you be *the* Lucifer?"

"I assure you, I was born with the name Frank and have been Frank Lucifer since I was a boy. I built my name and my business over many years. I do not appreciate someone running around claiming to be me. What did this man look like?"

The man groaned. "He had light brown hair. He was tall, though not quite as tall as you, and always dressed fancy like you."

Lucifer tamped down his frustration at such a generic description. "Anything else about him?"

"His eyes. They were dark and cold. Like he couldn't care if you lived or died in the next five minutes." The man's gaze darted around the room to each of them as panic seemed to be setting in. He seemed to have a clear grasp that he was in trouble and he may not have the information to get himself out.

"Well, you certainly don't have light brown hair, Lucifer. Though I suppose you could have worn a wig." Amelia sounded more normal now. He hoped that was a good sign. "Did the man have a beard at all?"

"No. Clean shaven every day like a gentleman," the man confirmed.

"Damn it all! It clearly wasn't you. But who was it?" She sounded as frustrated as he felt now. "Is there anything else? Anything different about the man?"

"No—wait! He talked funny. Didn't sound like any Londoner I've ever heard. Not even the fancy types like you all." The man looked at them hopefully.

Amelia turned a bit pale again. He was about to suggest she go upstairs when she cut him off. Reverting to her American accent, she asked, "Did he sound like this? Don't be too hard on yourself since you couldn't have known he was a liar."

Lucifer stared at Amelia in shock. She sounded like that bloody American he'd met recently. Her accent was perfect. "Aye! That's it! That weird accent. Kind of flat and strange sounding."

She pressed a hand to her stomach as if she might be sick. "I think I know who it is."

"Who?" Lucifer lurched toward her. She looked as though she might topple over at any moment.

"Not down here. We should go upstairs and speak. I have some things to tell you." She turned and headed for the steps that led out of the cellar.

Lucifer watched her carefully climb each tread and walk out of the space. "Gordie, call the doctor and get his finger set. Also, send some men to detain the Captain of The Sea Rose. We can't have the ship leaving until we get to the bottom of who was giving the orders. And, please take a guest room to clean up and get some sleep. We'll deal with this one in the morning."

Worried about what Amelia might reveal, he followed her upstairs and into his room. What was she going to tell him? Was she married? Had the bastard abused her and caused her to flee? He'd kill him if he hurt her. Or perhaps she had amnesia and suddenly remembered who he was? The not knowing was killing him. The what-ifs were worse.

Chapter Twenty-Eight

Amelia's head was spinning. She had been suspicious based on the description of the man, but when their guest confirmed the accent? There was no denying what she knew—Richard Mattingly was behind all of this. Of course, they had no proof, just her gut instincts and past experience. The door closed behind her with a soft click that nonetheless made her jump. She was on edge, had been for weeks, if she was honest.

"Amelia, what is it? Something has had you agitated for quite a while." He stood across the room, his shoulders set, feet spread, and his hands fisted at his side as though he was about to do battle.

She drew a deep breath. "Perhaps you'd better sit for this story. It's rather long and not a particularly sweet tale."

He cocked his head to one side as if considering her suggestion and then nodded before moving to one of the chairs by the fire.

Once he settled, there was nothing left to stop her. "My name is Amy VanBolton."

"Bloody hell!" Lucifer sat up straighter in his chair. "The missing American Heiress? I remember when she—you went missing. We all talked about finding you and collecting the reward money."

She nodded. "I came to London when I was sixteen years old. I was so very excited because it was my first time sailing across the ocean. I was certain it meant I was becoming a woman, though my mother was not quite ready to let me grow up. It turns out she had little say in the matter."

She took a deep breath and then sat in the chair across from him. It was that or pace, and she was frankly exhausted after everything that had happened. "It was truly a business trip for my father, so his partner was also on the trip with us. The man's name was Richard Mattingly."

"Mattingly? I just met a man with that name recently." Lucifer sat forward on the edge of the seat.

"Did you?" She wanted to say she was surprised but found she was not.

"I did, but please continue your story."

She nodded. "We were almost to London when something went wrong. My mother and I went up to the deck to meet my father for a walk after dinner. When we arrived where we were to meet him, he and Richard were arguing. My mother had told me to go back to our cabin, but I froze in place, terrified I would never see them again. I stayed and hid around a corner where I couldn't be seen. They were arguing about business matters, something Richard wanted to bring into their clubs but my father refused to consider it. I suspect Richard wanted to add prostitutes, but it was so long ago I can't be sure. When my mother arrived, it turned toward my parents' relationship. They were very much in love, but it seems Richard was also in love with my mother. Richard and my father had been friends since university, where they met my mother at the same time. But she chose my father. I guess Richard was still unhappy about that seventeen years later."

She paused for a moment and drew a deep breath. This was where things got difficult for her. "My father and Richard struggled. Then my mother screamed as my father clutched his side where Richard stabbed him while stumbling backward toward the rail of the ship. Richard pushed Father over, but my mother grabbed him as he dangled. She tried to save him, but in the end, he fell. Furious, she started to go find the captain and stop the ship, but Richard snarled something at her, and the next thing I knew, he pushed her over the side as well." Tears streamed down her face as she opened up her past. "I must have cried out when she went over the side because Richard turned and saw me. That was when I fled."

"Christ! Where did you go on a steamer?" Lucifer's eyes were wide with worry for the girl she'd been.

"I did what my mother had told me to do at the start. I ran to our cabin and locked myself in. I pushed furniture to block the door and waited until sunrise and our docking. Richard, of course, followed me and tried to get into the room a few times, but he gave up at some point. I somehow melded into a departing family to get off the ship, though I was still spotted at the last moment. But it was too late at that point. I ran. I ran through the damp streets of London until my side ached, and I couldn't run any further."

"My God, how did you survive? You were a girl alone." He looked anguished, his brows pinched and his fists still clenched.

"I was lucky. A washerwoman found me and took me in. She had no room and little enough food for her family, but still, she took me in and gave me a home. That was when I became Amelia Ketting. I have lived as her, and then Mistress Lash, for over twenty years. Eventually I gained work at The Market as a maid, and then had the opportunity to learn my trade. I've kept my secret all these years for fear that Richard would kill me as surely as he had my parents."

"Over the last few weeks, I thought I was slowly losing my mind. I kept hearing his voice in crowds, which truly terrified me. And then yesterday, as I stood in the salon downstairs, I saw him for the first time. He was older, his hair showing signs of graying, but it was him. It was as if someone had punched me in the stomach as I stood there staring at my parents' killer, and he stared right back."

The need to pace took hold, and she rose. "I don't know how or why, but it seems that Richard is behind these abductions. The man our guest in the cellar described is Richard, I am sure of it."

Lucifer stepped into her path and took hold of her shoulders, stopping her from pacing. "Whether or not it is him, the man is responsible for killing your parents. I promise he will not be permitted to get away with it again."

She smiled at him, though she felt as breakable as glass. "No, he'll not be allowed to get away with it again. I refuse to remain hiding in the shadows, to let him continue to govern my choices. It is time to fight back."

Lucifer nodded this time. "I doubt he'll be found at his hotel again. We'll search London for him. And I've already had Gordie send men to collect the captain of The Sea Rose."

Amelia smiled bitterly. "I wouldn't expect Richard to leave London yet. Not after we released the women, he'd collected. He'll be looking to get even with me."

"Perhaps. I suppose we shall see come the morning. We should retire for the night. Some rest would not come amiss after the day's events."

Exhausted, Amelia removed her clothing, glad for her men's trousers and easier-to-handle garments. She was tired, and the fact that she had no idea what to expect from Richard Mattingly had her on edge. But there was little she could do about it until morning.

Amelia dressed and arrived downstairs far earlier than she would have anticipated. Sleep had eluded her until she'd finally given up and dressed, leaving a sleeping Lucifer tangled in the sheets. She was sitting down to breakfast when a footman delivered a letter to her on a silver tray. It still struck her as strange to be treated as an honored guest in the elegant home, in large part, because she still struggled with the idea that Lucifer owned it.

Pushing her pointless musings aside, she opened the letter with unfamiliar writing on the front. A tremor ran through her hands as she read the contents.

Dearest Amy,

I am pleased to see you have become as beautiful a woman as your mother had been. Your parents' tragic loss at sea still haunts me to this day. When you ran off from the ship, we all feared for your safety. No one holds you responsible for what happened on the ship that night. I made sure it was documented as a tragic accident and not the result of your wild and unruly actions. It would be wonderful to see you properly if that might be possible, as I have much to tell you.

Your Friend,

Richard Mattingly

Her fingers went numb as the letter slipped to the floor in her shock. She assumed he would have made up some excuse to cover what happened. But that he alluded to the idea that he'd covered it up to protect her from her actions was outrageous. Could he have portrayed her parents' deaths as being her fault in some way? Her gut twisted, and the food laid out for breakfast no longer held any appeal. She sat there, stunned that he requested a meeting as casually as if suggesting they have tea.

"Good morning!" Lucifer stopped just inside the dining room door. Then he was kneeling at her side. "What has happened, Amelia?"

"It's Richard." She waved a hand toward the letter on the floor. "He wishes to meet with me."

Lucifer scooped up the note and quickly read through it as he remained at her side. The irony of the moment was not lost on her. For weeks, she'd waffled back and forth about Lucifer's role in all of this. Could he be the man she was looking for? Was he the culprit taking women and working with her to try and hide his actions? Distracting her with this unasked-for attraction. And now, just when she finally trusted him, believed that he truly was helping her because he cared, she was the one cast in shadows. She was the one who was being made to look as though she'd done something awful and had covered it up. Her stomach twisted and knotted, nearly causing her to cast up her accounts.

"I wish I could say I am shocked, but the man has no compunction whatsoever." Lucifer's statement came out dry and matter-of-fact.

She turned her head just enough so she could partially see him. "You believe me? Just like that, without a shred of evidence to attest to my innocence in the matter?" Her heart skipped a beat, maybe even three.

"Of course, I've never known you to lie. Withhold information, perhaps, but never outright lie." He snorted. "This man sat in my club and not only attempted—albeit poorly—to suggest I change how my operation ran so we could do business together, but he essentially tried to pull me into his abduction plot. And that was all before I refused and tossed him out. I assume that is part of the reason I was made to look guilty should he be caught in the end. So, yes. Without a doubt, I believe what you told me versus what this bastard has suggested in a few short lines of a letter."

Amelia's numbness began to wear off as her anger at Richard rose to the fore. Bolstered by Lucifer's faith and Richard's uncharacteristically sloppy work when it came to approaching him, she was furious that this bastard was once again attempting to shift the course of her life. She'd been too young to deal with him twenty years ago, but no longer. This business would come to an end. She turned more fully to face Lucifer, who still knelt at her side. "Thank you for believing in me, for not doubting me as I have done you over the last few weeks."

Lucifer reached up and cupped her face with one hand. "If this man is what you judged all men by, then it is easy to understand your lack of trust. But know this, I shall move heaven and earth to see this man called to account for his actions. Whether by my hand or that of the legal system, I care not, but he will answer for what he's done both in the past and more recently."

Despite everything seeming to crumble around her, this man was at her side and ready to fight with her. For her. Her heart swelled nearly to bursting as she smiled at him. It wasn't the time or place to say anything, but she knew now this was how her parents must have felt for each other. And she hoped that it was something she'd have forever. But first, they would have to deal with Richard. "What time should we have him come for tea?"

"We do not have him come over—yet. There are a few things we must address first." The softness that had shone from his gaze faded as a look of determination replaced it.

"Such as?" Worry and confusion warred with the hope swelling from deep within.

"We must arrange for our nuptials, and I need to speak with my brother. Once all of those things are settled, we shall need to visit Scotland Yard once more."

He'd rattled off a list of things to do that sent her head spinning. "Marriage? And the Yard? I don't understand."

"Before we can address the issue of Mattingly, we must first address your illegal status in this country. Marriage will quickly resolve that issue. Marriage to a peer of the realm who is related to a Duke will afford you even greater protections." He stated these things as casually as if he'd ordered dinner.

"Can we not simply tell him we're married?" Once again, it seemed Richard was causing her life to take an unplanned turn, and the familiar feelings of frustration, anger, and helplessness washed over her like a foul stench.

"I suppose we could, but do you not think he is the type of man who would follow up on something so critical to the success of his plans? I can't imagine that he didn't look for you by name once he discovered you were alive. He would have to know that you, or more correctly, Amy VanBolton, does not exist in England. Once he knows that, regardless of the facts, it is easy enough to cause you enough trouble to result in your deportation at a minimum. If he can find the right Justice, he could easily have you convicted based on his claims and deported straight back to America or worse, transported to Australia if he manages any other trumped-up charges." He took hold of her shoulders and looked her in the eyes. "Does any of that sound appealing?"

Fear choked her as she shook her head.

"I thought it might not. Let me help you with this." Hands squeezed her shoulders gently.

"But why? Why are you willing to do this for me?" Her heart raced at the wonder that he might feel for her as strongly as she did for him.

His face hardened. "Because you need the help, and no one should be forced to scrabble by on their own with no one willing to assist. I like to think that had my mother had a little help, she might have lived to see a better life than the one she had." He let go and turned away from her.

Well, that certainly wasn't a declaration of undying love. She was a bloody charity project for him. Sucking up the strange feeling of hurt inside, she tried to press on to practical matters. Time was short, and Richard had to be dealt with. "Very well. We can sort out how to dissolve the marriage after everything has been resolved. I am happy to be labeled the dissolute wife or adulteress if needed."

Lucifer glanced back at her from over his shoulder, and she swore she saw a moment of pain not unlike her own. But the moment was fleeting, and his next words left no doubt about where he stood. "There will be no divorce."

"That's ridiculous. We aren't marrying for love, so why would we remain bound?" What was this man thinking? She couldn't keep up with his mental twists and turns.

"You will have the protection of my name until the day you die. There is nothing further to discuss. Now, I need to go see my brother, and then I shall have to procure a special license. I suggest you focus on planning whatever amounts to a wedding in the next twenty-four hours. I can send Ros over if you wish." He was clearly brooking no arguments from her or anyone else.

She could be as stubborn as him. "Lucifer, I'll not marry you until we come to some agreement. Not even for my own protection."

He had turned and started toward the dining room door but stopped at her words. "As I told you previously, it will not be difficult to arrange for a priest to marry us without your agreement. Now, I have arrangements to make, as do you."

He stalked from the room, leaving her standing there as flummoxed as when he'd walked in. Once again, Richard Mattingly was the driving force behind the upheaval in her life. It was maddening that the man wielded so much power over her, and she could do little to stop him. And then there was Lucifer, who was apparently going to marry her, whether or not she wished it. What was she going to do? Could she refuse him at the altar?

She sighed. She was angry, but she was no fool. Marriage to a peer would afford her protection from Richard, but it would also change her entire life. Did she even want to be a Lady? She'd given up a life of privilege so many years ago. Did she wish to go back to that sheltered person? She wouldn't. She couldn't. She'd seen and done too much to ever again be that person. But how could she not marry him? This was ridiculous. She would marry him because she was no fool, and she would do her best to continue to be who she was—Mistress Lash. At least until she was certain Cat was ready to take her place. She bit her lip. Did Cat still want that? After all she'd been through, would she still want the future she'd been working toward?

Bloody hell! Once again, she found her life had been upended, and it was time to set things to rights.

Chapter Twenty-Nine

Lucifer stood in Flint's study once more, but this time he knew the conversation would end very differently than previous versions of this discussion. "Thank you for seeing me. I apologize for coming by unannounced."

Flint grinned. "You're family. You are always welcome. But I must say, I was surprised to see you. I figured with everything on your plate, you would be too busy for social calls for a bit."

"I was, but we have rescued the women." Lucifer sat down with Flint on a set of chairs close to the low fire.

"That's excellent news!"

"Yes, well, it is good news, and it was a close thing. They were nearly shipped off to America." Lucifer shared. "Which is related to my unaccountably early visit. It seems the man who is responsible for taking the women is a ghost from Amelia's past." He went on to explain how Amelia came to be in London. "So, I need to give her the protection of my name. I figure if I am going about all this to protect her, I might as well go all the way."

Flint whistled, having been quiet for the whole sordid tale. "That is quite the story. She is an impressive woman."

"Indeed. The foolish woman had the nerve to offer me a divorce before we've even married!" He groused. "As if I'd let a woman like her go once I convinced her to marry me."

Flint looked at him strangely. "Have you told her how you feel?"

"Well, not in so many words. I figure there is time enough for all that once we have everything settled. We need to make her as safe as we can and then catch Mattingly so that I can rest easy knowing she won't be hunted by this bastard," he growled. The idea that the man had tried to take Amelia, as well as the other women, made him wish to rend him limb from limb. But if he was going to become a peer of the realm, he knew he would have to change a few of his ways. The violence was one thing that would have to go—or at least appear to.

Flint shook his head and chuckled. "I take it she did not appreciate your business-like proposal?"

"She seemed amenable at first, but then she started banging on about divorces and causes. I told her there would be no divorce, that she would have my protection until she died, but that seemed to only agitate her more." He huffed. "I realize I did not fall to my knees offering declarations of my undying love, but isn't that a bit over the top?"

"Perhaps, but I find that our women respond better to hearing the words than to displays of manly prowess." His brother lifted one shoulder as if it was obvious.

"I'm not sure I would know what to say. I've never said such things to a woman before. In fact, I've always taken great pains to avoid those very discussions."

"I suggest you stop avoiding them if you'd like to have a harmonious marriage. All women desire to hear that they are loved." Flint's brow lifted in punctuation.

Lucifer sat quietly for a moment, absorbing his brother's advice. Could he make himself so vulnerable to another person? Could he tell her how he felt? "I shall have to consider your counsel."

Flint nodded but said nothing else.

Shifting uncomfortably in his seat, Lucifer knew the hardest part would come next. Well, hard for him. He expected that Flint would thoroughly enjoy this next part. "In addition to offering her marriage, I would like to take you up on your offer of a title. If it's still available, of course. While having a Duke for a brother is certainly a boon in this situation, I think also having a title might be of some value. I'd say it's inevitable that Mattingly attempts to follow through on his threats to cast her in the role of villainess."

He'd barely gotten started his little speech before his brother had started grinning like a Cheshire cat. "About bloody time you found a use for a title."

Flint stood and walked over to his desk, where he pulled out some paperwork. He crossed back to where Lucifer sat and handed it to him. He looked down at the Letters Patent officially conferring the title Marquess of Portridge on him. For a moment, he sat stunned. This went far beyond an offer of a courtesy title. "I don't understand. How did you manage this without my knowing? And when, precisely, were you going to tell me of it?"

Flint dropped back into his chair as casually as if he'd just handed him a loaf of bread and not a hereditary title with an estate. "You may be surprised by this, but being a peer is not much different from becoming a successful business owner. Once you have money and power, influencing people to do as you wish is far easier. It was a fairly simple matter, considering the title and estate are both old and rather neglected at this stage. The Queen's family was once quite partial to one of the former earls, and so, was thrilled to have the title dusted off and used once more."

"And when were you going to tell me of this?" Lucifer lifted one brow as he tipped his head slightly.

Flint chuckled. "I suppose I would have eventually found an opportune moment to convey the title to you. Once you were ready."

Lucifer couldn't help but laugh at his brother's obfuscation. But in light of the situation, it was a welcome surprise. "Thank you for this. It is far more than I came here seeking."

"My father was a bastard to the end. It was the least I could do to truly set things to rights. Of course, you'll need to present yourself to the Queen for everything to be right and tight, but that is a formality I can help you arrange. I also imagine a special license is on order. I can't imagine you wish to wait through the reading of the Banns."

"Indeed. I'd like to marry as soon as possible. I told Amelia she had until tomorrow to make arrangements for fear she would flee if I gave her any more time." Lucifer's gut clenched at the thought of returning home and finding her gone. He'd tear the city apart to find her if she thought of doing such a cowardly thing.

"I shall send Ros to her while we go procure that license." Flint rose once more and went to the door of his study. There, he paused and smiled. "Welcome to the family, Portridge."

Lucifer marveled at the sense of belonging that encompassed him as he sat staring at Letters Patent. It truly didn't change anything about him. He was still the man who had hauled himself out of the gutters of Seven Dials and built an empire with his bare hands and intelligence. And Flint had welcomed him as a brother right from the revelation of their relation, but somehow this gesture made real the notion that he had a family. He had finally achieved the one thing that had eluded him all his life—a true family. And soon, he would expand that family to include the woman he loved.

But still, the question lingered. Should he tell her how he felt? He'd always considered close ties a weakness. Something to be exploited. She'd not said anything to him, so perhaps she understood that he cared without his having to say anything? She certainly hadn't unburdened her heart to him. Staying the course seemed safer all around, at the very least, until the issue of Richard Mattingly was put to rest. Perhaps after that, he might consider exposing his heart if he thought she might love him back. That was a question worth pondering. Did she love him? If not, could he make her fall in love with him?

Chapter Thirty

Amelia stood beside Lucifer in the front salon of his home—well, their home, she supposed. The man cloaked in black robes looked solemn as he spoke the words that would bind them as husband and wife. She had ceased her arguing about getting a divorce. They could work that issue out later. Her soon-to-be-husband had been adamant that they would remain married even after Richard was dealt with. She foresaw a different outcome.

"Repeat after me. I, Frank Lucifer, take Amy Amelia Van-Bolton, to be my lawfully wedded wife." He paused as Lucifer's rich tone filled the space with a confidence and a calmness she did not feel as he repeated the vow.

Then the priest continued, "to have and to hold from this day forward—" and Lucifer repeated after him "—for better or for worse, for richer, for poorer, in sickness and in health, to love and to cherish." Another pause, "for the rest of my days until death us do part."

The priest turned to her and repeated the vows, adding in the obligatory obey and allowing her to recite them as well. As she uttered the last part she couldn't keep from privately tacking on, *mostly*. She suspected the obey part might be challenging at times. But then, he didn't truly seem to expect that of her. Or perhaps it would be more accurate to say he expected her to do as she pleased except under certain circumstances. Either way, there was only one way to answer the priest's question.

"I now pronounce you husband and wife." The man intoned. "You may kiss your bride."

Lucifer pulled her into his arms and kissed her as though no one else stood there watching. She couldn't help but respond by slipping her arms around his neck and meeting him thrust for thrust. After the chuckling around them turned to awkward silence, he finally released her mouth.

Behind them, the priest cleared his throat. "May I present to you the Earl and Marchioness of Portridge?"

Everyone clapped, covering her gasp of surprise at that little announcement. She turned to Lucifer. "What is he talking about?"

"I told you I was going to get a priest and a title." He shrugged.

"Yes, but I didn't realize it would happen so quickly. Aren't there steps to becoming a peer?"

"Apparently not when you are the brother of a duke." He grinned and walked her down the aisle. "Or at least one that does as he pleases, no matter your many objections."

Everyone moved to the dining room for the wedding breakfast as Lucifer led her down a hall and into one of the small sitting rooms nearby. "He had me named Marquess of Portridge in my own right. We now own a small estate two days outside of London near Shropshire, near where his ducal seat is."

"I see." She bit her lip and considered all the ramifications of this news. "I should think this would make a divorce harder to gain later on."

"Bloody hell! We've been married for not even two minutes. Woman, I've already told you there will be no divorce." He whisper-yelled the words at her.

"And I told you I didn't want a husband who was forced to marry me. And I certainly wouldn't have chosen a peer of the realm." She glared at him.

"No one has forced me to do anything. I chose to marry you." He frowned at her as his brows drew together. "And I'm as reluctant a peer as you are. I just have the good sense to understand the value the title brings under the circumstances. It will be far harder for Mattingly to make accusations against a peer of the realm, rather than a sex worker in a brothel, and make them stick."

Begrudgingly, she could acknowledge the sense of what he said. "You're not wrong about the title. But do not expect me to change who I am because of it. I'll not prance about and preen like some puff-headed twit."

He laughed at her. Outright laughed until he had to hold his stomach. When he finally calmed enough to speak, his smile remained. "And do you think Ros prances about like a puff-headed twit?"

"Of course not! She is eminently sensible and kind." She could see where he was going with this. And he was right, the infuriating man. "Fine. Your point has been made. Now, we should return to our guests?"

A gleam came into his eyes that she recognized immediately. "Not quite yet, *wife*."

He pressed her up against the door he'd closed until the decorative ridges drove her stays into her back, and then he kissed her. Perhaps she was feeling fanciful on her wedding day, but it was more than a simple kiss. He claimed her, possessed her mouth as thoroughly as she knew he would later possess her body. Their tongues met and tangled as a soft moan escaped her. He tasted like mint and whiskey at nine in the morning.

As they continued to taste each other, lost in the desire pulsing between them, he reached down and pulled her pale blue skirts up. He pulled back from the kiss for a moment. "Are you wet for me, wife?"

Wanting, no needing, his touch on her pussy, she growled low in her throat. He chuckled softly and returned to ravage her mouth as he ran his hand up her inner thigh. Finally, his fingers brushed the springy hairs covering her mound, and she whimpered in need. Her body ached for him in a matter of moments, cried out for him with a need that was startling in its intensity. He slipped a finger between her folds and slid over her clit, sending sparks of bliss shooting out as if warning her body of what was to come.

A knock at the door behind her sounded, causing both of them to pause. "My Lord?"

Lucifer rested his forehead against the door next to her and drew a calming breath, even as his fingers remained nestled between her legs. "Yes?"

"Your guests are awaiting you in the dining room." His butler sounded priggish at the best of times. Right then, he sounded positively sanctimonious.

"Thank you, Peterson. I am well aware of where my wedding guests are located." Lucifer ground out between gritted teeth.

Amelia had to stifle a laugh at the absurdity of the moment.

"This is not in the least funny," he whispered to her.

She couldn't hide her smile. "I think it's rather amusing, if slightly uncomfortable, for us."

"Slightly uncomfortable? I have a stiff cock that it seems I shall be sporting at my wedding breakfast in front of all my guests," he groused.

"And whose fault is that, *husband*?" She grinned saucily at him. "Besides, a bit of anticipation is good for you."

He groaned as he stepped back from her and let her skirts drop. "You truly are a sadist at heart, aren't you, my dear?"

"Don't be so dramatic. You have to know by now that I am no sadist. I merely appreciate the finer points of self-control." She shrugged one shoulder as though it was obvious.

"Do you?" Then he drew his fingers slicked with her juices into his mouth, riveting her gaze as he licked them clean.

Her breath heaved against her bodice as desire for her husband rushed through her once more. Her body tingled with wanting him, the buzz of desire coursing through her veins like a fine wine. Her legs trembled with desperation. For a moment, she considered flipping her skirts up and begging him to take her quickly.

"My lord, we cannot serve breakfast until you two rejoin the party." Peterson sounded positively aggrieved.

It seemed they had both forgotten the servant was standing inches away on the other side of the door. "We'll be there momentarily, thank you." Amelia managed to push the words past her closing throat as heat bloomed in her cheeks. Had he heard every word they said? She wanted to melt into a puddle of mortification. She was a lady now. She wasn't some nameless woman in a brothel any longer. She wasn't even the outrageously famed Mistress Lash. No, she was Lady Portridge. A bloody marchioness!

"Well, that will teach him to linger at doors where he is not wanted." Lucifer's brows drew together. "If he wasn't so damned excellent at his job, I'd sack him for interrupting us."

"He did nothing wrong. We were remiss in abandoning our guests." She pressed her hands to her cheeks in hopes they would cool, but to no avail. "We should join everyone before they send out reinforcements."

Lucifer chuckled. "I doubt very seriously that my brother or any of the men in the dining room would bother to come looking for us. It's not as if they don't know what we were likely up to."

Impossibly, her cheeks grew warmer. It was distressing to realize that she did, in fact, have the ability to be embarrassed about things of a sexual nature. Or, more aptly, a private nature. For so long, sex was not a personal, private thing between two people. It was merely another of the activities available at The Market. She drew in a breath. "Yes, well, in either case, we should return to the celebration. How's that cockstand coming along?"

"You impossible, wench. You've done nothing to aid me. How do you think it's coming along?" He pressed his lips together. Though based on his shaking shoulders, she was quite certain he was attempting to contain more laughter.

With that, they straightened their clothes and opened the door of the sitting room. A few short strides had them rejoining everyone despite her pink cheeks and his still obvious erection. They chose to ignore the obvious titters of delight from their salacious guests.

That afternoon, once the nuptial breakfast concluded and everyone had gone home, Lucifer and Amelia changed their clothes and headed down to Scotland Yard. It was time to acquire some official assistance in the matter at hand. Lucifer strode into the busy office of the Yard and looked about for a familiar face. Over the years, he'd met more than a few Peelers, but there was one man he knew from their days running the streets of Seven Dials. It had been a few years since he last saw him, but he didn't suspect Matthew Buckley had diverted from his chosen path out of the gutters. Seeing no one he knew milling about, he walked up to the sergeant, who sat at the rather imposing front desk. "Excuse me; I'm looking for Matthew Buckley. Do you know if he is about?"

"Sir, *Superintendent* Buckley is quite busy. Do you have an appointment?" The uniformed man, with an absurdly bushy mustache, looked down at them both with a pinched face.

"I do not, but this is a matter of vital importance. I promise you; he will wish to see me." Lucifer glared at the man until he huffed a little and walked off, presumably to let Superintendent Buckley know they were there. Superintendent! That was a surprise. That last he'd seen Buckley, he'd still been a lowly patrolman who walked the streets and helped with arrests when the Peelers were sweeping up an area. In the early days, he'd found himself caught up in a few more of those efforts than he'd liked. But he quickly figured out how to avoid such business and turned his focus to building an empire that kept him out of such activities.

Amelia looked at him, her confusion clear. "Superintendent? If you knew someone here, why didn't we simply come down here sooner?"

Somewhat uncomfortable with part of his own answer to that question—he certainly wasn't going to tell her that he'd wanted a chance to get to know her better—he shrugged. "I had no idea he'd come so far in the hierarchy here. Last I knew him, he was a simple patrolman."

A few minutes later, Buckley's blonde head appeared down the hallway. It was easy to see him since he stood easily a head taller than most of the other men in the building, even Lucifer himself. Of course, Buckley had always been lanky, even when they'd been practically starving as children.

"Lucifer? Is that you? What brings you to Scotland Yard when you aren't in custody?" Buckley shook his hand as he smiled, all while darting questioning glances at Amelia, who stood next to Lucifer, quietly taking everything in.

"I'd like to introduce you to my wife, Lady Amelia Portridge." Lucifer pressed his hand to her back and urged her forward a step.

Buckley took her hand and paused. "Lady? My, you have come up in the world. Does that mean I have to call you my lord now?" His eyebrows climbed up to meet his hairline.

"Indeed, I have come up. And yes, I'm afraid I have been pulled from the gutters and dusted off, so you may have to call me my lord, now and again." Lucifer couldn't help but glare at his old friend, who seemed to still be holding his wife's hand.

"I sense there is a story here. But first, tell me you didn't do anything nefarious to wrest this title of yours from someone.

Especially not this lovely lady." He bowed over her hand and even kissed it.

"A pleasure, Superintendent Buckley. And no, Lucifer did nothing to warrant the interest of Scotland Yard. Unfortunately, I am the cause of our visit." She offered his friend a tremulous smile.

Lucifer wanted to scoop her up and simply whisk her away from Mattingly and all that came with her past. But he knew from experience you could never outrun it. The past was maddening in that it always seemed to catch up with you.

Buckley darted a startled glance at him and then straightened up. "Why don't we head to my office, where we can speak in private?"

Chapter Thirty-One

Lucifer stood with Amelia in the front salon as they awaited their guest. They expected him at any moment. "Remember, you are my wife, Lady Portridge, now. I don't want him believing you are unprotected."

She rolled her eyes at him, but in his gut, he knew this man was unpredictable. Her being his wife offered her some protection, and the Peeler masquerading as a servant offered even more. Despite that, it didn't feel like enough to ensure she remained safe. It was maddening, but he had to let her handle this interaction. He'd done all he could to protect her for the moment.

"Mr. Richard Mattingly to see you, my lady," Peterson announced.

"Send him in, please," Amelia stated calmly as she settled on the settee across the room. He moved to her side to offer her his support as Inspector Brown nodded and took his place by the door as a footman. Lucifer reminded himself that around the corner lurking near the door so he could hear the conversation was his old friend Buckley, whose help they'd enlisted.

Mattingly walked in as though he was a long-lost dear friend. "Amy! It is lovely to see you after all these years."

He moved toward her as if to embrace her, but Amelia lifted a palm to stay his progress. "Do sit down, Richard. Let us not pretend a familiarity neither of us feels. I received your note and wish to hear what it is you wanted to speak to me about."

Richard's brows rose, but he inclined his head slightly. "Very well, right down to business. Perhaps you'd prefer to speak with me alone." He shifted his gaze to where Lucifer stood slightly behind her and then back over his shoulder at the lurking footman.

"I'd sooner stand in a pit of vipers than be alone in a room with you. My husband, Lord Portridge, is fully aware of the events of my past. You can say nothing he does not already know unless you choose to tell more lies, and my servants are paid well for their discretion," she replied.

Relief rocked him. Until she'd uttered the words, he hadn't been certain she would call out their marriage so clearly. Her back was ramrod straight. If he wasn't mistaken, she had shifted into her Mistress Lash persona the moment Mattingly had entered the room. Lucifer did not envy having to deal with her. Mistress Lash was quite a handful.

"Come now, Amy, let us not tell lies so soon. You do realize it is a simple matter of public record to see if you are married or not—and Lord Portridge? When did they begin handing out titles to guttersnipe? You do test the bounds of believability since you two have only just begun sharing a roof recently. I highly doubt you are legally married. Which, I'd like to remind you, places you in this country illegally." The man sat back in the chair she'd directed him to and looked around the room. "No tea? I was certain your invitation was to tea."

Amelia sniffed. "You misread my note, I'm sure." She paused for a beat or two as Lucifer suppressed a chuckle. "The matter of my marriage is, in fact, public record, as is the conference of the title Marquess of Portridge on my husband. The question at hand is, what do you want?"

He shrugged. "Very well, I want you and your—" he cast a glowering look at Lucifer "—partner to leave my business interests here in London alone. I had intended to wrap things up, but it seems some of my property was liberated the other night. I'll need that returned to me immediately so I can be on my way."

"I'm afraid I don't understand. How have we upset your business dealings? I wasn't even aware you were in London until I received your note."

Mattingly sat forward, eschewing his casual slouch for a more aggressive posture.

Lucifer took a step forward, drawing Mattingly's narrowed glare before the man pressed on with the conversation.

"Give me back the women you took, and I shall leave London and your secrets in peace. You two may continue in your *connubial* bliss while I go home."

Lucifer couldn't see her face, but he could practically feel her body vibrating with rage despite the calmness of her words. "Impossible, I'm afraid. Those women were taken against their will—one of whom happens to be a friend—and I shall not simply hand them back over to you."

Mattingly's face twisted briefly before he wrestled it back into control. "You should be careful, *Amy*."

"You will address me as Lady Portridge, or this interview will be over before it has truly begun." Amelia cut in to whatever he was about to say with a tone that brooked no argument.

Lucifer watched Mattingly's eyes narrow and his gaze shift from focused to a furious glare. But, once again, he managed to temper his response before continuing.

"You aren't a girl anymore. I can't keep protecting you from what you did. I was, of course, horrified when I stumbled upon the scene at the stern of the ship. You, arguing with your parents about your trip like the spoiled brat you were. And then, when your father put his foot down about a ball you wished to attend, you acted out. I'm sure you didn't mean to push him over the rail. But there he was, dangling as your mother tried to save him. And what did you do? You pushed her with him! When I tried to stop you, you nearly pushed me as well. I had to return to my cabin and lock the door until we docked for fear you might try to do me harm as well," he said, his voice choking up slightly even as he ignored her demand to use her title.

Lucifer wanted to reach across the room and strangle the lying sod, but he controlled his urge for the moment. Though, it was a near thing.

"A tall tale, to be sure. But here's the issue. You're a liar, Richard. A no-good gambler who lies as soon as his lips move. I wouldn't trust you to leave London if I gave back the women you abducted and five thousand pounds. So do your worst. I assure you I have connections in places you couldn't even imagine. You don't scare me anymore." Amelia stood, regal yet furious, with her hands fisted and tucked into the folds of her skirts.

"You should be scared of me, *Lady Portridge*. Don't make the same mistake your parents did in thinking I am the harmless family friend." His voice dropped to a menacing rasp. "Much has changed in the twenty years since I killed your parents. A few things have not. One or two more bodies on my conscience won't weigh any heavier."

The Inspector cum footman stepped forward as the door of the salon swung open. "We've heard enough, Lady Portridge."

Mattingly popped up from the couch and spun around as the door of the salon opened and Buckley, along with two more officers, stepped inside.

Mattingly's back was to them, but Lucifer heard the man growl. "What have you done, you meddling bitch?" Then he turned as he pulled out a pistol. Amelia's right arm whipped out as the police lunged over the settee, but she was far quicker with her whip than they could have ever hoped to be. By the time they reached Mattingly, his weapon was on the ground, and he held his hand as he cried out in pain.

"And you should not have made the mistake of thinking I was still a harmless child to be cowed by you." She recoiled her whip and glared at him.

Buckley still stood near the door, his eyes shining with approval at Amelia's handiness with her whip. Lucifer was quite pleased as well, considering he'd been about to push her out of the way so he could take the bullet on her behalf. But once again, his resilient wife needed no rescuing. They contained Mattingly handily, despite his furious struggles, and bustled him out of their salon.

As soon as the quiet after the storm enveloped them, his wife turned to him. "Well, I'm happy that bit of business is finished."

And then, to his surprise, she walked right into his arms. A lone tremor skated through her body as she stood there, strong and quiet. The woman had a depth of reserves he found unmatched in most men. The question remained now that Mattingly was dealt with. Would she choose to have him in her life and in her heart? Or would she go back to the way she'd lived her life for the last twenty years and isolate herself?

Chapter Thirty-Two

Amelia slipped from Lucifer's arms and smiled up at him. "Thank you for everything you've done to help me. I'm not sure things would have turned out so well without your assistance."

He reached up and cupped her face. "I wanted nothing more than to help you. It didn't start that way, but I was quickly ensnared by your intelligence and resilience. There are few women in this world who could truly be a partner to a man such as myself, but you are the one I want."

Her heart skipped a beat as she pulled away from him to put some distance between them. She wanted to say yes. She wanted to trust all she knew of this man and say yes. But one truth remained. He'd never said he loved her. She'd seen too many married men enter The Market cavorting with women who were not their wives, seeking pleasure wherever they could find it to replace something they did not find in what amounted to a business deal for most of them. She refused to have anything less than the love she saw between her parents. It was unconventional, but it made them both extremely happy for the time they were together. She wanted that more than anything else. "I cannot hold you to an arrangement that was not made based on love. You married me to protect me, to ensure I was safe from Richard. It was the gentlemanly thing to do, but I would not have you pay for that choice the rest of your life."

Lucifer growled as he advanced on her. She took a step back as she looked up at his furious countenance. And then he was on her. He hauled her into his arms and took her mouth with a savage kiss that claimed—it did not ask. It plundered—it did not seek. It commanded—it did not suggest. Their tongues twined and battled as his arms encircled her, as though he might never let her go.

As he continued to kiss her in the late afternoon sunshine of his front salon, all of her questions and worries faded away. This was the problem with Lucifer. When he touched her, she lost the ability to think rationally. He made her feel so deeply that she believed she could love him enough for both of them. That even without the words, she could stay.

He opened the back of her dress and then eased the fabric down her shoulders and free of her arms. Dropping the bodice on the floor, he started loosening her skirts. Once again, she wanted to curse the trappings of a proper woman. So many blasted layers! She pulled back from his kiss long enough to demand, "Cut them off me."

His eyes flared wide, and then he reached down into his boot and pulled the knife she knew he usually carried there. It took moments for him to slice through the remaining fabric. At least she'd opted to leave off the unwieldy hoops for today's meeting. Then he rose and pressed the blade to her back as he kissed her once more. One quick downward slice and her corset gaped away from her spine, held up only by his chest. The knife thumped to the thick rug they stood on, followed by her corset. All that remained were her chemise and drawers. He laid her down onto the divan they'd been standing near, pressing against her until she lay back for him.

There, he gripped the front of her chemise and ripped it in half. The delicate material gave way, exposing her flesh to his greedy gaze. He leaned over her and sucked one nipple into his mouth, pulling on it gently at first and then more strongly. As she arched up into the sensation, he worried the nub with his teeth until she cried out in pleasure. Only then did he switch to the other side.

Her hands cupped his head, guiding him to her other breast as he repeated what he'd just done. A welcome ache grew between her thighs as he continued, the need for him to fill her taking hold. She knew she was growing wet for him, wanted him seated deep inside. In that moment, it didn't matter that he'd never said the words "I love you" because he spoke them so loudly with his body.

She pushed at his coat, needing the heat of his skin against hers. He sat up and stripped it off, quickly followed by his vest and shirt. Then they were kissing again. Only this time, it was gentler, less combative and more like a melding of their tongues. She could taste the whiskey he'd clearly nipped earlier before Richard's visit. And the inherent sweetness that always seemed to be present when they kissed.

Despite the cooler air as the fire died down, unattended, she felt as though she were burning up. She pulled her mouth free and pressed it to his shoulder. Needing to taste him, to explore him. She tried to slide out from beneath him, but he was having none of it. "Stay," he ground out.

Did he mean for her to stay still, or was he asking her to stay with him? It didn't really matter because her answer was the same. Yes. For the moment, she would stay. Until it grew too painful to remain, she would stay. Because he might possibly say the words—one day.

Then he leaned up from her and opened his trousers to release his rock-hard cock. He'd ground it against her hip earlier, but now she could see it. Long and hard, swollen for her. She tried to slip down so she could take him in her mouth, but he used his knees planted on the cushion to block her movement. "No."

She looked up at him as he shook his head. And then he spread her legs wide and plunged inside of her. Once again, she rejoiced in her choice to wear her old-style drawers that left her pussy exposed. As he drove into her until his groin pressed to hers, she cried out and relished the feeling of fullness. The knowledge that, at least in this, they were one. He propped himself up on one hand, giving him room to both fuck her and reach down to work her clit. She twined her legs around his and joined his rhythm, lifting up to meet his every stroke as he slid a fingertip over her nub. Sparks flew, shivering over her body as she moved closer to orgasm. Reaching up, she tweaked her own nipples, pulling and pinching them as he shuttled in and out of her body.

"Amelia..." He called her name but then paused. Instead of more words, he increased the pressure on her clit and pumped harder as he filled her completely. "So, fucking beautiful."

And she felt beautiful. Felt like a goddess stretched out on an altar being worshipped. Then he strummed over her clit once more, and she exploded around him. "Oh, God! Lucifer!" Her body seemed to split into a million pieces as she lost all sense of solidness. All she could do was feel. The pleasure of him filling her, the surge of bliss from her head to her toes, and the way her body demanded more. More. More. Until she saw stars. Then, only then, did she float softly back to earth to find him straining above her, lost in his own release.

As they drifted slowly back to awareness together, she knew she loved him. And despite wanting what her parents had—that soul-deep connection—she knew she would give them a try. She would see if she could make him fall as deeply in love with her as she had him. After all, if she succeeded, she had nothing to lose and everything to gain. So, how did one make their husband fall in love with them?

Chapter Thirty-Three

May 1863

Amelia looked down at the blue silk of her ball gown. The front panel on the skirt created a triangle of deep blue. Then came a slightly darker blue panel on either side that was edged in a pleated ruffle up the front triangle and around the hem of the gown. The bodice nipped in at the waist, creating the illusion of a smaller span than she truly possessed. The neckline was a simple affair of gathered silk to emphasize her breasts, though it plunged rather daringly. The sleeves were a poof of the blue silk edged once again with a pleated ruffle to match the hem. It was a stunning Charles Worth gown that she'd splurged on after seeing a drawing of it. Despite having no place to wear it, she'd had to own it. Now it seemed a rather prescient purchase.

Lucifer assisted her out of the carriage and into Flint's home. The house was a hive of activity as both light and people spilled from the place. She drew in a deep breath and tried to remember some of the things her mother had taught her long ago as they had traveled to London. She could hear her voice reminding her to stand up straight, look people in the eye when she spoke to them, and remember that she may not be a peer of the realm, but she was a wealthy heiress in her own right. Except now she was a peer. Lady Portridge.

"Bloody hell, that's a lot of people," Lucifer mumbled beside her as they entered the home.

Amelia didn't have the heart to tell him that these were merely the early guests since it was barely ten o'clock. By midnight, the ballroom of the Duke and Duchess of Shropshire would teem with people. Flint's staff took their cloaks and ushered them to the ballroom entrance past the line of attendees awaiting their turn to be announced. As they entered, a footman's voice boomed out beside them. "The Marquess and Marchioness of Portridge."

All eyes in the room turned to them. Amelia's stomach flipped and then settled as she pushed the moment of unease aside. All those years ago, this is what she had come to London to see. A real ball, and now she was experiencing one. Flint and Ros stood just off to the side of the entry. As they entered the ballroom, their host and hostess nodded to them, and then Ros waved them over. "Welcome! Isn't this a magnificent turnout?"

Amelia smiled. "You will be nothing short of the hostess of the season. I am sure."

"Please, do not believe this is for us. I am certain everyone is here to see you two." She grinned as she lifted her brows in punctuation.

Stifling a moment of dread, she did her best to remain poised. "You may be correct. I suppose you two bringing us out in this manner makes this one of the more scandalous balls of the season."

"Scandalous? Don't be ridiculous. Infamous possibly, but Flint and I are above reproach, don't you know? If we've sponsored you, then you are officially of the upper echelons of the peerage."

Beside her, Lucifer groaned. "Dear God, don't say that, Ros. My reputation amongst the fast set will be in tatters."

They all laughed at his feigned distress, except Amelia heard a thread of worry in there. He hadn't planned on becoming a lord but had done so for her. Now the ramifications of that choice were coming to the fore. She decided he required a distraction. "Come, you must dance the first waltz with me once the music begins."

"Good heavens, Amelia! If you keep inviting men to dance with you, I shall most assuredly keep my reputation intact." Lucifer grinned.

"Of stuff it, Lucifer. I didn't ask men. I asked you." She winked at Ros, who tried to hide her laughter behind her fan, but failed.

"Go, enjoy yourselves. You are the guests of honor! Everyone will want to meet you." Flint said as he slapped Lucifer on the shoulder.

"I hold you responsible for all of this." Lucifer glared at his brother but ruined it with a smile. "Thank you for all you have done to help us."

For a moment, a small bubble seemed to seal around them, blocking the other guests out. "You're my brother. This is what being a family should mean. Does mean, now."

Amelia's throat tightened as the intense moment unfolded. Under her hand, she could feel Lucifer's arm tense, as though caught off guard by not just the words but the feeling Flint had imbued in them. And then the footman's voice boomed out, popping the bubble. "The Earl and Countess of Stonemere."

The rest of the Lustful Lords and their respective wives were announced, and she and Lucifer found themselves engulfed in their new family. Everyone chattered away, getting caught up on happenings since they'd last all gathered. It was a festive occasion that celebrated Lucifer's official introduction in the House of Lords, their debut amongst the Ton, and, for those involved, that Mattingly was safely imprisoned and no longer a threat.

"What has become of the women that were taken?" Lady Julia Wolfington asked her.

Amelia smiled. "Cat is officially supposed to take over Mistress Lash's clientele but has yet to do so."

Ros looped her arm with hers. "I hope she has recovered from her ordeal."

"Physically, yes." Amelia sighed. "I'm not sure she has fully bounced back mentally. Madame indicates she still holds herself responsible."

Ros nodded in understanding. "What happened was beyond her control. And she'll come to understand men are difficult creatures to control until you understand their deepest, darkest needs and will brook no arguments in seeing to them."

The three of them laughed delightedly.

"Perhaps I should take more of the upper hand with Wolf. He could use a good dressing down now and again." The gorgeous redhead grinned with a mischievous glint in her green eyes.

Amelia nodded. "I find all men need that once in a while."

And then it hit her. There, in a ballroom surrounded by a sea of people, she needed to be who she was. Lucifer may prefer to be in charge most of the time in the bedroom, but when he'd first come to The Market, he had been seeking someone to see to his needs. Somewhere along the way, she'd forgotten that. Perhaps it was time to remind him who was really in charge?

Lucifer watched his wife chatting with some of the wives of the Lustful Lords. It was odd to be absorbed into the group in such a fashion. He'd been studying them for quite a while, trying to decide if he should approach Flint. It had been sheer luck that Lady Brougham's brother had run up an enormous debt, bringing the entire group into his sphere.

Amelia laughed again, and he wondered how she was doing. He'd caught her darting brief glances at him as though checking on him. The idea that she cared created a warmth inside that sparked his desire. He looked around and realized that there were so many more people at the fete than when they'd first arrived. He sighed. There was no way he could steal her away from such entertainments early when they were the guests of honor.

The first strains of the musicians warming up sounded, and he decided to seek out his wife for the first dance. Having led her out onto the dance floor, he took her in his arms for the opening waltz and then pressed her indecently close. She looked up at him with a wicked smile.

"Do not grin at me in such a fashion, Lady Portridge, or you will find yourself in an alcove with your skirts up about your ears."

His playfully growled threat only caused her to grin wider. "Not quite yet, Lord Portridge. But I shall make you aware the moment I am ready to be ravished in a dark corner."

"And what makes you believe you have any say in the matter?" He enjoyed their naughty banter as he swept her into the flowing waltz.

She chuckled, low and sultry. He hesitated a half-second, nearly tripping over his own feet. His wife was up to something, but he did not know what.

"Do not be so foolish, husband. Besides, who says I shall be the one in the alcove being pleasured? Perhaps I shall drag you into one and push you against a wall so I can ravish you?"

He spun her around as they twirled through the dance. Her words slithered through him, causing need to prickle along his spine. Would she do such a thing at their first ball? At any ball? "I would be a fool to fight such an event."

She laughed again but fell quiet as they navigated the dance. Thoughts whirled in his head as he tried to imagine her doing as she suggested, and it wasn't hard to imagine it. To imagine her on her knees servicing him. After all, she'd done it before; only then she'd been blonde and masked. The music finally came to an end, allowing them to slip from the dance floor. Curious if she would follow through, he led them on a circuit around the edge of the ballroom. They nodded and said hello to a few people they knew, but mostly they were watched with curiosity by those of the Ton who had never had occasion to interact with one or the other of them.

Then they neared a spot where it was less densely packed, and those who were nearby were occupied watching the dancers. There was little in the way of conversation as the musicians were just above them on a gallery overlooking the ballroom, and the music was so loud, speaking was nearly impossible. Directly beneath the musicians was, in fact, a good-sized alcove with a convenient curtain to lend a bit of privacy. He waited, breath held, as they approached. *Would she?*

And then he felt the tug on his arm as she moved toward the space. To his surprise and excitement, she was acting on her words. Without question, he followed her into the hideaway, curious to see what she did next. Inside, she spun around and pressed him against the nearest wall, ignoring the cushioned bench seat tucked against the back of the space. It was just big enough to hold the two of them with the added volume of her skirts. That was his last mundane observation as her lips captured his and all his attention coalesced on her.

He wrapped his arms around her, loving the weight of her pressed against him as her tongue swept into his mouth. Her kiss was demanding and ardent, nothing tentative or shy. Instead, she took what she wanted from him. His body rose to attention. A cacophony of tingles started at the base of his spine and stretched out along his body as their kiss shifted to something more leisurely and sensual. If this was all she chose to engage in, he'd take it and consider himself a fortunate man until they were truly alone. The music for the second dance ended, and the next began. All the while, he leaned against a wall in a dark alcove, kissing his stunning wife.

As the opening measures of the music picked up in intensity, so did her kiss. And then she pulled away from him and lowered herself onto the bench. He moved to stoop down to her, to capture her lips again, when her hands whipped open the fastenings of his trousers, and she reached in to pull out his hardening cock. As he realized what she was about, all the blood in his body rushed to the very appendage she was currently stroking in her fist. As he'd said before, he would be a fool to fight such an event. And he was no fool. Settling in, he let his eyelids drift down as he watched her from where he stood. Amelia opened her lips and pressed the tip of his cock into her mouth as she swirled her tongue over the glistening tip. Watching her suck the precum off his head had his balls tightening and his cock ready to blow.

Determined to stretch this moment out, he began mentally reviewing his last inventory. She took his cock fully in her mouth. He had noted only five bottles of whiskey. He needed to add a case to his next order. He fisted his hands at his side, desperately trying to control the urge to sink his hands into her hair. She pushed his cock past the tight ring of her throat and swallowed him down until his balls were pressed against her chin. He mentally added two kegs of ale to his order. She worked him in and out of her mouth and throat, over and over, until he was pretty sure he was ready to order enough alcohol to stock his club for the next five years. It was a pointless endeavor to try and stave off the pleasure she wrought. Instead, he focused on the shaft of light that snuck through the curtain, exposing the creamy flesh of her bosom as she continued to suck his cock as though it might be the last time she ever did so.

And then she took him deep in her throat again and moaned. He couldn't actually hear her over the music, but the vibrations set off a chain reaction that had the pleasant tingles sparking off into jolts of pleasure that had his toes curling and his knees shaking. "Amelia!" He called out hoarsely in warning, all he could manage in the moment. And then he cupped her face and held her there as he pumped his hips, stroking his cock in and out of her mouth for a few strokes. "Fuck," he cursed on a strangled groan as he came. He sank as deep as he could into her mouth and let his load shoot down her throat. His incredible wife latched her hands onto his ass and held him firmly in place as he lost any prescient thought. His balls had drawn up, and his entire body felt as if he'd been struck by lightning. Or at least, what he imagined it might be like. As his orgasm dissipated, he moved to ease back against the wall and out of her mouth, but she held him still with one hand on his hip and the other wrapped around the base of his still hard cock. She gently licked him clean as he softened. In the aftermath of his orgasm, the sensation was almost too much, causing little jolts of aftershocks until she finally deemed his shaft ready to be tucked away.

As she rose from the bench, which had been the perfect height for such activities, she smiled up at him. "That, my dear, is merely a preview of what is to come later tonight."

Then his minx of a wife kissed him and darted out of the alcove, leaving him alone to regroup.

After taking a few deep breaths and willing his pulse to cease racing, he managed to step outside the alcove on somewhat solid legs. The air was just as stifling in the ballroom as it had been in the alcove, but he did not care in the least. He wanted to see that his wife was well and back with their friends. He arrived at the group in short order and found his wife smiling and chatting with Lord and Lady Brougham. Emily was animatedly sharing a story of some kind, and his wife listened raptly. Flint leaned over after glancing at his wife and then back at him. "I see you two found the alcove beneath the musicians."

Lucifer said nothing but stood there lustfully watching his wife, whose swollen lips and glowing cheeks reminded him of what she had done and what she had teasingly promised. It was highly likely that this would be a very short evening for them.

Chapter Thirty-Four

June 1863

Amelia paced the front salon of her home as six pairs of eyes watched her. "It's been three bloody weeks! Three!"

No one said a word as she made another pass, her skirts rustling angrily with each long stride.

"What does a woman have to do to get her husband to say he loves her?" she demanded of the group.

Lizzy offered a tentative smile. "Perhaps he has shown it in enough ways that the words are a mere formality?"

"Oh, I know the obstinate man loves me, at least in my head. There, I have no doubt. I mean, what man—who is not of a naturally submissive nature—would allow me to tie him up and do as I wish with him in bed? What man would see to my every need, even when I do not yet know it *is* a need? But I need to hear the words. I need to know in my heart that he loves me." Amelia plopped onto the empty chair and huffed. "I've tried everything short of tying him up and whipping it from him. But since I know that would merely be torture for him, I won't do it. So, what do I do?"

Theo looked at her consideringly. "Perhaps he needs to lose the very thing he loves?"

Amelia stopped and thought about it. "I suppose I could leave him. But would it be enough? Or should I file for divorce?" She worried her fingers as she thought about her options.

"I don't think you need to do anything so drastic right off. Perhaps an extended trip to Bath would be enough?" Marie suggested.

"That could be enough to disrupt his routine. The man is maddeningly regular about his schedule. You would think with the reputation he has that he would be more spontaneous and unpredictable. But no, he rises every day at nine, takes his breakfast, and then goes to his study to work. He's had all of his paperwork moved to the house. Around four, he departs for the club, where he works until eight. Then he comes home, has dinner, makes love to me, and goes to sleep. Then he does it all again the next day." Amelia allowed her frustration to simmer as she thought about it. But would Bath be the place *she* would go?

"Bath might be a bit stuffy for you." Ros offered. "Perhaps a holiday to Brighton might be in order?"

Amelia lit up. "Oh, that sounds perfect! Perhaps one of you ladies might like to join me?"

"Well..." Emily started just as others mumbled excuses.

Amelia laughed. "Yes, yes. You all are far too in love with your husbands to leave them for a few weeks. I certainly wouldn't go if I had another choice. But who can I take as my companion?"

"It might do Cat some good to go with you. Madame mentioned the other day that she was still recuperating at The Market and not seeing clients as of yet," Marie suggested.

Amelia popped to her feet. "An excellent notion. She and I need to have a chat about her future, anyway. I'm afraid I shall have to end our visit early so I can make arrangements and let Lucifer know of my plans this evening."

The ladies all departed after wishing her great success. They would be eager to hear how events unfolded when she returned from her trip.

That evening, as they sat in his study, Lucifer looked at Amelia and smiled. She knew precisely what he was thinking about since it was nearly eleven o'clock at night and dinner had long since ended.

"Are you ready to go upstairs, dear?" He set his book on the Theory of Supply and Demand aside.

"If you are." She remained agreeable. After all, she knew what delicious things he would do to her in their bed. She'd be a fool to deny him or herself one last time before she left for Brighton in the morning. So, they headed upstairs and began getting ready for bed. As they undressed, she decided it was time to tell him of her impending trip. "By the way, I had a visit with Cat today."

"Did you? How is she recovering from everything?" He was busy removing his shirt as he asked.

"Not terribly well, I'm afraid. I think a change of scenery would do her a world of good, so I've decided to take her to Brighton tomorrow." She made the announcement very casually.

"That's nice, dear." His murmured words came from just behind her as she stripped off her at-home dress. "I'm sure a jaunt to the seaside will do her a world of good." He planted a kiss on her shoulder just at her neck and helped her remove the rest of her clothing. That was his only comment on the matter before his hands and lips began roving over her body.

Arousal pulsed to life between her legs as he kissed and sucked on her neck while his hands cupped her breasts. Then he gently plucked each nipple until they'd grown to tight, hard nubs, and she ached for his mouth there.

Instead of doing as she expected, he patted her on her backside. "Get into bed on your hands and knees, please."

Curious about what he had in mind, she did as he asked. A few moments later, he joined her on the bed as he set a few things down. Climbing behind her, he smoothed his hands over her backside. "I've been wanting to sink deep into this arse for a while now. You said yes to me doing this before when I suggested it. Are you still amenable to such an exploration?"

His questing fingers stroked over her clit and up her slit to rub over her tight ring of muscle. Her hips flexed in demand. "Yes, I'll take whatever you wish to give me." And she cringed a little at how true the words were... or had been.

Something cold and damp swept over her crack, causing her to shiver. "Something to ease my way," he murmured as he pressed a finger past the muscles and sank it deep inside her backside.

Her body spasmed around his digit, a shudder of pleasure.

Then he added a second finger. This felt like more of a pinch and forced her to breathe through the tightness. She knew women enjoyed this as much as men, having heard a number of the ladies at The Market discuss the finer points of taking a man there.

"That's it; take the stretch, Amelia." His words were soft and encouraging, with an edge of excitement.

He added a third finger, and she felt so full back there. Full, but not full enough. She wanted more, deeper. And her pussy ached for attention. Pressing her forehead to her arms on the mattress, she tried to focus on anything else but the ache in her pussy. Then he removed his fingers, and something much larger pressed against her entrance. As he pressed his cock against her, she remembered the girls saying to push out against him to lessen the pain as he entered your anus. So, she did as they said, and with a sudden pop, he was inside her.

He froze, deep breaths rasping from his chest. "Fuck you are tight."

"More. I need more," she moaned as she tried to press back against him.

He growled a bit as he sank deeper, bit by bit, in answer to her demand. And then he was lodged deep inside her, making her backside feel fuller than she'd ever felt before. It hurt, but it also felt good. When he retreated slowly, a moan escaped her. And then he reversed course.

"Yes!" Her cry was muffled since her arms had collapsed, leaving her face buried in the mattress amidst a tangle of limbs.

He picked up his pace and worked in and out of her. She soon met him stroke for stroke as he pumped in and out of her backside. He was a tight fit, but she welcomed him. Wanted this. Was willing to give him all of herself in ways she'd never imagined before. The need to come grew with each stroke, but she wasn't really close enough.

As though he heard her thoughts, Lucifer reached down and around to stroke her clit. "Come for me, Amelia. Scream my name." His demand sounded raspy, as though he hung on by a ragged thread. As he dragged his finger over her sensitive bundle of nerves, jolts of sheer bliss fired off like sparks. At first, they were small and spread out, but quickly they built as he continued sliding in and out of her body, rubbing over places she'd never felt before. Her body heated and grew sweat-slick as they both kept moving. And then the fire caught. Like a raging inferno, her release ripped through her. "Lucifer! Yes!"

He fucked her harder, lengthened out his strokes, and kept strumming her clit as her body flew apart. She cried out incoherent things she'd never said before. Mumbled a string of thoughts and feelings that he'd never pulled from her. "I love you...love what you do to me...love how you make me feel... uuunnhh!"

He kept pushing into her until she felt his strokes grow shorter, more staccato. She was still riding high, but she heard her name on his lips. "Amelia!" And then he stiffened behind her. His hips continued on, though it was more of a listless movement, as he, too, floated back to the present.

He collapsed forward onto her back, and they tumbled to the side. Still joined, they lay there, recovering from such an intense orgasm.

Then it hit her. She'd said the words out loud. She'd told him she loved him. Her gut clenched. She'd said the words. He must have heard them. After all, they'd burst out in the moment, even if they were part of a string of other mutterings.

A soft sigh escaped her. She'd known he likely didn't feel the same way about her as she felt about him. He'd only ever offered her protection. But it still hurt to have it confirmed by his lack of response to her declaration, however spontaneous it may have been. Her trip to Brighton couldn't have come at a better time because she wasn't sure what she should do. Did she stay and hope time might help love grow, or did she rip out her heart and try to start over somewhere new?

The sun was high in the sky and blaring into his carriage as he headed home for lunch. Some unexpected deliveries that required his attention had drawn him to the club much earlier than normal. He stretched contentedly and remembered how delightful the previous night had been with his wife. She'd taken his cock in her arse and had loved every moment of it. He'd been hopeful, but then, when she was so tight it was clear she'd never had a lover there, he'd grown worried. It was one of his particularly favorite ways to take a woman, all that deliciously tight heat wrapped around him. His cock grew partly hard at the memory.

Even more unexpected than his wife's anal virginity was her declaration of love. Or at least he thought it was... she was mumbling, and there were so many things she was saying. But he was quite certain he had heard her say, "I love you." At least, he decided he would be—certain, that is. Of course, she loved him. She'd stayed. She was still his wife, and they were still under his roof. Wouldn't she have left him if she didn't love him? Didn't want him. That's what people did when they didn't love you.

He hoped to surprise his wife with his lunchtime visit and perhaps a quick round of loving before he had to return to the club to begin the evening. His carriage drew to a halt, and he hopped out. Happy and rather pleased with himself, he bounded up the steps and into the house. His butler looked up in surprise as he traversed the foyer, arms full of old newspapers. "Good day, Peterson."

The man attempted to bow as ceremoniously as he always did, despite his burden. "Good day, my lord."

"Where shall I find my wife on this lovely day?" He set his hat on the rack by the door and turned back to find Peterson looking at him as though he'd lost his bloody mind.

"Well, uh. Brighton, my lord." The man seemed to nearly stammer over the words.

"Brighton?" Lucifer stopped. What the hell was she doing in Brighton? Why was she not here to have lunch with him?

"Yes, my lord. Her ladyship went to Brighton for a visit with her friend, Miss Catherine."

Miss Catherine? Oh, he means Cat. But when did Amelia decide to go to Brighton? Had she told him she was going? "When is she to return?"

"She did not say, my lord. She did take a rather enormous trunk with her." Peterson looked distinctly uncomfortable delivering that bit of news.

"Very well. If you could let cook know I am home for lunch, I would appreciate it. Something light would be welcomed." Then Lucifer retreated to his study.

He racked his brain, trying to remember if Amelia had said anything about going to Brighton. He thought about last night. Something niggled at him. He remembered nuzzling her neck as she talked about having seen Cat yesterday. She'd smelled so delicious. He'd grown distracted by the need to smell her more deeply. He'd been nuzzling her neck and… yes! She mentioned going to Brighton for the day. But Peterson said she'd had a large trunk. What could she need a large trunk for? She'd not left him. She merely went for a brief holiday at the shore with Cat. He reassured himself that no woman who was as fully pleasured as she'd been the previous night would leave her husband.

Chapter Thirty-Five

Three Days! Amelia had been gone for three fucking days. Lucifer growled and just managed to keep from throwing his glass against a wall. A knock on his study door sounded, and then Peterson poked his head in. "The Duke of Shropshire and his friends are here to see you, my lord."

"Let them in." Lucifer flopped into the chair next to the fireplace. He glanced down at his wrinkled shirt and trousers, all that was left of what he'd worn to the club the night before. His cravat, vest, and coat lay strewn about his study somewhere early this morning when he returned home to discover his wife had yet to return from her trip. Her *day* trip. He knew that trunk had been bad news when Peterson mentioned it.

"Oh, my." Flint stopped short just inside the doorway, causing the rest of his entourage to crash into his back.

"Bloody hell, man! Speak up if you're going to stop." Cooper groused from the back of the group.

Flint shrugged and stepped inside, letting the rest of them see what had caused the short stop. Lucifer knew he was a bloody mess, but he didn't particularly feel like hearing about it. "The first one of you lot who says something gets planted a facer."

Stone snorted and sat down. Linc began to laugh uproariously as he hung on to Dunmere's shoulder. Flint rolled his eyes and sat down next to Stone. Cooper and Wolf followed suit, taking seats where they could, without further comment. The group sat there staring at him and not saying a word.

Annoyed by being the focus of their stares, Lucifer growled again. "Well, say something, damn you all."

"You just told us you'd plant us a facer if we said anything," Wolf pointed out reasonably. "Flint might still enjoy getting hit, but I, for one, will pass on that."

Flint rolled his eyes. "Really, Wolf? I haven't had a fight in months." He tugged at his cuffs, straightening his shirt. "A man can turn over a new leaf." He turned his attention back to his brother. "I take it you've not heard from Amelia?"

"Not a bloody word. I don't even know where she's staying." He crossed his arms over his chest. He knew he was damn close to sulking—fair enough, he was sulking—but what was a man to do? He certainly couldn't go chasing after his wife. If she wanted to leave him that badly, he should let her go.

Stone tsked and shook his head. "Really, Lucifer. I expected more from a man as determined as you. My God, you built a fucking empire, but you can't go find your wife and bring her home?"

Flint snorted. "He likely hasn't told her he loves her still, so going after her seems a bit daunting, I suppose. We've all been there."

Linc guffawed. "Speak for yourself, old man. I have yet to get caught in the parsons' trap, nor shall I any time soon. But what does telling her how he feels have to do with his ability to go after her?"

"Well, if he can't tell her how he feels, he certainly can't admit that he wants to go after her, much less act on it." Wolf stated what seemed obvious to everyone, including Lucifer.

A sigh escaped Flint. "I told you to tell her, you fool. Nothing good ever comes from not saying the words."

"They're just words." Lucifer groused.

"And yet here you sit looking as crusty as day-old bread," Cooper spoke up. "I have to tell you, I never expected to fall in love with Emily, but I must say it was far easier just embracing it and going after what I wanted. All this dithering about is ridiculous."

Lucifer looked at the golden-haired man and imagined punching him in the face. "Yes, well..." He really had no rebuttal for his friends. They were right. "Fuck!" He wanted to smash something as he let the word burst free from his chest.

Stone grinned. "I think he's getting it now."

"Getting what?" Linc asked, still amused and a little confused, it would seem.

"I bloody well have to go tell her I love her. It doesn't seem to matter that I work from home every day so I can take lunch with her or that I shower her with gifts and attention. Apparently, I have to say the fucking words for her to believe me. And I was too stubborn to listen to good advice weeks ago when it was given. Does that about sum it up, Flint?" Lucifer stood, exhaustion tugging at his body. He staggered forward a few steps before Flint rose and steadied him.

"Hold on now. I don't think you're in any shape to head anywhere but to bed for the time being." Flint stretched one of his arms over his shoulders.

Lucifer was quite sure it was the only reason he remained standing at the moment. "I have to go find her," he slurred the words a bit.

"How much have you had to drink," Flint asked.

"Just a few sips of whiskey." Lucifer managed to say, but then his eyelids started to slip closed. His body jerked, and then he opened his eyes again.

"When was the last time you slept?" Stone asked as he took up residence on Lucifer's other side.

"Not since 'Melia left." Lucifer struggled to stay awake, but the lack of sleep for three days was catching up with him rapidly.

He heard soft curses from the men around him. Then his brother seemed to take charge. "Wolf, talk to Gordie and have one of his men head out to Brighton to discover where Amelia is staying. He can send a telegram letting him know where to find her."

"I'll go see to that right now." Wolf stood and left.

"Stone, let's get him upstairs and into a bed before he collapses."

Flint and Stone moved him forward, but then exhaustion won out, and everything went dark.

Amelia sat in the lobby of The Old Ship Hotel and calmly sipped her tea as the chaos that was a bustling family resort churned around her. It was sort of comforting, in a way. Reminding her that life continued on in spite of everything. In spite of the terrible injuries humans may exact upon each other. In spite of her life pivoting in directions unknown. In spite of a slowly breaking heart.

"I can't tell you how good it is to be out of London and near the fresh sea air." Cat smiled as she sipped her own tea.

Amelia managed to smile because her taking Cat to Brighton had, in fact, been a good thing for her former apprentice. "I am heartened to hear it. Though, I am curious if you've decided what you wish to do now. I know Madame has given you some time to decide, but at some point, she will have to make a decision. Some of The Market's clientele need a firm hand with an excellent whip in it."

Cat let out a soft sigh. "I am aware. I just haven't known what to do since I was taken. I felt so helpless. How can I possibly make a good Mistress when I couldn't manage to save myself?"

"Why should you think your ability to become a mistress has a thing to do with your ability to save yourself? Did you fall apart, crying when you were taken?" Amelia let one brow drift up in question as she tilted her head to the side.

"No. I fought like hell to get away from those bastards. But I wasn't strong enough...." A tear slipped down Cat's cheek.

"When you discovered there were other women taken, did you look out for yourself and ignore them?" She probed further, knowing the answer she would hear.

"I couldn't. They were so... broken... and scared. Exactly how I felt inside, but they needed someone to hold them together. To help them through their ordeal, and there was no one but me to do it." Cat looked up, almost surprised by her own words. "I had to be strong for them."

"That need to be strong for others. To help people through whatever is plaguing them is what it takes to be a good mistress. It's not about how hard you can hit with the whip—you've been a deft hand since early in your training. It was your own inner strength you needed to discover." Amelia took a sip of tea and let her words settle for a moment. "I told you there was something missing. It seems as you gathered the other women and helped to protect them throughout your experience, you also found that inner strength and confidence you were missing. I would have preferred you discover it another way, but I suppose we each find that in ourselves through our own paths." Amelia couldn't help but look up at the entrance of the hotel once more to see if a familiar face might walk through the door.

"I know your path was not an easy one as well. But you have never let a difficult path stop you. Why are you doing so now?" Cat asked as she watched Amelia.

Her gaze snapped back to her friend. "What do you mean?"

Cat smiled at her. "Why have you taken such a passive approach to achieving what anyone can plainly see that you want? You have no more secrets to hide, and yet here you are with me doing precisely just that—hiding."

Amelia blinked, a little surprised by the observation. "I am here because you needed to get out of London, to get away from where everything happened and clear your head. And it turns out I needed to do the same."

Cat chuckled. "Are you sure you aren't running from what you want, what you've always wanted?" She hesitated. "It can be scary to realize the very thing you've always wanted is right in front of you. It was terrifying to agree to become your apprentice. The promise of financial security was both alluring and scary. The freedom to be myself and be seen was terrifying. And learning to read people's body language so I could understand what they really needed versus what they said they needed? Well, that was the hardest lesson of all."

Amelia had to look down to be sure Cat wasn't reaching into her chest to physically rip out her heart. It was like she had crawled inside her and mucked around a bit. "Bloody hell, you are an insightful creature."

"Well, I did have the best mentor there is." Cat grinned.

Amelia sighed. "I've been a fool. I was so focused on him not saying the words that I didn't realize I needed to focus on his body language. All the ways he was telling me how he felt without saying three little words."

"Just so." Cat took a sip of her tea.

Amelia turned her focus back to her friend. "So, you're ready to decide about The Market?"

"I am. I believe Mistress Cat shall be ready to see clients upon her return." She grinned and set her cup and saucer down. "I think I shall go for a stroll along the boardwalk."

Amelia set her own tea down. "Perhaps I'll join you."

Cat shook her head and stood. "I suspect you will be otherwise engaged."

Amelia wasn't following her meaning. "I don't have any plans that I am aware of."

"I know." Cat grinned and walked past Amelia toward the rear of the hotel, where the stairs were located that they had used during their stay.

"Amelia, we need to speak," Lucifer growled as he loomed over her like a dark specter conjured from her thoughts.

"Lucifer! Where did you come from?" she glanced around, utterly confused.

"London, of course." He shook his head. "I've come to fetch you home, where you belong."

Amelia's heart pounded in her chest. He'd come for her. Not even four full days, and here he was. She'd thought she would need to be gone for weeks when she left. Possibly forever. And, of course, just when she'd decided to return home on her own, he showed up. The man had impeccable timing. She stood. "I'll just go pack my trunk."

"I'm afraid I must insist you come with—wait, you said you'd pack your trunk? You're not going to argue with me?" Lucifer seemed nonplussed by her easy acquiescence.

"I am not." She stepped into his body, coming as close as her skirts allowed. The yellow silk enveloped his legs as she pressed her body to his. "I've missed you terribly. And I need you to know—"

"Absolutely not. You will cease speaking at once." He set her from him.

Hurt and confusion warred for supremacy as she stared at him. "But I—"

"I mean it, Amelia, not another word from you. I have something I need to say to you, and you need to hear it."

He growled more than spoke, but she supposed she had brought that on herself.

"I love you. I've loved you since I first met you at The Market wearing a wig and pretending to be a customer. You were so confident and sure of yourself. You didn't need me at all. I was merely there to appease your own wants. It was intoxicating for a man like me." He cupped her face in his big hands, his thumb idly caressing her cheek. "But then, along the way, as I discovered more about you, I became fascinated by you. Each new discovery of some facet of who you are.

Each new experience making love to you. The last four days have been hell and I never want to go back. I love you, Amy Amelia VanBolton, and I want very much to spend the rest of my life trying to make you happy."

Tears streamed down her face as she stared at him. Speechless. "I love you too, Lucifer." She jumped into his arms and kissed him soundly—to the sound of many shocked gasps and exclamations around them. Pulling back, she smiled at him. "I love you, and I promise never to run away again. We shall always talk about our problems, our wants," she gave him a naughty smile. "Our desires."

"Indeed, we shall, wife." He grinned broadly down at her. "Perhaps we should adjourn to your room and have one of those discussions this very moment?"

"I agree, husband. Though I should warn you, I expect to hear you say those words every day."

"What words?" He scowled at her playfully.

"I love you. I want to hear it every day." She looked up at him, her hands on his chest, and she knew she was right where she belonged.

"You may have to restrain me from saying it every hour. Now that I have done so, I am not sure I wish to stop." He smiled at her, his heart in his gaze.

"Then you'd best take me upstairs before the Management kicks us out of this hotel for indecent behavior." She glanced to the side where a man stood nervously waiting for a moment to interrupt.

Lucifer looked at the man and scowled, causing him to turn tail and scurry away.

Amelia smacked his chest. "Lucifer, you're terrible. Now take me to bed and prove to me how terrible you really are."

"I love you, Amelia. I'll never let you go now." He swept his arm around her and led her upstairs, where he proved that over and over again.

The End

About the Author

Sorcha Mowbray is a mild mannered office worker by day...okay, so she is actually a mouthy, opinionated, take charge kind of gal who bosses everyone around; but she definitely works in an office. At night she writes romance so hot she sets the sheets on fire! Just ask her slightly singed husband.

She is a longtime lover of historical romance, having grown up reading Johanna Lindsey and Judith McNaught. Then she discovered Thea Devine and Susan Johnson. Holy cow! Heroes and heroines could do THAT? From there, things devolved into trying her hand at writing a little smexy. Needless to say, she liked it and she hopes you do too!

Find all of Sorcha's social media links at
link.sorchamowbray.com/bio
~
or scan the QR Code

Read the Whole Series

His Wanton Marchioness
A Lustful Lords Novella

She waited her entire life to be married, and she refuses to let anyone interfere with her happiness...not even her new husband.

Elizabeth Grafton, the Marchioness of Carlisle just married the man of her dreams. Or he was. Now, he barely spends time with her. But most disturbing, he comes to her bed under the cloak of darkness—the man won't even light a candle!—and insists she keep her nightgown on until he leaves.

Alexander Grafton, the Marquess of Carlisle is deeply, madly in love with his wife. But, he wants to do things to her that a man could only do to his mistress. He's struggling to keep his baser instincts in check, and that was before his wife decided to seduce him. If she knew what he really wanted...she'd run away.

Armed with "professional" advice, Elizabeth sets out to thwart all of her husband's best intentions and show him just how shameless she can be. Can her wanton nature tempt her husband, or will he win their battle of wills?

His Hand-Me-Down Countess
Lustful Lords, Book 1

His brother's untimely death leaves him with an Earldom and a fiancée. Too bad he wants neither of them...

Theodora Lawton has no need of a husband. As an independent woman, she wants to own property, make investments and be the master of her destiny. Unfortunately, her father signed her life away in a marriage contract to the future Earl of Stonemere. But then the cad upped and died, leaving her fate in the hands of his brother, one of the renowned Lustful Lords.

Achilles Denton, the Earl of Stonemere, is far more prepared to be a soldier than a peer. Deeply scarred by his last tour of duty, he knows he will never be a proper, upstanding pillar of the empire. Balanced on the edge of madness, he finds respite by keeping a tight rein on his life, both in and out of the bedroom. His brother's death has left him with responsibilities he never wanted and isn't prepared to handle in the respectable manner expected of a peer.

Further complicating his new life is an unwanted fiancée who comes with his equally unwanted title. Saddled with a hand-me-down countess, he soon discovers the woman is a force unto herself. As he grapples with the burden of his new responsibilities, he discovers someone wants him dead. The question is, can he stay alive long enough to figure out who's trying to kill him while he tries to tame his headstrong wife?

His Hellion Countess
Lustful Lords, Book 2

A duty bound earl and a jewel thief might find forever if he can steal her heart...

Robert Cooper, the Earl of Brougham must marry in order to fulfill his duty to the title. He's decided on a rather mild mannered, biddable woman who most considered firmly on the shelf. But, her family is on solid financial ground and has no scandals attached to their name.

Lady Emily Winterburn, sister of the Earl of Dunmere, is not what she seems. With a heart as big as her wild streak she finds herself prepared to protect her brother from his bad choices, even if it means committing highway robbery. But marrying their way out of trouble is simply out of the question. What woman in her right mind would shackle herself to a man, let alone one of the notorious Lustful Lords?

Cooper's carefully laid plans are ruined once he must decide between courting his unwilling bride-to-be and taming the wild woman who tried to rob him—until he discovers they are one and the same. And when love sinks its relentless talons into his heart? He'll do anything to possess the wanton who fires his blood and touches his soul.

His Scandalous Viscountess
Lustful Lords, Book 3

Once upon a time, a boy and a girl fell in love...but prestige, power, and a shameful secret drove them apart.

Julia fled abroad after the death of her husband, Lord Wallthorpe. She has finally returned to England, but little has changed.

Except for her.

As a dowager marchioness, Julia lives and loves where she pleases. And the obnoxious son of her dead husband does not please. But what can an independent woman do? Why, create a scandal, of course!

Viscount Wolfington is no stranger to the wagging tongues of the ton. Between being a Lustful Lord and the scandal of his birth, he learned long ago that society had little use for him. So when he walks into The Market and finds the woman who once stole his heart being auctioned for a night of debauchery, he jumps at another chance to hold her—even for just a single night.

As Julia and Wolf unravel their pasts, will villainy win again, or will love finally conquer all?

His Not-So-Sweet Marchioness
Lustful Lords, Book 4

He's shrouded in shame, fighting with his demons in the shadows. Until she sets her sights on him...

Mrs. Rosalind Smith once followed her heart and love to the battlefield and left a widow. Spending the remainder of her life alone is enough... until she meets a man who's need for pain sparks an answering flame deep within her soul.

Matthew Derby, the Marquess of Flintshire is a fighter, it is all he's known since childhood. Throwing his fists is the only way to keep his need for pain at bay, and a certain gentle woman off his mind. She deserves a better man than him—Lord or not. Though when faced with the prospect of losing Ros, Flint realizes he has found something to fight for...something to live for.

To Ros' dismay, everyone around her believes her demeanor too sweet for someone like Flint. When his world begins to unravel and his dockside violence bleeds into the drawing room, a shocking family secret won't be the key to all the answers. Questions remain, can he solve the mystery, tame his dark needs, and still win Ros' heart?

His Reluctant Marchioness
Lustful Lords, Book 5

A notorious woman must rely on the devil himself for help. Too bad she learned long ago never to trust anyone...

Frank Lucifer is having one hell of a week. His gambling hell is short staffed after firing his floor manager, and his half-brother has offered him a title—one he doesn't need or want. Then the woman he's obsessed with dismisses him from her bed, and the problem is he doesn't know who the hell she is.

Mistress Lash has her hands full. Her apprentice is missing under sinister circumstances, and Scotland Yard refuses to lift a finger. A liaison with Frank Lucifer—however attractive she finds him—is something she no longer has time for. Besides, someone should take the arrogant rake down a peg or two.

She sets out to find her apprentice on her own, but everywhere she turns, up pops Lucifer. He's following her, and she's growing suspicious about why that is. When he suggests they join forces, she reluctantly agrees. After all, one should keep their friends close and their enemies closer... she's just not sure which he is. Yet.

Working together to find her missing apprentice, she worries about her ability to protect both her heart and her own secrets from the perceptive man. And as events play out, she must decide if Lucifer is the villain she is searching for... or just the devil who haunts her scorching hot dreams?

Other Books by Sorcha

The Market Series
Discover the series that started it all...

In this sizzling series The Market becomes the setting for Londoners of all walks of life to discover pleasure, lust, and even love. But can they do what is required to claim the ones they've fallen for?

Love Revealed (The Market, Book 1)

Love Redeemed (The Market, Book 2)

Love Reclaimed (The Market, Book 3)

The Market Series Books 1-3 (Boxed Set)

Love Requited (The Market, A Short Story)

One Night With A Cowboy

The One Night With A Cowboy series is a set of short stories linked by cowboys and Soul Mates Dating Service, a dating service with an uncanny ability to match up soul mates. These sizzling little treats are perfect for a quick hot read.

Claiming His Cowgirl (Book 1)

Taking Her Chance (Book 2)

A Cowboy's Christmas Wish (Book 3)

Roping His Cowboy (Book 4)

One Night With A Cowboy Books 1-4 (Boxed Set)

Stealing His Cowgirl's Heart (Book 5)

Made in the USA
Monee, IL
27 June 2024

60818246R00173